Praise for Andrew M. Greeley

The Bishop in the Old Neighborhood

"Blackie, with his quick wit and his fondness for Bushmill's, is his usual delightful self, and his many fans will enjoy this sojourn in the old neighborhood."
—*Publishers Weekly*

The Bishop Goes to The *University*

"Greeley interweaves both spiritual and educational topics into another supremely entertaining adventure."
—*Booklist*

The Bishop in the West Wing

"Blackie once again proves to be a loyal friend, a formidable foe, and a gifted spiritual adviser. An entertaining romp through the West Wing."
—*Booklist*

"Fun is the word for bestseller Greeley's latest, lively Bishop Blackie Ryan thriller. . . . [Readers] will appreciate the well-drawn characters, swift action, and logical resolution."
—*Publishers Weekly*

"Nobody has ever left the church because of an Andrew Greeley novel, but many have been attracted back to it by him."
—Reverend Ron Rolheiser, O.M.I.

THE
BISHOP
AT THE
LAKE

A Blackie Ryan Novel

—————◆—————

Andrew M. Greeley

FORGE®

A TOM DOHERTY ASSOCIATES BOOK
NEW YORK

This is a work of fiction. All of the characters, organizations, and events portrayed in this novel are either products of the author's imagination or are used fictitiously.

THE BISHOP AT THE LAKE: A BLACKIE RYAN STORY

Copyright © 2007 by Andrew M. Greeley Enterprises, Ltd.

All rights reserved.

Map by Heidi Hornaday

A Forge Book
Published by Tom Doherty Associates, LLC
175 Fifth Avenue
New York, NY 10010

www.tor-forge.com

Forge® is a registered trademark of Tom Doherty Associates, LLC.

ISBN-13: 978-0-7653-5502-7
ISBN-10: 0-7653-5502-7

First Edition: September 2007
First Mass Market Edition: August 2008

Printed in the United States of America

0 9 8 7 6 5 4 3 2 1

AUTHOR'S NOTE

During the summer in which I was thinking about this story, I watched many TV mystery films, featuring such skilled gumshoes as Lynley, Allen, Poirot, and Dalgleish. The English mysteries seemed always to involve a country house, of which that damp little island seems to have enormous numbers. I began to wonder whether the ineffectual and innocuous Coadjutor Archbishop of Chicago (with Right to Succession) might prosper in such an environment. Understanding that this purple-clad sleuth might not survive the dampness of the English countryside, I decided to create an English country house on a dune in the rain forest of southwestern Michigan. I therefore had to imagine such a house on an imaginary place between Grand Beach and Forest Beach, hereinafter known as Nolan's Landing.

Grand Beach, Forest Beach, New Buffalo, Stevensville, Saugatuck, and Michigan City are real places. Nolan's Landing, however, is fictional. All the men and women, lay and clerical, police and civilians, in the story are products of my imagination. The dunes are real, however, and date back to the Wisconsin Ice Age and to various levels of what the scholars call "Lake Chicago" and we call Lake Michigan.

—A

CAST OF CHARACTERS

S.P.I.K.E. Nolan (1923), Group Captain RAF (ret.), chairman of the Board of AVEL

Lady Anne Howard (1926), wife to Spike

John Nolan (1945–1972), Captain USMC, son to Spike and Anne

Most Reverend Malachi Howard-Nolan (1946), Archbishop (ad personam) Bishop of Laramie, son to Spike and Anne

Elizabeth Nolan (1948–1978), daughter to Spike and Anne

Philip Nolan (1950), son to Spike and Anne, CEO of AVEL

Loretta Healy Nolan (1952), wife to Philip Nolan (1975)

Eileen Nolan McGinity (1976), daughter to Philip and Loretta

Ignatius Nolan (1978), son to Philip and Loretta

Josephine "Josie" Nolan Kelly (1980), daughter to Philip and Loretta

Margaret Anne Nolan (1985), daughter to Philip and Loretta

Consuela Reynolds, wife to Ignatius

Gerald McGinity, husband to Eileen

Brendan Kelly, husband to Josie

Most Reverend John Blackwood Ryan, Coadjutor

Archbishop of Chicago with Right of Succession—
but NOT Apostolic Administrator
Mary Kathleen Ryan Murphy, MD, sister to Archbishop
Ryan
Cardinal Sean Cronin, Archbishop of Chicago, boss to
Archbishop Ryan
Joseph Murphy Jr., nephew to Archbishop Ryan,
jularker to Margaret Anne

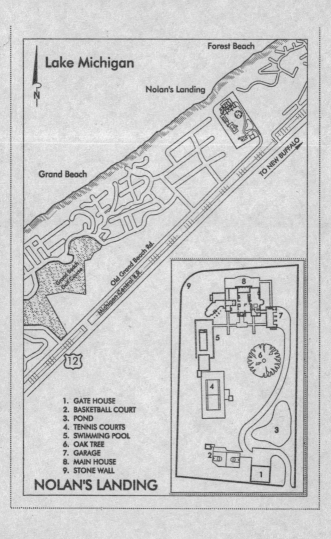

Lake Michigan

Forest Beach

Nolan's Landing

Grand Beach

TO NEW BUFFALO

Old Grand Beach Rd.

Michigan Central R.R.

Grand Beach Golf Course

12

1. GATE HOUSE
2. BASKETBALL COURT
3. POND
4. TENNIS COURTS
5. SWIMMING POOL
6. OAK TREE
7. GARAGE
8. MAIN HOUSE
9. STONE WALL

NOLAN'S LANDING

THE
BISHOP
AT THE
LAKE

1

"You're looking a little peaked these days, Blackwood."
Sean Cronin, Cardinal Prince of the Holy Roman Church
and by the patience of the apostolic see still Archbishop
of Chicago, leaned against the door-jamb of my study.

The game was afoot, Sherlock Holmes would have
said, only I had a sinking feeling that I was part of the
game. It was the nature of our relationship that I worry
about the Cardinal and he does not worry about me.
Moreover I didn't feel peaked at all. The Cardinal for
his part was the picture of health in his crimson robes.
A tall, trim man with white hair and a quick and charming smile, he looked like a Cardinal should look, a movie
star portraying, for example, Armand Jean du Plessis
Richelieu. Under the stern supervision of Nora Cronin
and his harmless Coadjutor Archbishop, he now consumed only one cup of coffee and one glass of Irish
whiskey per day. He also exercised every day and swam
in the Chicago athletic club twice a week. He was, I
venture to say, the healthiest-looking Cardinal in the
world.

"My sainted mother, the worthy Catherine Collins
Ryan, said I was born looking peaked."

"I suspect the dual obligations of a pastor at the

Cathedral parish and of my designated successor has been just a little too much."

Patently this was absurd. The pastor of any contemporary Catholic parish clings to his sanity only by his fingertips. However, as Milord Cronin well knew, the work of a Coadjutor Archbishop with the right to succession was nonexistent. He often said he would retire when he was eighty and I better pay close attention to the responsibilities that went with being Archbishop of Chicago. I would just as routinely respond to that if said Archbishop had the sense to appoint competent staff he would be able to play golf every afternoon in the week and spend three months in Florida as once was the custom among Chicago pastors.

He poured a cup of tea from my teapot and returned to the doorjamb.

"I'd look very bad," he observed with his manic grin, "if you die before I do. Therefore you really ought to go down to Grand Beach for a couple of weeks and get to know your family better."

"Arguably I already know my family too well."

Teacup in one hand he removed the computer output from my easy chair with the other and made himself comfortable—the Renaissance prince at his leisure.

"I am told that it is being said on LaSalle Street that your very good friend the Bishop of Laramie is currently in residence there."

"I barely know the virtuous Malachi Howard-Nolan, save for the intelligence that he is one of those persons who part his name in the middle, that he is alleged to speak with a noticeable upper-class English accent, and that he is in fact an Archbishop *ad personam* as we say in the mother tongue."

"There is a reason for that," Milord Cronin observed as he sipped his tea.

"Indeed."

"When I picked up my markers over in Rome and arranged the situation we currently have, among my other motives, was the fact that Malachi had set his sights on this archdiocese. I was not about to let that happen to Chicago or to the Church in the United States. Therefore, I intervened. Now he doubtless blames me for his failure to succeed here. I don't think he's quite given up yet."

"Heaven forefend," I murmured.

"So they gave him Laramie for which they intended you and the personal title of an Archbishop to soothe his pain. Malachi is, I suppose, harmless enough, despite his close relationship with the Companions of Jesus. Moreover, his campaign strategy has always been one of pernicious gossip and large gifts to curial officials such as a one-thousand-dollar mass stipend. He is in fact a pompous man as perhaps most of us are, but worse than that he's lazy. Chicago would be a reward for his great virtue and his lifelong service of the Church, by which he means the Roman Curia. He would enjoy wearing these goofy robes and parading around in a limousine but he wouldn't do any work. As I do not need to tell you, Blackwood, one must work very hard to keep this archdiocese from disappearing into the Chicago River."

"In which it would be freed of all its impurities by the good efforts of the Chicago Sanitary District as we used to call it."

"Moreover, you'd be walking down the streets of Laramie like a lonely cowpoke."

"This song suggests in fact that it would be the streets of Laredo."

"Regardless!" The Cardinal put aside his empty teacup and rose to his full seventy-four inches of height.

"Mal is up there at Grand Beach surrounded by the Ryan family and campaigning against you and Chicago and worst of all against me."

"I doubt that. Much more likely he is in the safe confines of Nolan's Landing, an enclave of the ineffable Spike Nolan. Grand Beach, or to call it by its more proper name Grand Beach Springs, has nothing to do with Nolan's Landing. We are loathe to associate with them and they don't associate with us."

"Reverse snobbery!" my Lord Cronin exploded. "Typical of your Southside Chicago Irish haute-bourgeoisie."

That comment was inappropriate and, sad to say, dangerously close to the truth.

"Besides," he continued, "as I've said before you wouldn't survive west of the Des Plaines River."

"As a point of fact," I responded, "you suggested that I wouldn't survive west of Bubbly Creek."

"That's why I want you to go down to Grand Beach and find out what Malachi is up to. Then you will report to me and I'll make calls to certain friends in Rome and that'll be the end of that."

"It may be that the new man in Rome will have some reservations about the deal you struck."

"The new man is on your side. In fact, he described you to me as being very interesting. That's the way you academics stick together."

I considered disputing the point but patently it would be a waste of my time. It would be similarly unwise to ask how I was supposed to spy on Nolan's Landing and its denizens from the perspective of Grand Beach. Perhaps I was supposed to send a mob of Ryan teenagers and young adults down the beach to assault Nolan's Landing in the dark of night.

That they would enjoy.

Milord Cronin turned at the doorway to my room and pointed his finger at me, the gesture which usually accompanies his final commands.

"Get down there and find out what Mad Malachi is up to and stop him. As long as I'm Archbishop of Chicago

I don't want somebody messing around with my archdiocese. Is that clear?"

"Blatantly."

"Good! See to it, Blackwood!"

2

"*It doesn't look* much like an English country home, does it, Uncle Blackie?" my nephew Joseph said, the last-born child of my sister, Mary Kate, and her long-suffering husband, Joe Murphy.

"No more than our dunes look like Sherwood Forest."

"It's a blend of a cottage on the lake and a fantasy about what an English country home was really like," he replied. "For one thing there are a lot more bathrooms in that house and central heating and air-conditioning. It's best just to admire it and laugh at it."

As a child and a teen Joseph Murphy was what his grandmother would have called a galoot—a large, awkward, quiet kid. He read a lot, failed in every sport he tried, and kept pretty much to himself. Sometime between seventh and tenth grade he became a man transformed, tall, strong, articulate, and a superb basketball player. First time I saw him after this transformation I scarcely recognized him. He had become six feet two inches of solid muscle and deep reflection. Scary fellow, I thought.

Now he is home from two Peace Corps years in Honduras, a serious, reflective, and a handsome black Irishman like his father, the ever patient Joseph Murphy,

MD—looking much like a suspect gunman of the Irish Republican Army.

"You've been in the house, Joseph?" I asked.

"Not exactly inside it, but they only use it for a month maybe six weeks at the most. So naturally Grand Beach kids sneak under the fence or climb over it and mess around on the grounds. We never did any damage. Our parents warned us that rich people can be very mean. We contented ourselves with hassling the two groundskeepers who live in one of the adjacent cottages. Their outside security system on the grounds is pretty good, the one of the house would be a challenge to the CIA."

"And they never joined the Grand Beach Social Club?"

"The real Grand Beachers would have been embarrassed."

"Not your mom and dad?"

"Nothing ever embarrasses them," he laughed. "They're cool."

"Patently."

"Spike Nolan has always been a little crazy people say. In 1938 when he was fifteen years old he went off to England on a tramp steamer, lied about his age, and joined the Royal Air Force. He fought in the Battle of Britain, collected a bushel of medals, married an impecunious young noblewoman, and ended up as a Group Captain, kind of like a colonel. He was twenty-three years old, my age. He worked at his father's company which made auto parts, inherited the company, and converted it to aviation electronics. Spike is more than a hero and more than just a crazy Irishman. It turns out that he is a genius. He intuited what kinds of equipment airplanes would need and was almost always one step ahead of his competitors. His latest invention is the plastic composite that Boeing uses in the 787. Aviation Electronics, as he still calls it, is now a multibillion-dollar worldwide enterprise. He owns two

Gulfstream jets, one for continental flights and one for intercontinental."

Joseph had done research on the Nolans. Fascinating.

It was a perfect Grand Beach day: temperature about eighty, clear blue sky, enough of a wind for the beach boats to be underway but smooth enough for the water skiers. The young people who had grown up in Grand Beach through the years felt that days like this were an anticipation of heaven.

"And he still runs the company?"

"Chairman of the Board, his son, the Archbishop's brother is the CEO. He's not a genius like Spike, but he's supposed to be competent."

My grandnephew knew a lot about the inhabitants of Nolan's Landing. But then he knew a lot about a lot of things.

"And the teenage English noblewoman?"

"Lady Anne Howard as she sometimes calls herself. Still very much alive. A lot of tragedy in their lives. Kids dying young, others running away, bad marriages, cocaine, embezzlement, the usual sort of stuff. It is said that they spoiled their sons and grandsons and overprotected their daughters and granddaughters."

"How did they do that?"

"They sent their young women to a convent school in Switzerland where the nuns kept a close eye on them and taught them good manners and French, Spanish, and Italian. Then when they came home to England or California or New York, wherever their home might have been, the family controlled their dating. Some of the husbands were already promising young men in the corporation. The young women were very docile and did what they were told. . . . Poor Spike."

"Where does the name come from?"

"Sean Patrick Ignatius Killian. He added the 'E' for Edward, his confirmation name. . . . They say his great-grandfather owned all the land between New Buffalo and Long Beach and began to sell it off at the beginning of the twentieth century. By 1950 that was a lot a capital to put into aviation electronics."

"Kind of a melancholy story, Joseph."

"A man like Spike Nolan, Uncle Blackie, comes along only once every couple of generations. From what I hear, no one in the family has ever been a match for him. Margaret may be an exception, too early to tell."

"Margaret Mary?"

"No, this one is Margaret Anne. The finishing school didn't have any effect on her. She came home and informed the family that she was going to go to university, indeed to the University of Notre Dame. Her mother and her sisters and her aunts were shocked—did she realize what kind of young men she would encounter there? They would pursue her for her money. There had been enough of that already in the family. Notre Dame was intolerable. There were a lot of nice young men in New York that she could date. She should stay away from drunken Chicago Irishmen at the Golden Dome. So her grandfather told her it was all right. She reminded him of Lady Anne as a teenager during the war. He rarely interfered in such decisions. So off to the Dome she went with her airplane."

"Airplane!"

"The Holy Cross fathers didn't know what to do. They never had a student who parked his or much less her Cessna at South Bend Airport. They forbade her to fly her friends to football or basketball games in the plane, though she had checked out on it. So when she was going to do that she simply hired herself a pilot. The Holy Cross fathers gave up."

"Sounds like a spoiled brat?"

"That image didn't last. She laughed, she sang, she danced, she wrote a hilariously funny column in the paper, she kidded the Holy Cross fathers, made fun of football players, and charmed everyone . . . also and for the record she's chaste and doesn't smoke or drink."

"A veritable *mulier fortis* . . . You knew her down there, Joseph?"

His response was smooth, too smooth by half, I thought.

"Everyone in Notre Dame knew Margaret, Uncle Blackie. Then Spike donated the new softball stadium. It was named after his wife who appeared for the dedication. Everyone said she looked just like Margaret. She seemed shy and quiet however. No one would use those words to describe her granddaughter."

"The toast of the Golden Dome?"

"I talked to her once or twice, no big deal, but she seemed vulnerable. Maybe that was the role she decided to play with me. Who knows what kind of games a woman like Margaret will play."

"What year is she in?"

"She graduated this year and informed the clan that she was going off to New Orleans to teach as an ACEr."

"When do Domers become ACErs?"

Joseph thought that was pretty funny.

"When they volunteer for the Alliance for Catholic Education. Well, when they're accepted. They're pretty strict about whom they accept."

"Ah!"

"They volunteer to teach at a Catholic School in the South for two years and take courses in education the summer before they begin to teach and the summer between the two years. They get a master's degree when they are finished."

"Ingenious."

"They get paid nine hundred dollars a month and live in their own little communities and pray together. There's lots of spiritual stuff in their training and during two years of work."

"Fascinating."

"Yeah, I figure the Holy Cross people are kind of setting up their own little religious order, limited terms of service, both genders, community life, that sort of thing."

"Ingenious."

The excellent Joseph had figured it out. Perhaps ACErs were an anticipation of what the religious life would look like in the next generation.

"Her parents hit the ceiling but she said she was going anyway and indeed she was going to fly her aircraft down there. Her mother and father told her she couldn't go; she told them that she was going anyway. Spike just kept his mouth shut or so they say. There is betting among her friends and people at the Dome on how long she will last."

"What is your bet?"

"I figure that Margaret will stay as long as she says she'll stay—for the whole two years."

"What will come next?"

"I hear that she wants to be a writer."

"Fascinating!"

The conversation was fascinating not just because Margaret Nolan did indeed seem like her legendary grandfather. My ex-galoot nephew knew more about her than I might have expected. Very interesting indeed. However, my purpose at Grand Beach was not to promote a romance in the Ryan clan but to spy on her uncle. I looked up again at the solitary house on a high dune and thought for a moment that there was something just a little sinister about it.

Joseph echoed my thought.

"There's probably a lot of tension and conflict up in that house, Uncle Blackie."

"Poor Margaret Anne."

"Yes, poor Margaret Anne."

Back at the apartment which his parents had added to their house at Grand Beach for me, I continued to reflect on Nolan's Landing and on the mysteries of human life. I didn't know yet what the tragedies were in Spike Nolan's nine decades of life. Perhaps sometimes he must've thought that he and his English war bride would be much happier if they had not come to the United States after the war, settled down in Chicago, and raised their children in a Chicago neighborhood. Maybe the success in their lives was also the cause of the tragedies about which Joseph had spoken. Milord Cronin would say that was the haute bourgeoisie South Side defending their own values. Tragedies are everywhere, even among the Grand Beach Irish as a walk down Lakeview Ave. would call to mind.

Poor Margaret, indeed.

I opened the dossier of notes on the Nolan clan which Mike Casey, sometime Superintendent of the Chicago Police Department and CEO of Reliable Security Inc., had collected for me. One couldn't tell the players without a program.

SPIKE—this acronym has become his real name and almost no one ever calls him Sean anymore, though the name has become popular these days—was born in 1923, attended St. Killian's grammar school in Chicago and St. Ignatius College (as it was called then, though in fact it had become a secondary school) for three years. Then without any warning to his parents and equipped with a couple of hundred dollars and his charming grin, he went to Canada and enlisted in the Royal Air Force. The RAF needed pilots desperately in the years before the war and wasn't too concerned about how valid Spike's passport might have been. He was trained in England just before the war began. He served in the RAF in the Battle of Britain at Fighter Command's Biggin Hill Station, a favorite target of the Luftwaffe Stuka bombers. In the noisy and hot, hectic summer days of August and

September of 1940 he earned a reputation as a fearless, not to say crazy, pilot. "I was too dumb to know any better," he later said. England awarded him the DSC and the DSO. He was recommended for the Victoria Cross, England's highest decoration, but the recommendation was never approved because of his citizenship and, he said, because of his Irish name.

Twenty years later the British government changed its mind—there had been a lamentable bureaucratic mistake—and awarded him the VC. He declined to accept the medal, though it was somewhere in one of his safes. He was not a hero of the Battle of Britain, he argued. "There were lots of heroes. I knew them well. And they are all dead."

He moved rapidly up the ladder of RAF promotions and ended the war as a Group Captain on the top RAF planning staff. For the first time in his life he was told he was brilliant. He didn't believe it until he heard the same thing from a very pretty and very young RAF rating named Anne Howard, a distant cousin of the Duke of Norfolk whose family had been the leaders of a minuscule English Catholic nobility since the Reformation. Lady Anne Howard (her real name, Blackwood, I'm not kidding) attended a convent school in England before she joined the RAF. She has therefore very little formal education and tends to be conservative in all matters, political and religious. Nonetheless, she seems to have been exactly what Spike Nolan needed in a wife—attractive, shrewd, loyal, and adoring. They were married immediately after VE Day in a civil ceremony. Anne was disowned by her parents and the Howard family. The Benedictine monk who served as the family priest refused to bless the marriage. However an RAF chaplain did preside at a Catholic marriage nine and a half months before the birth of their first son, Johnny. Spike still brags that it is thereby proven that they didn't have to marry.

Mike the Cop (as he is called in our family) had included a stack of clippings from newspaper and magazine articles, including pictures, about the "mercurial" (the favorite word of the writers of these pieces) rise of Spike Nolan. The thought occurred to me as I read the name that it could just as well been the name of a Capone-era gangster. The pictures of the young Spike and the young Anne and her newborn Johnny were very impressive, pictures filled with love.

The hero and his war bride and their adorable son were not welcome when they returned to the Brainerd neighborhood of Chicago and St. Killian's parish. His father and mother promptly disowned the whole lot of them, sight unseen. He should have served in the American Air Force, not the RAF, and he should never have married an English noblewoman. The couple had little money. The mustering-out pay for a Group Captain was nothing like that for a Colonel in the American army. They rented a small apartment over a drugstore at 87th and Loomis. Spike went to work as a baggage handler at United Airlines terminal at Midway Airport. That's when another mercurial rise began. In three months he was already a chief mechanic and thinking about electronics which would be needed for the new planes—the DC-6, which would shortly replace the DC-4, and then the jets which would come on line in the 1950s.

One Sunday afternoon when Spike was working overtime at Midway, Lady Anne put their son in a second-hand baby buggy they had bought for him and wheeled him across 87th Street into the tree-lined bungalow belt where Brainerd gradually blended with Beverly. The elder Nolans, both now in their sixties, were charmed by the grace of their only grandson and also by the poise and confidence of his pretty young mother.

When Spike returned to the apartment at 87th Street

he found his mother holding his son and his father beaming with joy. Anne, he would later admit, looked very proud of herself, "as well she should be."

Spike kept his job at Midway but studied very carefully the equipment and layout of the Brainerd Auto Parts Factory at 87th and Vincennes. Founded in the previous century to equip elegant carriages, the firm had prospered during the war by providing machine tools and parts for tanks, jeeps, and army trucks. They had converted smoothly to the postwar economy. Spike reasoned that, while they would continue to prosper in the enormous expansion of the automobile industry which was already occurring, the future for the firm was in the air. His father thought he was crazy but agreed to two brand-new engineers from Illinois Tech who knew something about airplanes, only on the condition that Spike would come back from Midway and work for the company.

"You'll have to pay me more than United Airlines does."

"You'll only be robbing yourself," his father said gruffly. "I'm leaving the whole mess to you when I die."

"The men in our family have long lives," Spike said confidently, "your father lived to be 90 . . . we're going to have another child and will need more room."

Spike promptly collected his wife and son and went looking for a house across the Rock Island tracks. In Beverly they found just what they wanted, a small cottage perched on a hill overlooking Longwood Drive, an old sand dune which is the highest point in Cook County.

His parents lived to see the birth of their granddaughter, Elizabeth, in 1948. The Sunday after her baptism in Christ the King's school-basement church, her grandfather and grandmother were killed in an automobile accident returning from the Notre Dame–Navy game. Spike was devastated. He and his parents were on the best terms they had been in his whole life: they now respected

*him as a bright and hardworking young man of whom
they could be proud, with the good taste to have married
a wonderful wife and father adorable children. They died
too young, he would often say in later life, knowing that
if they had lived Aviation Electronics, AVEL on the Dow,
would never have come into existence.*

*Spike's contemporaries from St. Killian's School and
St. Ignatius College were impressed by the transformation in his behavior. They gave the credit to his lovely
wife. Such changes happened to many of the veterans
of the war. But, as Anne would say when any of her
husband's friends remarked on his current abstemious
habits, "Oh, during the Battle of Britain Spike promised
God that if he survived he would not smoke or drink save
for the occasional glass of wine for the rest of his life.
Spike is a little crazy and I love him for it but he keeps his
promises."*

*Modesty prevented Anne from telling the whole story.
Spike made his promise to God only after he had fallen in
love with her the first time he'd seen her in the operations
room of his Spitfire squadron at Biggin Hill. He told himself that if he lived through the war he would take that
lovely young woman into his bed and stay with her for the
rest of his life. "To do that," he later admitted, "I had to
survive the war. So I made a deal with God."*

*They bought another home even higher up on Long-
wood Drive. They told their friends they would live there
for the rest of their lives. But that promise was made before Aviation Electronics purchased a much larger company in the British Midlands in 1955 and became a world
leader in its new field. Spike and Anne brought their family back to England and settled in a very elegant house in
Richmond on the River Thames. Spike commuted back
and forth from the new Heathrow Airport to Midway on
DC-6s and Lockheed Super Constellations with stopovers
at Shannon and Newfoundland.*

He promised his wife that as soon as the jets began to fly, the trip would be no more difficult than commuting to the loop on the Rock Island from the 91st Street Station. Their children went to English schools, English Catholic schools of the most conservative sort.

He poured all of the money his grandfather had gathered from the sale of the lots at Grand Beach into Aviation Electronics. He searched all over the country, and eventually all over Europe to find the most creative aeronautic engineers. He depicted for them his dream of what the company might do, and promised them that they would be part of it. He backed up the promise with a financial offer of salary and stock that the young men and the occasional young woman could not refuse. By 1954 Aviation Electronics was already ahead of the pack and would stay there for the next half century. Malachi was born in 1946, and Philip in 1950. Then a miscarriage and a bungled surgery ended Anne's reproductive years.

The family had spent a couple of weeks every summer in a rough and unheated summer cottage at Nolan's Landing. Annie once remarked that they all welcomed the peace and quiet of that little hut on the Michigan dunes. She went into something that we would call today postpartum depression after the miscarriage. Spike constructed his version of an English country house on the dune, though he had never been in an English country house. Some of the Grand Beach people would comment later when they saw it from the beach that it was a sort of Disneyland English country house. Anne pretended to be very grateful and came to love the place, especially since, as very minor nobility, she had never lived in an English country house as a child.

Spike's next major acquisition was a California company located only two miles from Caltech. So his trips from London to Chicago extended to Pasadena. Even a man of his agility and apparent immunity to jet lag had a *hard time keeping up with the pace. Then he decided to take the company public, which would produce enormous capital for further expansion and huge profits for his family. He insisted that the future now was in air safety. His lawyers and accountants argued that the corporation needed a headquarters which was not just in Spike's head as he wandered the world in scheduled jets or eventually in the company's private jets—two intercontinental Gulfstreams. He eventually qualified to pilot those planes, though he traveled with the usual crew of pilot and copilot.*

His corporate advisors suggested New York City, more or less equidistant to the plant in England and the one in California. So in 1960 the family moved to Manhattan. Spike rented four stories of a Midtown skyscraper for the company and assigned Annie the task of finding an apartment reasonably close to its new offices. The luxury apartment overlooking the East River she chose was too much for Anne. It was too beautiful, too expensive, crazy. But as she added, it's also Spike.

The accountants and lawyers who put the corporation together discovered that Spike's instincts had been sound. The components for the new corporation were in order. All they had to do was formalize it, produce organizational charts, and recommend promising young executives to head the various boxes on the charts.

The Nolan children were now cosmopolitans, part American, part English. Johnny, the oldest, was enthusiastically American. He planned to attend the United States Naval Academy in Annapolis, join the Marines, and become a Marine fighter pilot, following in his father's footsteps. Spike and Anne worried whether he would be as good a pilot in a modern jet as Spike had been in a Spitfire. Nonetheless, they sent him to a high school in Connecticut which specialized in preparing young men for Annapolis and the United States Navy.

Elizabeth, their second child and only daughter, could not identify with one country or the other and saw no need to do so. A strong-willed and strong-minded young woman, she announced to all that she was a sophisticated woman of the world and she identified with both countries and neither. Her mother sent her off to the convent school in Switzerland where the other young women in the family would eventually go. Malachi, who decided to be a priest when he was in prep school at Ampleforth Abbey in England, continued there and then enrolled at the Lateran University in Rome for his philosophy and theology. Spike made a donation to the archdiocese of Chicago and the Archbishop in return adopted Malachi as a student for the priesthood of the archdiocese.

Malachi was the opposite of his older brother. Johnny was a hard charger, a Marine before he reached the use of reason. Mal was inclined to be indolent, working only as hard as he had to. Spike and Anne were uneasy about his sexual orientation. However, he seemed to enjoy dancing with young women and romancing them casually. In fact, he barely escaped expulsion from Ampleforth because of an affair with a young woman from the countryside.

Philip, the youngest (named obviously after England's Prince Consort), was, like his father, a whiz at math. After graduation from the Benedictine Portsmouth priory school in Rhode Island, he enrolled at MIT. A young man with a keen mind, he anticipated that he would become his father's second in command in Aviation Electronics someday.

Anne would comment that once Spike owned a home he would so fall in love with it that he didn't want to sell it. "A house he thinks is very like a wife. You never want to let it go."

When they moved to New York, he also rented a home in the London suburb of Richmond. Later when the Aviation

Electronics site in Pasadena expanded, he bought a beach house on the Pacific Ocean.

"So we have five homes," Anne would admit, "one on the Pacific Ocean, one on the East River, one on the Thames, one on Lake Michigan, and one on Longwood Drive. When I wake up in the morning I'm not sure where I am."

Which was her favorite? "The one on Longwood Drive of course and after that the old house on Nolan's Landing where we all used to get together for a precious month in the summer."

I thought I heard melancholy in her words. Lady Anne, I believed, would have been perfectly willing to spend the rest of her life on Longwood Drive with her husband, a successful professional man, and her family in one piece going to Catholic schools in Chicago. She might even have wondered if such a scenario for their lives might have been far happier than their actual life course. Yet she loved Spike, and realized that he was a great man, and continued to adore him. If Aviation Electronics had remained a small Chicago firm and they still lived on Longwood Drive, they would've built a small house on Nolan's Landing and easily fit into the Grand Beach community. Well, that was not to be.

Mike Casey had provided a stack of pictures of the Nolan children as they were growing up, attractive little rug rats, handsome teens, and beautiful young adults, even the somewhat portly teenage Malachi, in his Ampleforth scholar's gown. More pictures showed Anne and Spike with Jackie and Jack Kennedy, one shot even on the Hyannisport sailing craft, four handsome young people with bright visions of the future.

Then the children's wedding pictures, Johnny in a Marine officer's blues with his blonde movie starlet bride, Martina Adams, in 1970; Elizabeth in 1968 with Edward

Macduff in front of the Chapel of Christchurch at Oxford, both of them in informal dress; Philip with Loretta Healy and a massive wedding party against a background of St. Patrick's Cathedral in 1975.

Elizabeth and her husband slipped into the counter-culture of the late 1960s and avoided all contact with her parents, whom they described as capitalist blood-suckers and war criminals, though they were only too happy to live off the income of the trust funds Spike had set up for all his children. That money enabled them to become heroin addicts, move to Katmandu, and die in one of the tiny back streets of the city in 1978 with their throats slit. Elizabeth had been raped before she was killed.

Her brother Johnny was already dead for six years, missing in action over Hanoi in 1972, survived by his wife, Martina, and his six-month-old son, Martin. Martina, now described as a "movie star," demanded that the memorial service be in Los Angeles. In a hysterical scene at a Presbyterian Church she blamed his father for her husband's death. "He was a reckless flyer because he was trying to live up to your fucking reputation," she screamed. "Now he's a fucking hero. Does that make you fucking happy?"

When they returned to Chicago, the Nolans organized a discreet memorial service in the new Christ the King Church.

Despite his contacts with military aviation, Spike was never able to learn the details of Johnny's disappearance. All the Navy would tell him was that his son was missing in action. He continued to be missing in action for thirty-five years.

Six months later Martina remarried, a Hollywood agent by whom she had a daughter she named Taylor. The agent was not successful in promoting her career, but he didn't mind living off her trust fund money. When Martina Adams found out that he kept a couple of mistresses, she dumped him and together with Marty and Taylor moved in with the lead singer from a rock band, a liaison which was never formalized by marriage. Her next relationship was with a man twenty years older than she, a major producer of independent films. Eventually they were married and according to reports from Spike's friends in California they seemed reasonably happy. Spike and Anne never saw their grandson again. He went to UCLA for a couple of years and then joined the California State Police. He rebuffed all attempts by his grandparents to get in touch with him. Like his mother, however, he continued to spend trust fund money, though very cautiously.

Malachi was ordained the same year by a cardinal in Rome, returned briefly to Chicago, turned down a parish assignment, went back to Rome to enroll in the School of Noble Ecclesiastics, which trains priests for the papal diplomatic service. He rented a large and comfortable apartment in the Piazza Cita Leonina where he entertained lavishly. He didn't quite make it into the diplomatic service but became a minutante, a clerk, in one of the curial congregations. He returned to Chicago occasionally to display his monsignorial purple and whisper the latest Roman gossip. He was mostly English but partly American. One of his favorite jests was "I am too much a Brit for the Yanks and too much of a Yank for the Brits . . . to tell the truth I rather like it that way."

He bounced around the various congregations, and moved up incrementally in the curial bureaucracy. He became more and more like an Anglican in his deportment if not in his affiliation. He served in a minor role during papal visits to England and Ireland. He confided to his parents and family at one of the reunions at Nolan's Landing that he would soon be named a bishop.

In fact, in 2002, later rather than sooner, he was named "substitute" (undersecretary) of a minor Roman congregation and waited eagerly for a major appointment in the United States, quite possibly, he suggested to his parents, Chicago, when they finally decided to get rid of Sean Cronin. Unwisely perhaps, he shared his prediction with his priestly friends in Chicago, a small group of men who routinely reported to Malachi Cardinal Cronin's alleged misbehavior, especially his close relationship with his foster sister and sister-in-law Nora.

Where, I wondered, did Mike the Cop pick up that choice bit of information? I never heard it. My Lord Cronin surely had picked it up. Perhaps it didn't bother him because he simply didn't care. Yet he knew who the despisers were in his own archdiocese and probably warned them in a late-night phone call.

The sixties were a bad time, Spike would occasionally remark. Those of us who had kids growing up in that era didn't know what we should do. I guess we blew it. His good wife, however, disagreed. They had free will, she insisted, they knew what they were doing.

Philip, their last child, became their pride and joy. He graduated from MIT with honors, went on to earn a PhD in aeronautical engineering at Caltech, and became his father's right-hand man in Aviation Electronics, a coconspirator in all his father's visionary schemes. He was, truth to tell, something of a nerd, devoid of Spike's wit and flare. He also became a major contributor to the Republican Party but never argued politics with his father because as he said to his wife, Loretta—also a Republican, "I would certainly lose."

Spike credited him with major responsibility for the development of composite material which would replace aluminum on the fuselages of jet planes and notably decrease the weight and the fuel costs of the jets of the twenty-first century. In 1999 Spike stepped down as CEO and Phil succeeded him. Spike remained Chairman of the Board. Aviation Electronics' value on the New York Stock Exchange did not waver. Spike and Anne continued their philanthropy to worthy causes all around the world especially if they were Catholic. Spike favored the more liberal Catholic causes and Anne the more conservative but they did not argue about the grants, at least not in public. Notre Dame was a frequent beneficiary of his generosity—including the Anne Howard Nolan Softball Stadium. Anne favored the various Catholic charity services around the country especially in big cities like Chicago and Los Angeles. Both contributed heavily to Latino projects and strongly supported immigration reform. Spike refused to serve on the board at Notre Dame but accepted their honorary degree with a proud announcement: "Even though I didn't graduate from high school, now I am an educated man, ain't I?"

In the next ten years Phil and Loretta produced four grandchildren much to the delight of the grandparents— Eileen in 1976, Ignatius in 1978, Josephine in 1980, and finally Margaret Anne in 1985. The kids' parents exercised much closer control over these four children than Anne and Spike had over their offspring, though as Spike told his wife it was easier to control kids because the 1960s were over.

Iggy chose Fordham for his college and picked up his law degree at Fordham Law School while he worked in the city courts in New York. Then he joined the law department in the Aviation Electronics skyscraper. Eileen, Josephine, and Margaret attended the same convent school in Switzerland, now somewhat updated, which Aunt Elizabeth had attended. The two older sisters showed no particular inclination to continue their education or to develop career paths of their own. They both married, in the year after their twenty-fifth birthdays, two promising young men from Aviation Electronics selected by their father and mother and brother. Eileen's husband was Gerald McGinity from Fordham and Harvard Business School. Josie married Brendan Kelly from Holy Cross and MIT. Ignatius waited till he was twenty-eight to marry and chose as his spouse Consuela Reynolds, Josie's convent school roommate. In each relationship, the grandparents sensed that there had been some casual fornication leading up to the engagements and weddings, no public co-habitation and no pregnancies or known abortions. The young people were too cautious to risk rocking the boat, for fear it might sink. The three couples were handsome and looked quite lovely in their wedding pictures in The New York Times, *with St. Patrick's in the background. All three young women were spectacularly beautiful, the Nolan women, like their mother, statuesque redheads.*

"I think that Phil and I have done a good job preparing for the future of the corporation," Loretta whispered to Anne and Spike at Josie's wedding reception.

Both grandparents made sounds of agreement, something that they had learned long ago to do with Loretta.

"They're nice kids," Spike said as a limousine was driving them back to their apartment on the East River. "Yet to tell you the truth, Annie love, they're just a little dull."

"Rather," his wife agreed.

"We didn't sleep together," he continued. "Through no fault of my own, I might add. Yet I think we were crazy in a sense that they would never begin to understand."

"Different times in different places, my darling. The world seemed much different in the ready room at Biggin Hill. They'll have their own challenges."

In due course Eileen and Josie both produced great-grandchildren and at the present moment Consuela is

*alleged to be in an early stage of pregnancy. All three
agree that they will have two children at the most.*

*Margaret Anne Nolan is another matter. She was the
only woman in the family history thus far who insisted on
attending a university after she returned from Switzerland.
She was adamant that she would go to the Golden Dome
and would do so after her twenty-first birthday with the
income from her trust fund whether her family approved
or not. There was shock among the other women in the
Nolan clan at this decision. The Nolan women do not need
a university education. Look what happened to your Aunt
Elizabeth when she went to Oxford. You want to end up in
a back street in Katmandu raped and with your throat
slit?*

"I don't do drugs and I'm not going to Katmandu."

*"You go to Notre Dame, you'll fall in love with some
drunken South Side Chicago Irishman."*

*My source does not tell me how Spike Nolan reacted to
that slur. However, the bias against higher education for
women is so obsolete that one wonders why it was pushed
so strongly for Margaret. Probably because she was so
clearly a dissident and a trouble seeker. Nothing good
could possibly come from granting her the freedom of
contemporary college life even if the college was Notre
Dame, especially if it were Notre Dame.*

*Spike made the final decision, as he always did in fam-
ily matters, with the advice and consent of his wife who
is usually silent in these battles.*

*Anne responded without hesitation. "If it hadn't been
for the war, I would have gone up to Oxford."*

*"If Margaret wants to go to college let her go to col-
lege," Spike agreed. "I've always regretted that I never
had a chance to get higher education."*

*"You've done very well," Loretta said, "for someone
who did not go to college."*

"The final decision is up to her parents," Spike said

quietly. "Still, if you want to know what I think, I think
Margaret belongs among the fighting Irish."

How had Superintendent Casey obtained the information contained in the last several paragraphs? His Park
Avenue contacts must be very good indeed. He had added
a report on the financial status of the family.

Spike was clever enough to create generous trust funds
for all his children. The trust funds have grown enor-
mously in the previous half century. The income from
them is sufficient that his children and eventually his
grandchildren probably would not have to work an hon-
est day for the rest of their lives. There were no strings
attached to these trust funds. Martina Nolan would con-
tinue to live off the family treasures as long as she was
alive. When she died the fund would go to Marty Nolan.
After his death the fund would dissolve. Moreover the
fund provided for a generous monthly payment to Marty
while his mother was still alive. Thus the children of Phil
and Loretta were already receiving a monthly payment
and could look forward to a nice inheritance at sometime
in the future.
The Feds, IRS, and SEC especially kept pushing Spike,
mostly because he was there to push. But their much-
publicized investigations, detailed at great length in the
pages of The Wall Street Journal, *never produced any re-*
sults, though a couple of them are still ongoing. Ignatius
had a tendency to gamble and in fact had run up some se-
rious debts. But Consuela and his mother had delivered
ultimatums and he had quit, temporarily perhaps, gam-
bling and even joined Gamblers Anonymous. His mother
and his grandmother continued to worry about him. Josie
went on occasional shopping binges. If there were any in-
fidelities in the family they are well-kept secrets. There is
no reason to believe that there is any serious pathology,

much less any criminal records among the surviving
members of the Nolan clan.

I closed Mike Casey's dossier—an American family
history told with vigor and imagination by an American
storyteller, even if he were a cop and a painter. I didn't
need all this information. It was the sort of report that
Mike would have made if I was trying to understand a
murder. I wasn't embarking on an investigation of a
crime. I probably knew more than I wanted to know
about the summer residents of Nolan's Landing, Richmond, Ocean Beach, New York City, and Longwood
Drive. However, some of the background might be useful
in understanding what Mal Nolan, or Mal Howard-Nolan
was up to. Besides, in the event of romance between a
younger member of our own clan and one from their clan,
I might be called upon to render an opinion, not that my
opinion would necessarily influence any decisions. Mary
Kathleen Ryan Murphy and Anne and Peggy Anne Nolan,
should they ever happen to meet on the beach or somewhere else, would instantaneously bond against all possible opponents. I was prepared to remark, "It takes one
shite-kicker to know another."

3

"*I presume you* will not have to wait long for your pallium," Archbishop Malachi Howard-Nolan informed me as we sipped our drinks and pondered the meaning of the Lake's glittering silver sheet beneath us.

"I lay awake at night dreaming about that priceless woolen stole," I said with a modest irony he would miss.

"It must be difficult," he said with his trademark genial grin, "to have been Sean Cronin's errand boy for all these years."

"I was barely able to cope."

My conscience, never an insistent dimension of my soul, murmured that I should be ashamed of myself for pulling the archiepiscopal leg of such a willing victim.

The Archbishop and angel to the church of Laramie is a large man, not obese but big and overweight. He was dressed in garb appropriate for leisure time in the country—light blue slacks, dark blue blazer, and a yellow shirt opened at the neck. He moved with the grace appropriate to its office, solemn, ponderous, stately, even if Laramie was only something more than the cow town it had been in the time of Wyatt Earp and similar distinguished personages. He spoke with the drawl which marks the English upper class (and offends me, Irish nationalist that I am). One of his priest admirers in Chicago, a man not without some wit, remarked to me it sounded so authentic that he's gotta be faking it. He was smoking a large cigar which had Cuba written all over it and sipping slowly from a shining martini glass. His porcine face and self-satisfied manner suggested that he knew what was really happening in Rome. He was a man who had spent much of his priestly life in the service of the Roman Curia, knew all the gossip, and was willing to whisper it to you, so long as you kept it to yourself.

Not exactly the kind of man who would fit in with the real and would-be cowboys in Laramie.

I on the other hand was clad in my usual solemn high-summer clothes—jeans, a black T-shirt, and Chicago White Sox cap and White Sox windbreaker. The dinner invitation on the telephone from Spike Nolan's secretary said dress would be casual. She didn't quite mean that casual but since the Nolans were unquestionably the wealthiest family at whose home I had ever supped it was my solemn obligation to take a stand for South Side Irish populism.

"I hear it said," Malachi sighed, "that Chicago is a terrible mess. I'm afraid you'll have to clean it up and that will be hard, you being a native Chicagoan."

"That's what they always say about Chicago," I sighed just as loudly. "I don't suppose there's any more of a mess than it's always been."

"Then there is the problem of a woman. It's a shame but I don't think there's any way it can be kept quiet after he's dead."

"What woman?"

He was talking about Nora Cronin, the Cardinal's foster sister and sister-in-law.

I sighed again.

Malachi was a nasty man. From his redoubt here or on the shore of Lake Michigan he was collecting information about the archdiocese of Chicago and Cardinal Cronin to report to his friends in Rome and say that it was a shame that they had not forced Cronin to resign on his seventy-fifth birthday. It was also unfortunate that they had accepted the idea of a coadjutor with right to succession. Bishop Ryan, he would say, was a nice little man, very clever but not the one to clean up the mess. It's too bad something can't be done about the situation.

He would talk to a few laypeople and a few priests in Chicago and collect comments from them that would support his slander. It would all be matter-of-fact and very sad and at least some people in Rome would take him seriously and regret that they had not sent him to Chicago as Bishop. I was surprised that he was so stupid as to display his cards in the game to me. He must have thought that I would not be on the phone to Milord Cronin that very evening.

His schemes wouldn't work. Sean Cronin's clout in Rome was too powerful to be destroyed by insidious passive-aggressive gossip. But he could create problems that my Lord Cronin did not need.

I was not looking forward to the responsibility of becoming Archbishop of Chicago but I was not about to permit this creep to get any closer to Chicago than the Michigan dunes.

We were sitting in the library of Nolan's Landing, an English manor house built on the dunes of Lake Michigan. The manor house effect was weakened by massive picture windows on the fronts and the sides of the building. It was necessary to pretend that you were an English country squire but on the other hand you didn't want to lose the views of the splendid Lake, a compromise that I found acceptable, given Spike's intention to please his wife.

Since we don't want to depend on the unpredictable Lake for swimming we also spoil the manor house effect with a large pool, not quite Olympic size, just outside the library window and one floor down. The women of the house, some of them quite attractive, had arrayed themselves in various forms of dress and undress—all arguably modest, but not unrevealing—and smeared their trim and disciplined bodies with thick layers of sunscreen. As my sister Mary Kathleen Ryan Murphy insisted, you don't see many obese rich women. They have the money to spend on trainers and diet managers.

They too were sipping beverages, brought to them by a Latino servant woman in the usual black dress and white apron. They huddled under umbrellas in case the sunscreen did not protect their carefully nurtured skins from injury. Only one of them, a very young woman, was attacking the water with a ferocious and graceful crawl. This one I assumed was the legendary Margaret about which my nephew had spoken. Interesting.

"So I'm afraid you won't have an easy time of it," Malachi continued. "Still it's Chicago and you'll get a Red Hat almost immediately, won't you?"

"I might surprise them and decline it."

He was horrified.

"Blackie," he said, "that simply isn't done. No one refuses the Red Hat."

We were not alone in the room. A young, dark-skinned priest in neatly fitting clerical suit had been introduced to me as Malachi's "chaplain," an Anglican term for the bishop's secretary. Come to think of it there was a touch of the Anglican about Malachi, including the purple sox. Most Catholic Bishops had given up that privilege long ago. The so-called chaplain responsibilities included refilling Malachi's martini glass whenever that was required. He looked like an Aztec priest about to cut out the heart of a cowering captive. His face seemed frozen in marble, his eyes glared with implacable hatred. Doubtless one of these Companions of Jesus.

"Lovely day, isn't it?" Malachi asked. "I'd like nothing

more than to go down there and walk on the beach. However, I'm allergic to hornet bites and this seems to be a season for swarms of hornets."

He spoke in the aggrieved tone of someone who was aware that the world is conspiring against him but will nonetheless bear that conspiracy bravely.

Then he returned to his principle theme—the mess in Chicago.

"There is of course the sexual abuse problem you will have to deal with when you finally replace Cronin. I'm told by my friends in Chicago that many priests have been unjustly accused and that there is general dissatisfaction among the laity and the clergy over this fact. There is even talk of a systematic appeal to Rome to reopen the cases of those who have been expelled from the priesthood. They argue that there is no room for forgiveness in a church governed by Sean Cronin."

Why was the man doing my work for me? Why was he outlining his plan to replace both the Lord Cronin and his unworthy coadjutor? Was he so confident of a success that he felt no need to keep it a secret? Or was he an incorrigible gossiper who could not resist the impulse to share the gossip with anyone who would listen?

"The zero tolerance policy was adopted by the American bishops and approved by the CDF," I replied. "I hardly think the present Pope will reverse himself."

"The new Pope believes strongly in forgiveness," he lectured me. "We will have to see what happens."

Outside the swimmer climbed out of the pool, a lithe young woman in a modest brown two-piece swimsuit. This was doubtless the fabled Margaret, radiating the predicted vigor and determination. She wrapped a large towel around her shoulders, seized a Diet Coke can from the cooler, walked over to the umbrella where her grandmother was sitting, kissed her on the forehead, and then strode out of the pool area and back into the house.

"That is Margaret Nolan," the Bishop of Laramie informed me. "The youngest child of my brother Phil and his wife Loretta. She is a serious problem to her parents. As you surely noted, she is quite innocent of modesty."

"I am told that she greatly resembles her grandmother."

"Her grandmother is a distinguished English noblewoman far superior to that little hoyden . . . however, I do not want to bore you any further with what people are saying about Chicago these days. I'm sure you will welcome an opportunity in another archdiocese where you would not inherit Sean Cronin's sad legacy."

In his mind, befuddled now by a few too many sips of martini, his fantastical plot had already become an accomplished fact.

"Every diocese has an imperfect legacy. In my experience Chicago's is far better than most of the other dioceses of the same size."

"The great problem there, as my Chicago friends tell me, is that Cronin has ruled far too long and the extension of his rule has created very serious problems."

The other women at poolside were gathering up their clothes, their lotions, and their drinks and adjusting their swimsuits with a tug here and a tug there to improve the illusion of modesty. They were strikingly attractive women and fully aware of that truth. After the others had left, a diminutive white-haired woman in a light blue shift emerged from under a vast red umbrella, and, book in hand, exited the pool area with elegant grace. Doubtless this was Anne Howard, long ago an RAF rating in a frantic operations room at the Biggin Hill station just outside of London. I would dearly love to know what she thought of these womanly descendents. However, she would doubtless be too discreet to express her opinions to anyone.

"Well, enough on the boring subject of ecclesiastical politics, Blackie. It is time to prepare for our preprandial drinks. I should warn you that Father permits only one drink before supper. He is rather proud of his own virtue in these matters and expects the rest of us to imitate him. We Catholics are not Puritans are we? . . . If you don't mind waiting a half hour here in the library I will come to escort you to the drawing room. . . . Father Alfonzo, would you accompany me to our rooms?"

✓The Archbishop *ad personam* of Laramie wavered a bit as he rose from the chair and left the room, Father Alfonzo supporting his arm. Not only was he a gossiper and a clumsy conspirator, he was also a souse. His schemes were fantasies spun out of alcohol-induced dreams. Nonetheless, he still might be dangerous. In his martini-dulled brain, he had created a picture of the archdiocese of Chicago that was obscenely false. Even if Milord Cronin was not willing to make a fight (a most improbable supposition), his harmless, ineffectual, and almost invisible little coadjutor would mount the barricades on Michigan Avenue.

I must be in my declining years if such a small jar of the creature would turn me into a raving militant. What was it the French said at Verdun as they were destroying a whole generation of young men? They (the horrid Hun) shall not pass!

No way, not at all, *never*!! I waited forty minutes for my brother from Laramie to reappear. Then a young woman in white slacks and a blue shirt with a Golden Dome emblem on it appeared in the door of the library.

"Hi, Archbishop Blackie, my Gramps said I should take you down to the drawing room for drinks."

"You are, I take it, the legendary Margaret."

"That's one of my names. I'm also Margie, Margo, Margaret Anne, and Peg. I don't mind all the names, because they make me more of a complicated woman than I really am but would like to be."

"And that you are capable of such a thought indicates

that you are a more complicated woman than you really are."

"I love it! I totally love it! An Irish bull. I knew that four years at Notre Dame would really expand my horizons!"

"Should you be a member of my clan, you would certainly be called Peggy Anne."

"I'd like that!"

She did not affirm whether she would like to be called Peggy Anne or like to be a member of the clan Ryan. Perhaps both.

"Remember, Archbishop Blackie, Gramps says only one drink or conversation at supper becomes too wild."

"So I have been told, though I hear there is another reason for his restraint in the drink taken."

"Isn't that a neat story, Archbishop Blackie? He promised that he would never drink more than a glass of wine and not smoke at all if he lived through the war and married Gramms. Totally cool."

"Apparently she was worth it."

"For sure! . . . Gramps, here's Archbishop Blackie!"

I should not have been surprised by Spike Nolan, but I was. He was a white-haired, delightful leprechaun, with dancing blue eyes, an impish grin, and a quick, disarming smile. The thought flashed through my head, occasionally inclined to Romanticism, that I'd fly a Spitfire behind that man.

And be shot down the first day.

"Archbishop! It's good of you to come down the beach and join us for supper!" he said as he shook hands vigorously. It would have been an insult to his energy to describe him as spry. He might be eighty-three years old, but his enthusiasm would keep him forever young. Doubtless he and Margaret Anne got along just fine.

"I'm afraid, Group Captain, that I didn't come down

the beach but drove over in that retro cruiser which de-
files your parking area."

A memory of the groundskeeper who had met me at
the electric gate which blocked the entrance to Nolan
flashed into my head. A lean, bald man with haunted
eyes, he had stared suspiciously at me.

"Archbishop Ryan," I told him.

"Not a very distinguished car for an Archbishop," he
had said. "But you're only a Coadjutor Archbishop, so I
suppose it's all right."

Was he joking? Hard to tell from his frozen face.

"With the right of succession," I added.

The gate swung open. I heard a sound from him that
might have been a laugh. Then Spike's voice recalled me
to the dining room.

"This is my most recent wife, Annie. She runs the
family of course."

Anne Howard-Nolan was wearing a light blue dress,
not unlike the shift she'd worn at poolside, set off with
discreet—and very expensive—silver jewelry.

I was enveloped in a sweet smile.

"You're most welcome, Bishop Ryan," she said, as she
tried to kiss the bishop's ring that I was not wearing. "I
believe your family lived on Longwood Drive so we
must've been almost neighbors."

"You have my sympathies, Lady Anne," I said, kissing
her hand. "My late father, Ned Ryan, always said that it
is not an easy thing to be surrounded by the South Side
Irish."

Her husband laughed.

"She's always said that our days in Christ the King
parish were the happiest of our lives."

In the back of my head I heard the drone of the Spitfires as they took off from Biggin Hill more than sixty
years ago and Anne Howard was a sixteen-year-old RAF

rating charmed by an Irish-American hero for whom she recited the rosary to herself as the aircraft took off. She was still slender, still pretty, still charming, and still very much in love with her crazy pilot.

"What can I get you to drink, Archbishop?" Spike asked me.

"I'm sure the conversation tonight will be brisk so I will have nothing more than a glass of iced tea, if you don't mind."

"Very wise decision, very wise indeed! Margaret Anne, will you find a large glass of iced tea, surely of the spiced kind, for the good Archbishop, while I introduce him to the rest of the family?"

The women in the family (except for the youngest and the oldest) had made a collective decision that they would wear thin, loosely fitting, summer dresses which fell to their ankles. Such garments require little in the way of underwear and are both cool and comfortable (though the house was air-conditioned) while at the same time provide discreet hints of well-preserved figures. Four such women in the room at one time suggested a spirit of summer abandon in which almost anything might happen, but only if one were on the French Riviera and characters in a French film.

Phil and Loretta, now in their middle fifties, were living proof of Mary Kate's dictum that the rich don't become obese. A tall, solid couple, with disciplined bodies and radiant good health they had designed themselves, with the advice of expensive hairdressers and cosmeticians, to appear ten years younger than their chronological age. They were the heirs of the firm and the assistant patriarch and matriarch of the clan. I suspected that Loretta at any rate resented her secondary position. They were polite to me of course. After all I was a Catholic Archbishop. But they were not particularly friendly. I didn't look like an Archbishop and didn't act like one, not that their own was much better. It would have been quite a feather in their caps if Malachi had succeeded my Lord Cronin.

Ignatius and Consuela were next, he perhaps the second in line after his father. Yet they both seemed silly little blond people, she giggling over her pregnancy and he clutching his drink like he was afraid Spike would take it away from him. All the other men save for Sean Cronin's trusted espionage agent were wearing sport coats. Iggy however wore only a short-sleeved sport shirt and kept his arm around his wife's expanding waist through the whole cocktail hour. They regarded me, I feared, as someone who would make the dinner even more boring than it ordinarily would be.

Eileen and Josie, like their mother, were striking, full-bodied women with long red hair and dangerous eyes. Their husbands, admitted to Aviation Electronics and the Nolan family by marriage, were quiet and good-looking and obviously very intelligent, carefully chosen consorts for the two archduchesses who were expected to say very little. Unless my experience with the lower levels of the Catholic aristocracy had completely deceived me, both these marriages would someday be in jeopardy, though not unsalvageable if Loretta stayed out of the conflict, which seemed improbable.

"Might I ask you a question, Archbishop Ryan?" Ignatius asked. "What exactly can a Coadjutor Archbishop do?"

Smart-mouth little punk wanted to put me on the spot. Not the first one to think that the bumbling little cleric was a pushover.

"He can and indeed must do many things—preside over the Eucharist, hear confessions, such as they are these days, visit hospitals, officiate at weddings, minister to the sick, bury the dead, console the bereaved, pay the bills, keep the records, answer the phone, encourage the lay staff. He never lacks tasks to keep him out of trouble."

"But any priest can do those things, can't he?"

"Can and should."

"Then how are you different? You don't have the responsibilities like Uncle Archbishop has in Laramie."

"I have the greatest respect for the Bishop of Laramie and his great responsibilities. In Chicago, I am like the backup quarterback. I wait on the sidelines until there's an emergency. Then, doubtless terrified, I try to do my best."

"The backup quarterback is always desperate to get his chance."

"The backup Archbishop, if he has any sense, knows how unqualified he is in comparison with the starter he has to replace. Otherwise he wouldn't be backup."

"Bravo!" Spike Nolan exclaimed.

"Bravo," his brother Malachi agreed, though I doubt that he knew what I had said.

Just then Peggy Anne appeared with a huge glass of iced tea, lemons and limes impaled on the rim, saving the day for her brother Ignatius, whom I was about to ask what was the point of his question.

"You and your grandmother seem to be violating the dress code." I suggested.

"Mom loves to flaunt herself," she replied. "None of them are, like, sensitive enough to get it that Gramms disapproves. She's like, it makes the dining room look like a bordello. And I'm like, Gramms, how do you know what a bordello looks like? And she just laughs and tells me how wonderful I am."

My brother, the angel to the church of Laramie, had appeared supported by his chaplain. He ordered another martini, which was provided by the servant in charge of the bar, despite Spike Nolan's obvious disapproval.

"Gramms goes, that kind of dress is perfectly accept-able on the beach or on the deck or at poolside, but not in a dining room that's air-conditioned.

"And I go, Gramms, you are just an old-fashioned Puritan like Gramps. And she goes, do you really think so Margaret Anne and I go no way. I've seen those pictures of you at San Tropez. And she just sniffs and laughs."

No one paid any attention either to their Archbishop or to his chaplain. The stone face of the latter displayed total and systematic disapproval.

"I think it's time that we go in for supper," Spike announced. "Archbishop Ryan, at the insistence of my daughter-in-law, we eat healthy here—a green salad, and a very healthy omelet, which by way of compromise will include ham, cheese and mushrooms."

Omelet for supper! They had to be kidding!

"I'm supposed to take you into supper, Archbishop Blackie," Peggy Anne informed me. "Besides the very healthy omelet, they plan to make a meal out of me. You better stay out of it. I can take care of myself."

I reserved judgment on that.

The dining room was pure Disney, an English country dining room right out of *Upstairs, Downstairs* or the Trollope novels or Jane Austen on three sides. The fourth side was a sweeping panoramic view of Lake Michigan turning silver with whitecap frosting as the sun raced toward the horizon and the Chicago skyline. I'm afraid I gasped.

"I know it's kind of gross," Peggy whispered, "but it's also totally gorgeous."

"Totally," I agreed.

"It will not be necessary to bring in your drinks to supper. We have put several bottles of Anita Chablis on ice—from our vineyard in California. You may note, Archbishop Ryan, that it compares favorably to the Chablis from the Cakebread Vineyard . . . Will you say grace, please?"

Everyone seemed to know their assigned place at the table. Peggy Anne led me to a place next to her own. Her Gramms was on the other side of me. The Alpha and the Omega, I thought as I began my prayer.

"This is a grace that is attributed to Saint Brigid of Kildare, who may not have been a priest but seems to have been fully convinced that she was a bishop ... Bless the poor, bless the sick, bless the whole human race, bless our food, bless our drink, and all our families please embrace. Amen."

Those around the table responded with a fervent "Amen."

The green salad was served first. It was innocent of salad dressing. Spike Nolan made a face. This was not his idea of healthy eating. The white wine was excellent. I sipped from my Irish crystal glass cautiously.

"Might I ask you a question, Group Captain, about the Battle of Britain?"

"Spike."

"Blackie."

"No one asks about that anymore, Blackie," he said with a manic grin. "It was a long time ago and nobody cares much about it anymore. So I'll be happy to answer your question."

"As I consider the received wisdom from such informed sources as the History Channel it seems that Hitler quit too soon and that if he had persisted longer he would have won the Battle of Britain, and England, its army devastated by the evacuation at Dunkirk, would not have been able to stop him."

"And you tend to disagree with the received wisdom?" he asked, his blue eyes sparkling with mischief.

"I know that the Luftwaffe's loss of aircraft was half again higher than yours, that you were producing three aircraft for every two they manufactured, and that their aircrew losses were seven times higher than yours—two thousand one hundred versus three hundred approximately."

"I think I knew most of those three hundred men. They still come to me at night when I'm asleep."

"They're usually friendly spirits now aren't they, love?"

"Usually."

Around the dinner table there was solemn silence. Perhaps there never had been any family conversation about those days. The Ryan family had never spoken around the table about the Battle of Leyte Gulf, where my father and his squadron of destroyer escorts had turned back a flotilla of Japanese battleships.

"If Hitler therefore wanted a campaign against Russia, he had to protect the Luftwaffe from even heavier losses. Moreover, one may be able to load a tank on a barge or an artillery piece and a team of horses that pulls it onto another barge. But, how does one unload such material on what England with some exaggeration deigns to call beaches, especially if you have no experience with amphibious operations?"

"You have to capture a seaport, presumably Southampton," Spike said softly.

"One has had considerable success with one's paratroops in Norway and Holland. Therefore one mobilizes paratroops in France and flies them across the channel in planes and gliders and seizes Southampton. What could be more simple?"

"What could be more simple indeed?"

"However, Hitler did not know that your people at Betcheley Park had broken the Enigma code and would be able to inform the RAF of the day and the hour that invasion force would take to the air. Nor did he really believe that your radar picked up German planes as soon as they left their airports. I assume that the RAF was prepared."

"Did you read somewhere, Blackie, that I was part of the planning for that eventuality?"

"No, but I kind of suspected."

"We would have thrown every fighter aircraft we had into the battle to stop them." As he spoke, Spike Nolan's face began to glow and his voice became animated. "We would've attacked in groups, not wings, three hundred planes in each wave, with defensive cover in the air above us against the 109s. It might have been the end of fighter command, but England would have been saved. We would've hit them while they were taking off at dawn, we would have shot them down before they reached the channel. These weren't bombers, these were slow and unarmed transport planes carrying parachutists or towing gliders. We would've suffered a lot of losses but theirs would've been much worse. We would probably have finished them off over the channel. And what was left of them the Royal Army would have mopped up at Southampton. Then Bomber Command would have gone after the barges in the gulf and the channel ports. Perhaps the Royal Navy would have worked up the nerve to appear in the channel. As young people like Margaret Anne say, he would have creamed them."

"And a lot of you would be dead," his wife said sadly. "Probably including yourself."

"Maybe, but I had made a deal with God about drinking and smoking and you would have been saying the rosary to yourself in the operations room at Biggin Hill."

Unless my eyes were playing tricks on me, he placed his hand on the thigh of his wife. Well, why not?

"It's a moot question. Hitler would have had to postpone his invasion of Russia for another year. I'm glad it didn't happen. Too much death. I was a kid then, I didn't think about mothers and children, wives and sweethearts. . . . Most of those airborne troopers would die in Russia eventually, I suppose."

He stared out at the Lake, lost in thought. Was it the channel he was seeing?

"Later I felt guilty about the Germans I killed in the Battle of Britain. . . . It was a kid's game. Many of their aircrew bailed out and spent the rest of the war in His

Majesty's prisons. . . . They were the lucky ones. . . . Was Hitler capable of invasion?" He spoke thoughtfully. "Marshal von Runstedt who was supposed to lead it didn't think so. So your friends on the History Channel are wrong."

"What's Biggin Hill?" Consuela asked with a characteristic giggle.

"An RAF fighter station on the fringe of London in those days, one of our command centers. The Stukas, German dive bombers, raided us almost every day. They'd shut us down one day and we'd be open for business the next day.

"They really bombed London!"

"Yes, Consuela dear," Anne replied. "Our pilots would come back from their flights and often have to rush into the station to dig us out. Your grandfather saved my life one day when a wall fell on me."

She began to weep, softly and silently.

"Gross."

"In the early days when I was flying across the Atlantic, after Croyden closed and before Heathrow opened, I used to fly out of there. There were a lot memories . . ."

"Your deal with God, Gramps"—Margaret Anne broke the ice—"must have included Gramms too."

"That's what I tell her."

Loretta, whom I had started to dislike intensely, had to intervene to defend Consuela who was her creature.

"I don't think war stories are appropriate for the dinner table."

That was a rebuke to me!

Anne responded on my behalf.

"Quite the contrary, Loretta dear," she said in her most upper-class English tones, "some stories should be repeated around the supper table so we'll never forget them. If poor Spike had come five minutes later, I would have died of suffocation. None of us would be here now."

Loretta went into a sulk that lasted a good five minutes.

Philip tried to change the subject. "Too bad they had to close down Croyden and Biggin Hill. They would be great for in-town flights around England."

No one said anything after that.

Peggy Anne whispered in my ear. "Mom has to dominate. She can hardly wait for Gramms to die, so she can take charge of frigging everything."

"Only if you die too," I whispered back.

"I never talked dirty to a Coadjutor Archbishop," she said. "Sorry, Archbishop Blackie."

"No, you're not."

The omelet was served and delicious it was, though I doubted whether it could be called healthy. What kind of crazy people served omelets at dinner in a house on the dunes? I glanced around the table. This was one weird bunch of Irish.

I sipped the Anita wine cautiously to make it last. I dared not ask for a second glass. I would be driving home along Old Grand Beach Road, which was dangerous in full daylight.

Outside the setting sun had splashed a broad gold ribbon on the Lake.

For some reason I remembered the groundskeeper I had met on the way in. I knew him from somewhere, of that I was sure.

My fellow successor to the apostles had fallen asleep.

Our dessert was fresh Michigan raspberries, polluted with skim milk.

Loretta squared her shoulders for another attack.

"I think we should discuss Margaret Anne's plans," she said, madam chairperson taking charge.

"Nothing to discuss," my table partner bristled. "I'm working as an ACEr in New Orleans."

Maybe she should have walked out. On the other hand, she probably would enjoy the fight.

I had been on occasion trapped in one of these bitter Irish family fights, orchestrated to force me to take sides. Senseless and tasteless encounters. I wanted no part of this one.

Eileen opened the assault.

"Why do you have to make so much trouble for the rest of us? Are you still trying to draw attention to yourself like when you were a little brat?"

Josie joined in.

"Do you want to get yourself raped and murdered in a back alley of the French Quarter?"

Ignatius, a bit player, finished up.

"You never think of anyone but yourself."

Consuela joined the fray.

"You swim naked in the Lake every night. I've seen you. That shows how little concern you have for us."

"I don't swim naked, but that's not a bad idea. I may try it some night."

"Slut!" Eileen said.

This was a scene from the work of the late and much lamented playwright Eugene O'Neill. In fact these people were worse than his characters.

I noted that her father said nothing. His face was locked in an agonized frown. He didn't like the game.

Loretta did not let him evade his paternal responsibilities.

"You haven't said anything, Philip."

Blackwood, you might have married a woman like that.

No way.

He struggled for the words.

"I wish you wouldn't do it, hon. I don't see what it accomplishes."

"Weak words," his wife sneered.

Did she want to destroy their marriage? Did they have a prenuptial agreement?

"Malachi, what wisdom do you have from your years of pastoral service?"

My brother apostle struggled to wake up.

"Upon my word, I believe, my dear child, that you do not devote enough consideration to the well-being of your family and your father's firm."

"And you Bishop Ryan, with all your wisdom what would you contribute to this discussion?"

She had sandbagged me, caught me unprepared. You don't do that to the ineffectual coadjutor.

I addressed the titular man of the house, whose normally mobile face was unreadable.

"Spike, I have two observations for your attention. The first is that it violates all the standard norms of hospitality to permit a family discussion like this in the presence of a guest. The second is that it is gratuitously rude to attempt to draw the guest into the discussion. I will not offer an opinion as to what the admirable Margaret Anne should do. However, on the basis of my years of attempting to moderate such family conflicts in the rectory office, I will predict what she *will* do. Regardless of what is said here tonight she will go to New Orleans. The only impact of the current discussion will be to strengthen her resolve. Moreover, it is likely to increase her motivation for the work, no matter how much she might come to dislike it. Further deponent sayeth not."

Loretta, her face red with fury and her carefully cultivated beauty obliterated, started to say something.

Spike intervened.

"As the host I might be indulged to express my own opinion, Archbishop Blackie. I agree completely with you. Margaret Anne is of age and surely has the right to follow her own inclinations as to how to spend the next two years of her life. . . . Go with God, Margaret Anne. What did the man say in *Star Trek*? Be well and prosper."

"Thank you, Gramps."

"You're quite welcome, dear. Now as to Archbishop Blackie's complaint about the norms of hospitality, I must offer my most sincere apology. My doubtless well-intentioned daughter-in-law has been intolerably rude. I trust that you will forgive us all."

"Certainly," I said nodding my head.

"Senile old fool!" she cried and left the table sobbing with rage.

No one said a word. Father Gomez helped Malachi rise from his chair.

Finally, Spike stood up.

"On that note I think I might adjourn this gathering. Margaret Anne, will you escort Archbishop Ryan back to the library whence you brought him. Your grand-mother and I will join him in a few moments. Philip, a word with you, please."

"Well," my escort said once we were ensconced in the library, "I'm glad they got it out of their craws. It had to happen sometime. Sorry you had to endure it."

The others had filed into the drawing room.

"That is the story of your life?"

"Pretty much. I was the youngest child, probably un-wanted, adored by everyone outside the family, resented by my sisters and my mom. I didn't fit, I fought back, I made trouble. My dad tried to help me. Didn't do much good. I can be pretty obnoxious, Blackie, when I want to. Once I screamed at my mother, 'If you didn't want me, why didn't you abort me!' "

"Peggy Anne!"

"Well, I was a brat. In for an inch, in for a mile . . . but she has to control everything, poor woman. She made up the *healthy* menus for the week and gave them to the cook without telling Gramms. I think she's in real trouble now. So is Dad."

"One does not mess around with Spike Nolan?"

She laughed. "No way . . . She's been trying to take over the company. She sails into the offices in New York and bosses everyone around. She wants Gramps to appoint her and Iggy to the board. . . ."

"Why?"

"She has some kind of power thing. . . . I don't know. . . . She can be so nice, as long as you do what she wants you to do. . . . Thanks for your support, Archbishop Blackie. You were like totally great."

"The one who was truly great was your grandfather."

"Good old Gramps. He doesn't like being pushed off the throne while he's still alive."

She laughed softly and wiped the tears off her face.

The Lake had quieted down and changed its color scheme from purple to deep black. The moon had risen behind us and begun its nightly task of bathing the Lake in its serene glow.

"I saw you and Joseph Murphy down on the beach a couple of days ago. You were staring up at this house, making fun of it, I suppose."

"The stalwart Joseph did remark that it was the kind of summer home that Mr. Disney would have created if he had the money."

"That's pretty good," she exclaimed with a laugh that exorcised the tears which had been streaming down her face.

"You knew Joseph when he was at Notre Dame?"

"Sure I knew him! Everyone, like totally, knew him when he was a senior. He was a local hero on campus, the big quiet kid they brought up from the intramural league when they had lost two of their point guards. Then the first day he was in uniform they lost the third point guard.

Joseph Murphy took over and scored twenty-five points. He led us all the way to the NIT championship. We were all so totally proud of him. Were his brothers and sister and parents proud of him too?"

"Proud and astonished. We hardly recognized him in that melodramatic final at Hartford. I presume you flew your airplane to the Hartford airport for the game."

"You know about the aircraft? That was pretty dumb. I should never have brought it to South Bend with me. And when I couldn't find a pilot to take us to Hartford, well I had checked out and had a certificate to fly the aircraft so I just did it, that's all, and landed without any trouble at Bradley Airport, despite the snow. I found a pilot to take us home after the game, but I almost got expelled from the school anyway. The Holy Cross fathers were so happy with the victory that they gave me a pass."

"Not too swift, Peggy Anne."

"Not too swift at all. But I was only a sophomore then. The editor would not let me write a humorous column about the trip because he said that would rub the administration's nose in it."

"But like you say, you were only a sophomore."

"So Joseph told you all about me?"

"He spoke a few words and only with admiration and respect."

"I bet."

"Coadjutor Archbishops always speak the truth. I cannot guarantee, however, what happens when they become real Archbishops."

"Joseph is home from the Peace Corps?"

"Indeed."

"How did he like Honduras?"

"As you've said, Joseph doesn't talk very much. However, he claims to have matured during his two years there."

"I don't see how he could be more mature than he was when he was a senior at Notre Dame. . . . So what's he doing this summer?"

"I believe it might be said that he is reading and considering his options."

"Aren't we all? I hope one of his options is to return to Notre Dame and go to the law school maybe and use the last three years of his basketball eligibility. He'd be a cinch for the NBA."

"In all honesty, I must confess that his family is unaware of that eligibility. Joseph likes to play basketball. But he does not like organized sports and particularly bigtime sports. I'm sure he would hate the NBA."

"What did he say about me?"

"As I've already said, he spoke of you with respect and admiration."

"Hmfp! Did he say that we had talked at Notre Dame?"

"I believe he remarked that he had spoken with you a couple of times."

"Did he tell you that I interviewed him for over an hour to do a piece about him for the paper? A funny piece?"

"Did he find it funny?"

"He sent me an e-mail in which he said it was hilarious and thanked me for being such a perceptive interviewer."

"How clever of him!"

"He's clever all right. And very bright. And I thought very mature. Despite what everybody says I didn't find him quiet at all. He gave me some of the funniest lines I used in the article."

"I don't believe that his parents ever saw the article."

"They'd hate me for making fun of their little boy."

"I very much doubt that, Peggy Anne."

"Well, say hello to him for me when you see him."

"I surely will. . . . tell me, who presides over the Eucharist here for your family?"

"An elderly priest comes over from the Dome on Sundays. Uncle Bishop claims that he does not say mass on vacation. We certainly wouldn't let that horrible Father Gomez offer the Eucharist. But we can't understand a word the Domer priest says. We think it might be Latin."

"On Saturday afternoon at five-thirty Chicago time I preside over the Eucharist on the dune in front of the Murphy residence. The whole clan comes of course and a lot of our friends. You'd be most welcome."

"You sure?"

"Totally sure."

"Well, if I have time I might ride over on my bicycle. It sounds kind of cool."

It was an interesting test. If she joined us, she would confirm what I was beginning to expect. There was a soft spot in young Margaret's heart for my nephew. Oh yes, she would want to see how Bishop Ryan said mass and would perhaps want also to fulfill her Sunday obligation (which did not seem to trouble many of her generation). But she would also like to say hello to Joseph Murphy, and perhaps meet his family.

There would be no risk in that, would there?

No, Margaret, no risk at all. All that would be at stake would be the rest of your life. And, arguably, the rest of Joseph Murphy's life. Would the risk be worth it? The good Lord knew and he wasn't telling. His local representative, Blackie Ryan? Toss the dice, young woman. You may never have a better option. Go for it.

Spike and Anne entered the library, anything but serene. The two women embraced, the younger one now sobbing.

"Margaret Anne, you are not a slut," Spike said. "I can affirm that your sainted grandmother on several occasions has entered far less salubrious waters than our Lake out there without any clothes on, much I might say to my delight."

"She was just trying to seduce you, Gramps."

"Well, dear, as I always say, there is a time and place for everything. Nothing wrong with a nude swim with your beloved on certain occasions."

"I'll leave you with Bishop Blackie."

"Just a minute, Margaret Anne," her grandfather said, reaching out to block her departure. "I have a question for you."

She frowned. Too much heavy stuff tonight.

"Big-deal question?"

"Not really . . . I intend to nominate you to the board of directors of Aviation Electronics. Do you think you might accept? You don't have to answer now."

"My Daddy know?"

"He will support the appointment."

"I can still go to New Orleans?"

"You shouldn't have to ask that, Margaret dear," her grandmother said.

The worry on Peggy Anne's face was erased by a look of pure mischief.

"Do I get my own Gulfstream III?"

"Not quite yet, we'll send one of them to pick you up when we have a board meeting, unless you want to fly your Cessna 177."

"I'm planning to sell the Cessna. I should never have brought it to Notre Dame and I certainly won't want it in New Orleans. I'm not a sophomore anymore. I can pile up my qualifying miles at some local airport down there. . . . See, Archbishop, how mature I am?"

"Totally mature!"

"She's the best of the lot," Spike said as she bounced out of the library.

They both sat down on the leather couch from which they saw the Lake turning pale under the charm of the full moon. They were suddenly a dejected, elderly couple who had endured a painful experience.

"Our sons let us down, Blackie. One died, another turned out to be a lush. Phil has lost control of the women in his family. . . . Might Malachi really have succeeded Sean Cronin?"

"I think it unlikely, but strange things can happen in the Catholic Church."

"Is that Incan his catamite?"

"I don't think so."

"I told Philip that he would either control his wife or I would. She is not to appear at the company offices again. Margaret Anne will be the only one of them that will ever join the board. She will not give the cook her own menu again."

"She was such a sweet lovely young woman, wasn't she, dear? We missed something about her."

"It's fortunate that she wanted a prenuptial agreement." Spike lifted his shoulders in a hint of despair. "She'll get some money, but there won't be a public scandal and we can afford the money."

"There will be a divorce?" I asked.

"Phil has been fed up for a long time," Anne sighed. "We didn't raise him with the skills he needs to fight a controlling woman. He just doesn't know how to deal with her."

"Sad," I said.

"Very sad . . . Anne and I own enough of the shares in Aviation Electronics to control the board. We had planned to leave them to Phil. Who else? Now I think we will leave them to our granddaughter. Do you think she can cope with that responsibility, Blackie?"

"Well, she's not a sophomore anymore!"

We all laughed.

"We can never be sure what our kids will be like when they're forty. I hazard the guess that she's a pretty safe bet."

"She's in love with that nephew of yours, isn't she?" her grandmother asked. "The one she wrote that very funny article about?"

"It was a cleverly disguised love letter," Spike insisted.

"Sophomore crush," I said. "We have her own word for it that she's mature now. . . ."

"Does he feel the same way about her?"

"How could he not?"

"The money and power won't frighten him off?" Spike wondered.

"Certainly not. Nor will he be tempted by power. He lives in a different world."

"They are awfully young," she sighed.

"Older than we were, Annie."

"Those were different times."

"Were they really?"

"Of course."

"Forgive me for sounding like a doddering old ecclesiastic. Should they decide that they want to spend the rest of their lives in the same house and the same bedroom, it would be an unwise investor who would sell short on such a union."

We all laughed. They walked with me down to the door of the house. Anne hugged me. Spike shook hands.

"Hope we see you again, Archbishop."

I agreed.

The moon had slipped behind a cloud bank. Muffled thunder rumbled in the distance. The media weathermen who said that we needed rain would have their way.

"A big fight in there tonight," said Michael the caretaker, as I stopped at the gatehouse.

Where had I seen him before?

"You have the house wired?"

Again that sound which might have been a laugh.

"You can tell when she has her dander up."

"Who?"

"Loretta, who else?"

Interesting. Perhaps.

It was a fast-moving storm. Lightning crackled above me. Heavy curtains of rain pounded my retro cruiser. Even in clear sunlight, Old Grand Beach Road was perilous— or so I was convinced. I placed myself in God's hands— and those of Serafina, my guardian angel.

I finally arrived safely at the Ryan-Murphy summer home, a veritable miracle for which I thanked the good Lord and all his angels and saints and especially Serafina. Then the thunder ceased, the lightning disappeared from the sky, and the rain stopped.

Some joke.

In my secure apartment I reported to Milord Cronin.

"Cronin," he said when he picked up his private phone.

"Blackie."

"So?"

"There's bad news and there's good news. The bad news is that your good friend from Laramie is indeed plotting much along the lines you anticipated. The good news is that he is an inept and ineffectual plotter."

"So?"

"The themes of the plot are as follows: Chicago is a mess and the mess needs to be cleaned up. Cronin has been Archbishop there too long. The arranged succession merely continues present administration. Cronin's relationship with his foster sister is creating scandal. Ryan is a nice fellow but incompetent. Morale is low in the archdiocese because of Cronin's treatment of accused priests. It is said that there is no forgiveness in Cronin's Chicago."

"Is that all?"

"I think it should be enough. There is a coterie of Chicago priests who report these problems routinely to our mutual friend. I'm sure he passes them on to his friends and to the friends of his friends."

"Nothing much that I had not expected. . . . and the good news?"

"The good news comes in two forms. He is so inept in his scheming that he does not hesitate to review it all to me, by way of demonstrating his sympathy for me. Moreover, it is very much to be feared that he is a lush. In my presence he consumed four martinis and several glasses of a quite distinguished California Chablis. I am further assured that has happened every night of the week since he's been down there at Nolan's Landing."

"Poor man."

"Additionally, he is accompanied by a certain Father Gomez of the Companions of Jesus, a man who reminds your humble correspondent of an Aztec priest about to engage in human sacrifice."

"He has always been close to those fellows."

"Even within his own family there is some suspicion that Father Gomez is his catamite."

"Is he?"

"I doubt it. Much more likely he is his babysitter."

There was silence on the other end of the line.

"It makes me feel unclean just to hear about this stuff."

"I share your reaction."

"I assume that these issues have already arisen in Laramie."

"Doubtless. Presumably you know which clerics are his spies in Chicago. You probably can make one of your patented late-evening phone calls and scare the living daylights out of them."

"Oh yes, as you would say, Blackwood."

"Your friends in Rome, good men and true, you can warn about the dangers of such conspiracies, especially when they are accompanied by excessive drinking."

"Certainly I can. I feel sick now and I'll feel even sicker when I do that. It is probably not necessary. On the other hand one cannot afford to take chances."

"In the present condition of the church, there do not seem to be any alternatives. One, alas, must fight fire with fire, even if the fire doesn't seem very dangerous."

Milord Conin was silent again for a long time.

"As the man said in the play, Blackwood, I may vomit. This sort of thing should not happen in the Church."

I might be the only one of his priests who would catch the reference to *The Man Who Came to Dinner.*

"I should add there is a good deal of volatility in his family environment. I don't believe he is the cause of this volatility. Nevertheless, it's worth watching. I sense that almost anything could happen."

"I learned long ago, Blackwood, not to question your instincts. Hang around up there and see what happens. See to it!"

That made it official.

4

I walked outside from my apartment and saw lightning once more cutting across the sky. This was the real storm, the other had been just a prelude, a warning.

I rang the doorbell to the main house. Joseph opened the door and let me in.

"Major storm warning, Uncle Blackie. It sounds like a big one. On the radar screen it is heading directly for us."

In the parlor of the "big house" the radar screen loomed on the silent television set. Truly the big red blotches were heading right at the border between Indiana and Michigan.

"Nice evening?" My valiant sister Mary Kathleen Ryan Murphy, clad in a Grand Beach sweat suit, asked as I joined her in the parlor.

"I wouldn't say so . . . where is the stalwart Dr. Murphy?"

"It is his turn for night duty at the unit," she explained, "poor dear man."

"Was Margaret there?" Joseph asked casually. Or trying to sound casual anyway.

"She was my dazzling dinner partner."

"What did you think of her?"

"Remarkable."

My good sister's suspicions were aroused.

"Who is this Margaret?"

"A girl."

"A young woman," his mother corrected him.

"Of the Golden Dome variety," I said by way of clarification.

"Somebody you went to school with, Joseph?" his mother demanded.

"A couple of years behind me. I talked to her a couple of times. No big deal."

"When someone says to me that something or somebody is no big deal, I immediately assume professionally that it is a very big deal. Is she attractive, Blackie?"

"I would certainly not describe her as unattractive, but what do I know about such matters? . . . She did, in fact, ask me to say hello to you, Joseph, which I hereby do. She also wondered if you were going to return to Notre Dame to use your remaining three years of basketball eligibility. I told her I thought not."

"A beautiful young woman from Notre Dame hardly a mile down the beach, Joseph, and interested in you and you haven't even bothered to talk to her on the telephone. I don't understand young men these days."

The good Mary Kathleen did indeed understand young men these days.

"No big deal," her son responded.

We abandoned that subject and returned to Joseph's experiences in Honduras, about which he had been very reluctant to talk, and his future plans. Included among them was a possibility of enrolling at the University of Chicago Divinity School and studying under David Tracy, the great Catholic theologian there, a man about whom I had written a book once upon a time. In most Catholic families in our social circle such a temptation would be enough for the parents to summon an exorcist. The Ryans

were different however. Mary Kate thought that might be
a very good idea.

The radar screen showed the big red splotch sweeping
ashore between New Buffalo and Michigan City. The
wind cried in outrage, trees outside waved and shook and
bent, thunder exploded over our heads, and the lights
flickered and went out.

Then they blinked back on.

"Drat!" my good sister said. "I'm going to have to re-
set all the digitals."

The phone rang, its sounds almost drowned out by a
roar of thunder and a burst of lightning that seemed to be
in front of us on the beach and maybe creeping up the
dune toward us.

"Dr. Ryan." She grabbed the phone which was right
next to her on the floor, just in case her husband might
call from Northwestern University Hospital.

"Yes, Margaret . . . How terrible! . . . Yes . . . We'll be
right over, dear. . . . Of course Bishop Ryan will bring
the holy oils. . . . Immediately!"

"Bishop Nolan has been attacked by a swarm of hornets. He is experiencing convulsions with an allergic reaction. I'm going over there with the antihistamine that
I keep in the fridge. Blackie, she asked that you bring the
oils."

The lights went out in the house and this time stayed
out.

"The entrance to their home is off Old Grand Beach
Road, is it not, Blackie? It will be a swamp now. We better
take the Lexus. You'll drive, Joseph?"

He would indeed.

Old Grand Beach Road must have been a drainage in
some earlier glacial age. It slopes downward toward a
lower drainage which was probably obliterated when the
New York Central tracks were laid down. Then later U.S.
12 was constructed on the far side of the tracks. Old

Grand Beach Road fills up during a storm and then spills water back into the woods. Joseph Murphy drove through the darkened streets of the village with speed and skill, almost as if the street plan had been impressed on his brain long ago. Then he turned down Old Grand Beach Road, already under several inches of water and lighted only by the occasional lightning bolt. Joseph and the Lexus were having a great time. His mother and his ineffectual little uncle were terrified.

Somehow he knew where the turnoff to Nolan's Landing was. He flipped the wheel, spun a vast wake behind us, climbed up the road, raced through the open gate, and skidded to a stop in the driveway of the great house, a much greater house than ours at Grand Beach.

The door was open. Peggy Anne and the caretaker were standing with battery-operated lanterns in one hand and an umbrella in the other.

"Margaret." Peggy extended her hand.

"Mary Kate," my sister said, shaking hands with the young woman as though she were equal. "You know the Bishop, you may remember my son Joseph."

"Uncle Bishop is upstairs. The convulsions are pretty bad. Thank you all for coming."

Peggy Anne was in charge, both of the house and her own emotions. Tossing aside her umbrella and holding her lantern high, she led us up the stairs. Michael the caretaker, as mysterious as ever, followed with his lantern.

"Please be careful. This house was not built for wandering around in semi darkness. . . . Are you all right, Bishop Blackie?"

"Just fine."

Fortunately the dependable Joseph Murphy caught me before I fell down the stairs and dismantled myself.

We heard Malachi Nolan's choking gasps as soon as we turned into the corridor. Illumined by candles, flashlights, and repeated bursts of lightning, his room might have been a surrealistic setting for something from Dante's *Inferno*. It smelled of blood, bug spray, urine, and human sweat. On the floor next to his bed, Malachi clad in flaming red pajamas, was twisting and turning and pounding his head on the floor.

"Very serious convulsions," Mary Kate said, tossing aside her raincoat. "We must act quickly."

She opened her black bag (the kind you can't be a doctor unless you have one of), pulled out a syringe, attached a transparent container onto it, knelt on the floor next to Malachi, and filled the syringe.

"Woman," Philip Nolan demanded, "are you a qualified physician?"

"Go to hell," she responded, with considerable restraint under the circumstances, I thought.

Just as she was about to inject the saving antihistamine into Malachi's butt, Father Gomez shoved her arm.

"You may not do that!" he bellowed. "What is in that syringe?"

"Get out of my way you frigging asshole," she snapped. "I'm trying to save his life."

"You cannot call me that," he screamed. "I am a priest!"

Lightning exploded just above us, followed instantly by a deafening roar of thunder. The redoubtable Joseph lifted Father Gomez off his feet and literally threw him out of the room.

"Most priests are frigging assholes," she replied as she pushed the plunger on the syringe. "Margaret, dear, you did kill all the hornets, didn't you?"

"Yes, ma'am," she replied meekly.

I knelt on the other side of Malachi, made the sign of the cross on his forehead with the sacred oil, and recited the brief version of the last rites.

"Malachi Nolan, I absolve you of all your sins, in the name of the Father and of the Son and of the Holy Spirit, and by this holy anointing and his most tender mercy may

God forgive your offenses, in the name of the Father and the Son and the Holy Spirit, and by the authority granted to me I bestow upon you the papal blessing, in the name of the Father and of the Son and of the Holy Spirit."

Mary Kate snatched her stethoscope from her bag and listened to Malachi's heartbeat.

"Dangerously irregular," she muttered. "Blackie, will you hand me my blood pressure gauge?"

I did so, lest I too be written off as a frigging asshole.

"Margaret, dear, did you call anyone else? . . ."

"The New Buffalo fire department ambulance . . ."

"Good, put in a call to St. Vincent's Hospital in Michigan City and tell them to be ready for a man with an allergic reaction from a hornet's bite. Say that Dr. Mary Kathleen Ryan is caring for him and will accompany him to the hospital and fears serious cardiovascular effects. Got all that?"

"Yes, ma'am."

"Surely we can avoid a one-horse hospital in Michigan City." Philip tried to reassert his control. "We will medevac him over to Northwestern."

"Who are you?" Mary Kate demanded.

"I am Philip D. Nolan, his brother."

"Well, Mr. Nolan, I happen to be on the staff at Northwestern and we don't medevac patients during thunderstorms. Now will you please shut up and let me do my work . . . Blackie, he's improving. I'm going to give him another shot to see if I can bring his pressure down."

"Thanks, Blackie," Malachi whispered.

"Will our son die?" a woman's voice asked gently.

"I don't think so, Lady Anne. Maybe Bishop Ryan will lead us in the recitation of the rosary."

I had not noticed the senior Nolans, standing quietly by the window, classy people that they were.

Mary Kate injected her second vial of epinephrine.

I began the first sorrowful mystery. There were only a

handful of people in the room—Spike and Anne, Philip, Michael the caretaker, Joseph. In the room next door there was the biblical sound of wailing and gnashing of the teeth.

Peggy Anne reappeared.

"They'll be waiting for you, Dr. Ryan."

"Good! Did you call the police, hon?"

"The State Police in Bridgman and the Sheriff in Stevensville."

"I will not tolerate any more of this interference in the privacy of our family," Phil blew up. "Surely we can deal with this matter inside the family."

Mary Kate drew a deep breath.

"Mr. Nolan, I am obliged by law and the ethics of my profession to report serious felonies when I encounter them in my medical practice."

"What felony? I don't see any felony."

"When someone intrudes a hornet's nest into the bedroom of a person with a history of allergic reaction to the bite of such an insect, there is prima facie evidence of attempted murder."

"Philip," Spike spoke for the first time, "please shut up. You are making a bad situation even worse. Thank you very much, Dr. Ryan, for your generous assistance. . . . His blood pressure?"

"Going down . . . Mr. Nolan?"

"Spike . . . My wife is Annie, I think we were neighbors on Longwood Drive long ago."

"You make me cry, Spike!"

Like all the Ryans, my sister is both a romantic and a sentimentalist.

"Bishop Ryan," she managed to say, "please continue with the rosary. . . . Joseph, will you find a blanket to cover Archbishop Nolan?"

Margaret Anne arranged the lanterns in a circle and we continued to pray. None of the other family members joined us.

5

The rain continued to pound against the big picture windows of the house. But the pyrotechnics gradually diminished and the wind no longer shrieked through the trees. The worst of the storm was over and there remained only a long night of rain.

We continued to pray, then we heard the frantic wail of a fire department siren.

"New Buffalo has finally found its way to Nolan's Landing," Mary Kate remarked. "Peggy, hon, will you and Michael greet them at the door? Spike, it might be best if you were down there to fend off any objections to the removal of your son, whose vital signs are improving, by the way, to St. Vincent's Hospital."

"Yes, ma'am," Spike responded promptly.

"Blackie, I'm going to accompany my patient to the hospital to supervise treatment. You may want to stay here for a time. Joseph, will you drive Uncle Blackie to Grand Beach?"

"Yes, ma'am," he answered, perhaps imitating Margaret's docility.

My sister replaced the medical instruments in the black bag and donned her raincoat.

"Let's see what happens downstairs, Blackie."

"Yes, ma'am," I said, not daring to depart from what had become the standard answer.

New Buffalo medics in yellow rain slickers were already inside the door.

"I am Dr. Ryan. My patient is Archbishop Malachi Nolan. I will accompany him to the hospital."

"Yes, ma'am," the senior medic, a youth of no more than twenty-five years, replied.

He knew the script too.

"He suffers from an allergy to hornet venom. I have injected him with two vials of epinephrine and stabilized the convulsions. He would benefit from oxygen underway into the hospital."

"Yes, ma'am."

Peggy and Michael led the three firemen upstairs.

"Yes, ma'am."

My sibling grinned at me. "Punk, you are incorrigible."

Peggy reappeared, wearing now a dark blue Notre Dame Windbreaker and carrying an umbrella, which somewhere must bear the insignia of the Golden Dome.

"Where do you think you're going, young woman?" my sister said, striving for a stern tone.

"Someone from the family has to go to the hospital with Uncle Bishop."

"Fair enough," Mary Kate said with an approving smile. Margaret Anne Nolan had clearly won her approval, like totally.

Just then, with Spike and Anne holding the lanterns, the New Buffalo firemen appeared carrying Malachi Nolan down the stairs on a stretcher. The inevitable Michael the caretaker accompanied them.

For a brief fraction of a second I remembered where I'd seen him before and then was blindsided by surprise and promptly forgot.

Loretta Nolan and her other two daughters crowded into the foyer, adorned by luxurious robes.

"Why are they removing him? The convulsions have stopped, have they not? He has not died, has he?"

A touch of hysteria infected her voice.

"They are taking him to St. Vincent's Hospital in Michigan City for further treatment," Spike replied curtly. "Now please get out of the way, so we can get him into the ambulance."

Philip Nolan entered the foyer to add to the blockade.

"I want to confirm for the record, Dr. Ryan, that we have not contracted with you for our brother's medical care."

Mary Kate laughed in his face.

"I'm not planning to send you a bill, Mr. Nolan. In point of fact, however, when your daughter summoned me for emergency treatment, she opened a contractual relationship. Now will you please permit these stalwart New Buffalo fire personnel to carry your brother into the ambulance?"

My gallant nephew Joseph gently but firmly dispersed the blockade, removed the umbrella from Peggy's hand, and raised it above her head as the stretcher bearers lifted Malachi Nolan into the ambulance. Mary Kate climbed into the ambulance, Peggy followed her, and Joseph closed the door.

The fire siren wailed again and as if in response more sirens screamed. With some difficulty the Buffalo ambulance avoided a crash with the Berrien County Sheriff and the Michigan State Police car.

"The police!" Loretta screamed hysterically. "Have you lost your mind, Spike?"

"No, Loretta, but I am losing my patience. Will all of you please go to your bedrooms and let me deal with the police myself?"

The foyer was reoccupied, immediately, by four cops. Two in the blue uniforms of the Michigan State police and two in civilian clothes from Berrien County's Sheriff Department. None of them bothered to wipe their feet before they entered and tracked rain and mud in the house.

"What's going on here?" demanded the state trooper with sergeant stripes on his jacket. "Was that the deceased being removed from the house without our authorization?"

He was wearing the Spanish-American war hat, which state troopers around the country seem to think made them cowboys in white hats, though the Michigan cowboy hat was in fact blue. An overweight man with a face that was always prepared for sorrow, he carried in a holster a .45-caliber six-shooter and attached to his broad belt a cell phone, a BlackBerry, and a Mace spray. He seemed fully prepared to disperse a mob of frenzied Iraqi Shia.

"No, Sergeant," Spike Nolan said firmly, a Group Captain once more. "My son, Archbishop Malachi Nolan, is being removed to St. Vincent's Hospital in Michigan City for further treatment."

"That's out of our fucking jurisdiction. You should have sought our fucking permission."

"We have jurisdiction in this case," the deputy sheriff interjected. "This is our case."

"The fuck it is," the sergeant snarled at him. "This is our fucking case!"

"Gentlemen, I leave you here to resolve your problem. I am a retired Group Captain of the Royal Air Force. I will await your decision in the office to your right. I am not impressed by noncommissioned officers who use vile language to establish their masculinity. I would ask you to refrain from it when we discuss this case of attempted murder. I would also ask that you wipe your shoes on the mat we have provided so that you will not track mud all over my house. Is that clear?"

He turned on his heel and walked toward his office.

"Blackie, would you care to join us?"

"I wouldn't miss it for the world, sir. I think my shoes are clean, sir. If it pleases the Group Captain, sir, may I sit down, sir?"

"Bravo, Captain!" his wife cheered. "You put those jerks in their proper place."

"Fucking huns!" Spike laughed. "A sip of Baileys, Blackie? I've always considered that as wine. If it had existed that day I made my solemn oath, I would've excluded Baileys from the category of liquor I was foreswearing. . . . Lady Anne?"

He removed a large bottle of Baileys from his desk and poured each of us a modest drop. We toasted each other.

"Dr. Ryan told me," I said, "that she believed she had the allergic reaction under control. But she worried that there might be some cardiovascular involvement."

"I shouldn't wonder," Anne responded. "Poor Malachi eats too much, drinks too much, and doesn't exercise at all."

"I would like to make two suggestions, Spike, if I might."

"Certainly, Blackie."

"Who handles your legal affairs in Chicago?"

"I believe it's Schwarz, Sullivan, Solare, and San Martino."

"AKA Triple S and S. A very high-priced firm, and of course with the required ethnic names. I would suggest you call them tonight. They will have some kind of clerk on duty to answer the phone. Ask him to send two of their best and toughest criminal lawyers to Nolan's Landing. The cops out there are idiots. They will try to intimidate your family into answering the questions the way they, that is the cops, want them answered. I don't think you can afford to let them do that."

"Very wise advice. I'll call them at once."

"I assume your security here consists merely of the

ever present Michael and one of those pleasant smiling Latinos who serves the drinks?"

"We need more? Reliable Security takes care of us when we're in Chicago. They're real pros. How many more do we need?"

"For the next several days at any rate, four on three shifts. Three around the house to fend off the media and the curious, one outside the Archbishop's bedroom at St. Vincent's Hospital."

"Of course." The leprechaun grin spread across his face. "I'm afraid I don't have a night number for Mike Casey."

"I as a matter of fact do have such a number. I'm not without some clout at Reliable Security."

"Why am I not surprised?"

"I would propose the following tactic. You phone the four S firm and I will go out in the hallway and call Mike Casey on my cell phone where his number is programmed and I'll also notify Milord Cronin of these events."

I awakened my unfortunate boss from deep sleep.

"Cronin," he mumbled, clearly wondering where he was and what was going on.

"Blackie," I announced myself.

"What day is it? Blackwood, where am I? What's happening?"

"It is Thursday morning, you are in your bedroom in the cathedral rectory, sleeping the sleep of the just man, and I am going to report a somewhat singular development in the matter of our mutual friend Malachi Nolan."

"What the hell has he done now?"

"He has barely avoided being murdered, in, you should excuse the expression, a locked room."

"Of course, in a locked room," he growled. "Where else?"

"He is allergic to a hornet's venom, a fact that was well known in his family. Tonight several hours after all had retired he was attacked by a swarm of hornets. Someone had introduced them into his bedroom. One of his nieces who had been swimming in Lake Michigan heard the sounds of his convulsions, collected a hornet-killing spray can, discovered the door to Malachi's bedroom was locked, and summoned her father and her brother and a caretaker to knock down the door. The same virtuous and perceptive young woman had the great good sense to summon Dr. Mary Kathleen Ryan Murphy to convey a vial of epinephrine to this house and convey me and my holy oils to administer last rites. We responded at considerable risk to life and limb because of the rainstorm that is presently assaulting the southeastern end of Lake Michigan. The injections stabilized Malachi's convulsions, but Dr. Ryan took the prudent step of transferring him to St. Vincent's Hospital in Michigan City. She was concerned about a possible cardiovascular involvement—in layman's language a heart attack. The local gendarmes are in the foyer at this moment doing a dance about questions of jurisdiction, as is their wont. I remained at the scene of the crime to protect, as I always do, the interest of the Church."

"I think I'll be able to remember all this in the morning. If not I'll call you on your cell phone. What time is it again?"

"Unless my watch is inaccurate, which as you know it often is, it's seven minutes after four and still raining."

"Yeah . . . thank Mary Kate for me. And also the alert granddaughter."

"And when you awake in the morning, remembering that they are on Mountain Daylight Time, you might call the Chancery office in Laramie and report the situation. I'm sure you will not neglect to inform the papal nuncio."

Then I called the Riley Gallery and awakened Annie Riley who, upon hearing my voice promptly gave the phone to her husband. He agreed that he would send a band of his finest across the Lake to our segment of Sherwood Forest.

During both phone calls I was distracted by the noisy exchanges in the foyer between the local representatives of law and order.

My cell phone rang almost immediately after I disconnected the call to Mike the Cop.

"Blackie."

"Your sister with a report on Archbishop Nolan's health. Blackie, his alcohol content was point two-two. That's certainly aggravated the impact of the venom. He is resting comfortably now and we are monitoring his heart condition carefully. He's a very sick man."

"In several different ways, I suspect. I will pass your information on to his family."

"I am having a very pleasant conversation with the remarkable young woman that apparently took charge of the house. She's actually quite impressive."

"Oh yes, she is that. And might I remind you, good sister, that she should not be a patient. No psychotherapy tonight."

She laughed and hung up on me. The trouble with your shrinks is that they always want to analyze everybody with whom they speak. In this case that would hardly be appropriate. The two state cops were waiting in the office when I returned.

6

"*Archbishop Ryan, may* I introduce to you Sergeant Leonard Munster and Corporal Jeanette Prybl of the Michigan State Police." Spike was still the Group Captain. "Sergeant, Corporal, I have asked the Archbishop to remain here both to represent the interests of the Catholic Church and also provide me with any advice that he might deem appropriate."

"We don't recognize any right of the Church to intrude itself in one of our investigations," Sergeant Munster said, now in a very carefully controlled voice.

"I will not intrude in the least, Sergeant. My role will be only to listen. However, if in the morning you asked Captain Arne Luther Svensson about me, he will assure you of my prudence and discretion."

I had hoped that Arne would have come with the first wave of cops. However, even the mention of his name would probably guarantee a civilized conversation.

Spike described who he was, what he did for a living, why they owned the summer house at Nolan's Landing, how long they expected to be here. He listed the names of the members of the family and their addresses and their relationships one with another; he also listed the names of the servants and told the police that all had the requisite papers.

"In the present situation in this country, Sergeant, a man in my position, whatever he may believe about appropriate immigration policy, cannot afford to be perceived as violating the law of the land."

The sergeant, who obviously did not like to work with the families of the superrich, grunted unpleasantly.

"We should seal the room where the assault occurred. Corporal Prybl will affix crime scene tapes to assure that no one violates the crime scene till our forensic people arrive tomorrow morning."

The corporal produced a large wheel of yellow tape, large enough to tape all of Nolan's Landing from the beach to the road. Spike led the two cops up the stairs. They followed with the sergeant's booted feet thumping heavily on the stairs, impressing them with the weight and solemnity of his office.

Both the cops wore thick boots, not unlike those affected by storm troopers.

"Who the fuck are you, punk?" he demanded.

"My name is Joseph Murphy, I'm Archbishop Ryan's driver, and he asked me to sit at the head of this corridor to make sure that no one left."

The sergeant grunted again.

As the law of Southwestern Michigan tramped down the corridor to the only room with an open door, Joseph whispered to me, "Michael the caretaker told me that Father Gomez split just after the cops arrived. He was driving a gray Toyota with a New Mexico license plate number 347-982."

He handed me a slip of paper with the license number. Joseph was proving to be an effective and imaginative assistant. In fact, I had never suggested that he monitor the corridor.

"Fucked-up mess," Sergeant Munster growled. "A lot of people have trampled around this place. You should have prevented that. You have any idea how many of them there were?"

"I believe," Spike replied, "they would include my wife and I, my son Philip, his daughter Margaret Anne, who was the first to notice the cries coming from the room, Dr. Murphy who administered the antidote, Archbishop Ryan who performed the last rites of the Catholic Church, and three firemen from New Buffalo who carried my son to the ambulance. Do I have them all, Blackie?"

"Father Gomez, the Archbishop's secretary, who my assistant has just informed me saw fit to leave within the last half hour."

"Nobody was supposed to fucking leave!"

Spike had not mentioned Michael the caretaker, who had at least participated in pushing the door open. I presented the sergeant with Joseph's slip of paper.

"What the fuck is this?" The sergeant groped for his thick horn-rimmed glasses, stared at the paper in confusion, and looked like he was going to lose his temper permanently.

"It's a description of Father Gomez's car. You may want to put out an all-points bulletin on him."

"I don't need no priest to tell me how to do my job," the sergeant shouted. "Corporal, call the station on this."

"Yes, sir," she said uneasily. "Right away, sir."

"Sergeant Munster," Spike Nolan said mildly, "if your abusive language does not stop immediately I will call state police headquarters in Lansing and ask them to replace you."

Sergeant Munster was patently an elderly officer who had been thrust into his task because of a shortage of competent senior officers at the time the assault had been reported to Stevensville. He couldn't see very well; he couldn't think quickly. He was not the kind of investigating officer a complex case like this required.

"I don't see any hornets around here," he grumbled.

"That's because they are all dead, Sergeant," Annie Nolan said in her most plummy of British voices. "I can count twenty of them on the floor or on the bed."

"How did they get in here?" he demanded. "Was the window open? Did someone close it afterwards?"

"The house is air-conditioned, Sergeant, and of course the windows were closed as were all the windows of the house in this terrible rainstorm."

I attempted to clarify the poor sergeant's thinking by pointing out the core dilemma of the case.

"That, I believe, Sergeant, is the essence of this case. Archbishop Nolan doubtless entered this room about the same time as everyone else went to their bedrooms. It was fully an hour and a half later that young Ms. Nolan heard the convulsions, summoned her father and brother to push in the door, and then disposed of the hornets. From examining the doors of the bedrooms—" I walked over to the door and held up the broken locks, which still clung to it. "—I conclude that when these doors close they automatically lock, unless the little button is pushed out, like so. Thus some time between ten and eleven-thirty the hornets' nest was inserted in the bedroom. Archbishop Nolan may have opened the door and his assailant might have thrown the hornets' nest in, slammed the door shut, and taken his leave. Thus we have something of a locked-room mystery. Unless the Archbishop when he recovers can tell us who came to his room after he went to bed—you must remember that he was wearing pajamas when the other members of his family rescued him—and threw the hornets' nest at him, we are faced with a baffling locked-room mystery."

"I'm not interested in any locked-room mystery," Sergeant Munster growled. "The crime scene team will take a look at that tomorrow. What I'm interested in is what happened last night."

"There is also the issue," I continued, "of what happened to the hornets' nest. The criminal must have brought the hornets here in some container, most likely their nest or hive as it is sometimes called. At nighttime hornets, like humans, sleep. One might have removed the nest from wherever it was affixed, put it inside of some container, and then tossed it through the open door of his room. It seems most unlikely that we cannot find a trace of the nest or whatever container the criminal used."

Sergeant Munster was not interested in these issues.

"I'm not interested in such speculations," he muttered. "I am interested in closing this case."

I told my compliant conscience that it was innocent of all responsibility in the matter of Sergeant Munster. The elder Nolans had witnessed his stupidity and would certainly denounce him to his superiors. He was probably near retirement anyway and his only likely punishment would be a suspension and the loss of any further salary increases.

He and the good Corporal Prybl blundered around the room, messing up the evidence even further for the crime scene team that would arrive in the morning.

Finally he ordered the corporal to tape the room, and, as he said, "everything in it.

"We can't do anything more here until the forensic boys show up tomorrow morning. We'll probably have to ask permission of the Indiana police to interview the victim in St. Vincent's Hospital. We will return here in the afternoon to interview all the suspects."

"At the risk, Sergeant, of putting too much emphasis on a single word, no one in this house could fairly be claimed a suspect at this point in time," Spike Nolan said firmly. "It might be much more discreet if you describe them as the other members of the family."

The sergeant stomped around a bit more, growled and snarled and then tramped down the stairs, without a word, obviously intending to retreat from the field of battle.

"I'll want to interview you too, punk," he snapped at my totally innocent grandnephew. "Everyone in this house is a suspect."

"Sure." Joseph favored the sergeant with his most winsome smile. "But I was the one who drove Dr. Ryan over last night and was at my own home in Grand Beach when the crime occurred, if there was a crime."

"Regardless! And Mr. Nolan, I want everybody who was here last night to stay here until I give my permission to leave. Is that clear?"

"Certainly, Sergeant."

The sergeant and his trusty corporal went out into the downpour without another word.

"Pleasant fellow, isn't he," said my valiant nephew.

"The poor dear man," I suggested, "has watched altogether too many FBI programs on television."

"I'll have my attorneys call Lansing about him first thing in the morning," said Spike.

7

Somewhere out there in the deep darkness a telephone rang. If I knew where I was, I would reach for the place where the phone ought to have been. Alas, I did not know where I was, I did not know what day it was, I was only moderately certain who I was. I opened my eyes. Astonishingly the outside world was not, in fact, dark at all. Bright sunlight was pouring through the window, so patently it was no longer nighttime. I began to suspect that I might be at my apartment in Grand Beach. I lifted the telephone, which was on the wrong side of my bed. No one. Then I tried my cell phone, which was in the pocket of my jacket. Finally by process of elimination I decided that it had to be the phone on the wall that enabled the denizens of the Ryan Murphy house to establish contact with me.

"Blackie," I said, still mystified. "Go away, please."

"Sorry, sorry, Blackie, I know you had a long night. However, your very good friend Mary Alice Quinn is outside with her camera. She has been denied access to St. Vincent's Hospital so she wants to talk to you."

It was the gentle voice of my brother-in-law Joe Murphy, who with considerable effort preserves his Boston accent despite his longtime marriage to my sister and his long association with a family who spoke only South Side Chicago English. As the good Mary Kate has often remarked, the only thing seriously wrong with Joe Murphy is that it's impossible to be angry with him.

"What do you hear from your good wife on this morning, it is morning, isn't it?"

"It still is morning, indeed only ten o'clock in the morning. She reports that her patient is resting comfortably and his vital signs are improving. She will remain at the hospital for a couple hours more. I rather think she's enjoying playing the role of a PCP, one she has not played for a long time."

My sister Mary Kathleen, the primary care provider. Not bad for a past president of the American Psychiatric Association.

"If you would, Joe, tell the good Mary Alice Quinn I'll be with her in about fifteen minutes."

I allowed myself perhaps twenty-five minutes to prepare to face the Chicago media. I even donned a black clerical shirt and found a Roman collar to go with it. Alas I had no crozier or pectoral cross to establish that I was in fact an Archbishop. Those emblems of office would not, however, make much difference. I would just look sillier.

"What the hell is going on, Blackie?" Mary Alice fired her standard opening line at me as I emerged from the door of my apartment. Her posture vis-à-vis the archdiocese was always one of suspicion about a cover-up, though in fact we had abandoned such a strategy many years ago because, among other reasons, we had discovered that just didn't work anymore.

"Late last night, my sister Mary Kathleen Ryan Murphy and I were summoned to Nolan's Landing where the good Archbishop Malachi Howard-Nolan, Bishop of Laramie, had suffered from an attack of hornets. Since he suffers from a known allergy to such stings, Dr. Ryan injected the Archbishop with an appropriate counteragent, epinephrine, I believe. I administered the last rites of the Catholic Church. The convulsions came under control. Nonetheless it was deemed prudent to remove the Archbishop by ambulance to St. Vincent's Hospital in Michigan City. I immediately informed His Eminence Cardinal Sean Cronin who in his turn I presume has already informed the Papal Nunciature and quite possibly the Vatican. The most recent information I have is that the convulsions have ceased and that his vital signs are improving. I do not feel qualified to make any further comments."

"It all sounds like another Catholic cover-up."

"Ah?"

"I mean isn't it an interesting coincidence that you happened to be here at the time of the attack and your sister happened to have the histamine injection handy."

"The proper name of the counteragent is epinephrine."

"Whatever. Wasn't it an interesting coincidence that she had some of the stuff on hand."

"Some might say providential coincidence. Like the valiant woman in the Book of Proverbs, Dr. Murphy is always prepared."

I smiled, bowed, and withdrew. Ms. Quinn, always a good loser, smiled back.

I noted, with some pleasure, that despite broken tree limbs and some puddles on the street, summer had shrugged off the autumnal storm and proposed to award us another glorious August day.

"Does your sister routinely keep such medication in your house here?"

"My sister believes that like the valiant woman in the Scriptures she should always be prepared. And as a prudent mother she maintains in this house a wide variety of medications to fend off all the ills that summer may inflict on her children or anybody else's children. Her prudence may well have saved the good Archbishop's life last night."

"Will you visit him today? Will Cardinal Cronin?"

"As soon as I eat my breakfast I will pay my respects. I will not try to predict the Cardinal's schedule for today."

"Is it just a coincidence that you happen to be here when the Archbishop suffered this assault from the hornets?"

It was not a coincidence at all, in point of fact. I was here because Cardinal Cronin wanted me to spy on him from a distance but I'm not about to tell you that, Mary Alice Quinn.

"As coincidental as the thunderstorm that hit all of us last night."

At that point I begged to be held excused so that I could partake of the breakfast that I knew was waiting for me.

The stalwart Joseph produced bacon, pancakes, orange juice, and tea, doubtless as his mother had instructed him to do. No raspberry Danish, alas.

"Did you sleep well, Uncle Blackie?"

"Well enough, but not long enough."

"Crazy night, wasn't it? . . . What did you think of Margaret?"

"What Margaret?"

"You know what Margaret, Uncle Blackie."

"Ah, you mean the Golden Domer?"

"Yeah."

"I found her to be a very attractive young woman with her head attached properly and firmly to the right place."

"Yeah."

That was the end of that conversation.

As I was finishing the last remnants of my breakfast, aware of my late mother's constant reminder of "waste not, want not," the phone rang with, as it developed, Joseph's own mother on the line wanting to speak to me.

"Sister."

"Your very good friend Archbishop Howard-Nolan is doing about as well as can be expected. They have a good cardiologist on the case. He insisted that the Archbishop be kept in the hospital for a couple of days though he doesn't think an immediate cardiac arrest is likely. Eventually we are going to medevac him to Northwestern and reevaluate his condition."

"It seems reasonable."

"If you want to see him yourself, Joseph will be happy to drive you to the hospital especially since it will give him a chance to talk to this remarkable young woman."

"You mean Peggy of the Golden Dome?"

"Good name. If I don't see you, I'll see you."

My good sister's prediction was uncannily accurate. Joseph was only too happy to transfer me from Grand Beach to St. Vincent's Hospital in Michigan City.

Perhaps because I was still wearing the proper accouterments of my office, we were promptly directed to the third floor of the hospital, the intensive care unit, if I remember correctly. (All I lacked for the full array was my bishop's ring, a remarkable silver piece created by my cousin Catherine Collins Curran. I rarely wore it save for the most solemn moments for fear of losing it. I have a terrible record, only partially exaggerated, for losing things. Nonetheless, I was wearing Catherine's St. Brigid's pectoral cross of which I was inordinately proud and which is somewhat harder to mislay.)

Upon emerging from the elevator we encountered not only the fair Margaret of the Golden Dome but also, more surprisingly, Cardinal Sean Cronin, Prince of the Holy Roman Church. They were engaged in animated conversation with much laughter on both sides, charm encountering charm. Milord Cronin was always charming with women, more especially so when the woman in question happens to be young and pretty.

"This lovely young person is explaining to me, Blackwood, how you wondrously administered the sacrament of the sick last night. I had never thought liturgical ceremony was one of your strong points but I guess I must accept her word for it. It sounded like a harrowing night. And, Joseph, the last time I saw you close up you were about two feet shorter. I hardly recognized you at that historic triumph in Baltimore. Congratulations!"

The young Vietnamese-American off-duty Chicago cop who was sitting on a chair at the door to Malachi Nolan's room was grinning. Asian women have a propensity to smile, but this particular smile was a broad grin. She too enjoyed the charm confrontation.

They shook hands vigorously, while the stalwart Joseph blushed and the ineffable Margaret smiled proudly. Milord Cronin was clad in his tailor-made black cassock with scarlet buttons and wore a scarlet cummerbund and zucchetto. The effect, which he surely intended, was to illumine the quiet, dull, and impeccably clean hospital corridor.

"Cardinal Cronin," Margaret said proudly, "said mass for us and for all the nuns in the hospital in Uncle's Bishop room. Uncle Bishop was so pleased."

"I understood from this young Golden Domer that under the circumstances the most you could do was the abbreviated version of the sacrament of the sick. So I substituted all the other ceremonies before I presided over the Eucharist. I trust you are not offended?"

"It was the appropriate thing to do," I said piously. "There is certainly a healing component to the full ritual of all the sacraments. I'm sure it gave comfort to Archbishop Howard-Nolan in both mind and body."

My sister emerged from the hospital room, exhausted and happy, as she always is when she's achieved a major accomplishment.

"He's doing well," she reported. "It was very good of

you to drive out here, Sean. It meant a lot to him. He needs to sleep now but he wants Blackie's blessing before he does."

Remarkable.

"Blackie." The Bishop of Laramie looked up at me with a grateful smile. "You and your sister are simply wonderful. Thank you so much. I don't think I would've made it without you two. I'll never forget your courage and your grace. Now if you give me a blessing, they tell me I need a long sleep."

"Certainly, Malachi." I then imparted one of my favorite Irish blessings, which ends with the marvelous wish that the blessed one be in heaven half an hour before the Divil knows he's dead.

Malachi liked that.

"One short question, Malachi, about last night. Did anyone knock at your door after you went upstairs?"

"No, I don't think so. I was quite worn out from my travel and fell asleep almost immediately. The first sound I can remember was of those terrible insects. One thing I've learned from this incident is that I must always carry a syringe with the antidote when I travel."

So it was clearly a locked-room mystery. Fair enough. Subsequently we agreed that the Cardinal would join us at the Ryan-Murphy manse for lunch and Joseph would drive Margaret back to Nolan's Landing, where "your grandparents will surely be concerned about you, Peggy Anne."

The name change had occurred already. My sister had made up her mind that this was to be her new daughter-in-law.

8

(Joseph)

"You were wonderful last night, Joseph."

"Thank you, Margaret. I was enormously impressed with the way you took charge of the whole scene."

I was embarrassed by her compliment and even more embarrassed by my inept response.

"Your uncle is totally cute," she continued, "and your mother is a remarkable woman. . . . And don't try to repay the compliment. I'm ashamed of my family, not for the first time."

"Your grandparents are a wonderful couple, still deeply in love no matter how long they've been together."

She touched my arm gently, sending a jolt of electricity through my whole body.

"I come to this reunion because of them. My dad is all right, he's a very good business executive. He worked very closely with the University of Delaware to make this composite stuff we're putting on the 787. But my mom is totally out of control and makes all the decisions. She means well, but she just doesn't see the world the way I see it. My sisters and brother have never been given a chance to have a single thought of their own. I'm sure it's not that way in your family."

"Well, Mary Kate has strong opinions about everything,

and she loves to argue but she only wins about half of her arguments and that proportion has gone down steadily through the years. So she's fun."

"Wonderful fun! I think she's got you all figured out, by the way."

"You talked about me?"

"Naturally we talked about you, Joseph. What did you expect?"

"She likes to psychoanalyze everybody," I protested, my face red-hot at the thought that these two women would talk about me and without my permission. It was embarrassing. But kind of nice too.

"Well, I don't care! She liked me, that's what counts!"

"That shows that she still hasn't lost her good taste."

It was Margaret's turn to be embarrassed.

"Thank you, Joseph," she said quietly, "that's a very nice compliment."

A powerful urge came over me to take Margaret in my arms and overwhelm her with passionate kisses.

Not quite yet, I told myself. It's too early for overt sexual moves. Besides I don't think I'm quite ready to take that step. Still it would be nice.

Instead I asked her whether she water-skied.

"Sure, I learned how in Europe when I was sixteen. I'm the only one in the family that skies."

"We have a 195-horse Century. I could pick you up on the beach. Blackie would drive and my brother Peter and his wife would come along. Would you ever want to join us?"

"I'd love to . . . Do you swim at night?"

We turned into the Grand Beach entrance from Red Arrow Highway and crossed over the Michigan Central tracks. Only a few more minutes to talk . . . Two long years.

"Several times a week. It helps me sleep. . . . Do you?"

"Same."

"Maybe we could meet some night halfway down the beach. I stay pretty close to shore."

"So do I."

We paused as we both realized that this might not be a good idea. What could happen on a starry night . . .

"Would you consider letting me take you for a ride in my Cessna? I'm a pretty good pilot."

"I've heard about your landing at Bradley airport the day of the NIT game. I'd trust you to fly me anywhere in the world."

"I'll sell it before I leave for New Orleans. It wasn't really a good idea to bring it to South Bend. I won't make the same mistake this time. I can build up my hours with rented planes down there and it won't bother anyone."

"Growing up is hard," I said lamely.

And we were all too quickly at the elegant driveway at the back of Nolan's Landing, where it seemed like Inspector Morse might pull up at any time.

I felt like I had blown it again.

"Thanks for the ride, Joseph. It was good to talk to you after all these years. Cool car."

Three of her fingers touched my cheek, a light tap of affection. Maybe I hadn't blown it at all.

There's no rush, I told myself on the way back to the village. At least we had agreed to water-skiing.

9

"*Sergeant Munster and* a thug from the LaPorte County Sheriff's office pushed aside the security guard and the nurses, shoved their way into my patient's room, and attempted to interview him," Mary Kate reported. "My patient was very upset. He had to be sedated."

"Sergeant Munster et. al," I answered, "will be toast by the end of the business day tomorrow."

"I called Mike Casey. He proposes to arrest both cops, if they try to barge into Northwestern. He will also seek disciplinary action against both of them and is confident that he will get it."

Her husband, youngest son, and I were sitting on the deck consuming the pizza which Joseph had collected for us from Brewster's in New Buffalo. She had driven back to St. Vincent's after Cardinal Cronin had returned to Chicago.

"You will medevac the patient to NU tomorrow?"

"First thing. His vital signs fluctuated wildly when we finally pushed those pigs out on the street. He's calmed down now. I'm still worried about a serious heart attack."

"I should call Spike Nolan," I said. "He must protest very loudly to Lansing."

"Can I have some of your pizza, Joseph?" she asked.

"No extra charge. I'll warm it up for you. Get you an Amstel Light too."

My sister trailed after me into the house.

"Their forensic team has been here all day," Spike told me. "They're very professional, courteous, and pleasant. One of them commented that the muddy footprints on the floor are certainly the Monster's—their name for him. He said he'd put that in the report. I wonder if he tracked mud into St. Vincent's. . . . He promised me that he'd wind up the investigation tomorrow. He'll be back about one in the afternoon. Would you mind coming over, Blackie? I want you sitting in on every interview."

"Aren't the lawyers there yet?"

"They certainly are. I will insist that you be present in addition, if you don't mind."

"I'll be there."

"I'll talk to your sister to give my oral permission for the medevac, if she wishes."

I handed the phone over to her.

"Thank you, Spike. We'll have the best cardiac team in the country look after him. . . . Oh, we'll sedate him before the trip. I don't want another series of traumas. . . . The nuns called the Michigan City Police. They got rid of them."

"Were you present at the interview?" I asked after she had hung up.

"Certainly!"

"What did they want to know?"

"Who came to the room after he had gone to bed. He said no one. They insisted that Margaret visited him. He denied it vigorously. . . . Are they trying to frame that poor child?"

Poor in the lexicon of Irish mothers is not a statement of economic status.

"I wouldn't be surprised. However, they will not get away with it."

I called Stevensville to ask when Captain Arne Luther Svensson would be back in the office. Tomorrow about noon.

I joined the family on the deck and stole another slice of pizza, so deftly, if I may say so myself, that the theft could be attributed to the leprechaun that occasionally follows after me consuming food and drink without my consent. The family was discussing Margaret, or Peggy Anne, her proper name in the context of my virtuous sister's decision.

"The serious question, Joseph, is whether you're going to marry that woman."

"What woman?"

"Margaret Anne Nolan, who else?"

"Whom else?" I corrected her.

"You stay out of this, punk. This discussion is between Joseph and his parents."

"I can talk too?" Joe Murphy asked with a sly Boston grin.

"You think I should marry her?"

"You could live a long time before you find anyone better."

"I think I know that. She's the best one I've met so far."

"So?"

"I know, I'm not getting any younger. Yet if I remember family history both Margaret and I are a lot younger than when you decided you were going to marry Dad."

"We both knew, as soon as we met one another, at the psych unit at Little Company of Mary, this was it. Seems to me that you and Margaret know the same thing."

"Times were different then," Joseph protested, using one of his mother's favorite clichés. "Give us time."

"A young woman that beautiful and that gracious will have all the swains she wants unless you give her some hint that you're interested."

"Yeah."

"You certainly have to admit that she's drop-dead gorgeous."

"Margaret? There are a lot of young women around the Golden Dome who have pretty faces and nice figures without being called drop-dead gorgeous. She's cute, smart, and has a great sense of humor. I suppose she showed you the article she wrote about me after the NIT game."

"And the e-mail you sent to her about the article. I thought they were an exchange of love letters."

"Nobody down at the Dome saw that," he argued.

"Skillfully concealed love letters," Mary Kate sniffed indignantly.

"Sophomore crush," I interjected. "On a great athletic star."

"Whose side are you on, punk?"

"Punk" is my name from childhood when I was the last and patently the least of the family. The matriarchs of the family had decreed at my ascent to the archbishopric that it was time to give up the diminutive. They slipped back into the usage only when they were impatient with me. I never minded the nickname however. It fit my persona perfectly.

"Margaret's."

"I learned from Margaret," Joseph said slowly, as if he were trying to articulate a complex notion, "what it means that real beauty comes from inside out. Margaret is radiant, vibrant, filled with life and energy and enthusiasm, she can't hide it and she doesn't try to hide it. It's simply her. Margaret is fire, white fire. I'm a moth afraid of the fire."

"Oh," said Mary Kate.

"Oh," said her husband.

"There's a lot of things I have to do, and she has to do,

before we make any decisions. She will be locked in at New Orleans for two years and she's entitled to that. Afterwards, well we'll have to see how we feel."

"Her family is off-the-wall crazy." Mary Kate was now changing her strategy.

"I've noticed, but she's not."

"Magic Child syndrome, maybe?" his father murmured.

"She sure is magic," Joseph agreed.

"Your father is talking about a phenomenon about which there has been some discussion in the literature, a highly dysfunctional family from which one extraordinary young person emerges despite all the abuse from everyone else."

"There's usually some outside link with reality," Joe Murphy said. "Aunt, friend, perhaps a priest."

"Or a grandparent?"

"Indeed, yes."

"I'll have to read that literature sometime," Joseph said, frowning thoughtfully. "Not just yet."

General silence, as though a family agreement had been reached. Now someone must bring closure to the conversation.

"I'll pencil in a Saturday afternoon two years from now," I offered.

"That would not be a bad idea, Uncle Blackie," my nephew replied. "I know I'll have to get up enough nerve to ask her by then."

"You have some doubt as to how she will reply?"

He thought long and carefully.

"Not really . . . I'm going to take her water-skiing one of these days and she's probably coming over here for a Saturday evening mass. Will that do as a cautious beginning of courtship?"

The next afternoon it became clear that the Monster was preparing to charge Margaret Anne with perpetrating the attempted murder on her uncle. He showed up confident and enthusiastic—our interventions with Lansing had yet to bear fruit.

"Our forensic boys did a fine job, like they always do," he informed Spike and me. "We pretty much figured out how it went down. By the end of the day I'll be able to wrap everything up and bring the perpetrator up to Stevensville for a meeting with the prosecuting attorney."

No, you won't, I thought to myself, not at all, no way, never.

"Did your forensic team find a hornets' nest?"

"We don't need no hornets' nest," he sneered, "we have a perpetrator."

The first one to be interviewed was Loretta Nolan. So that's the way it was going to fall out. A great witness on the stand Loretta would make—until a defense attorney asked her a question that drove her round the bend and over the wall. The interview room was the library. Present in the room were Sergeant Munster; Corporal Prybl; Loretta Nolan; Sumner Butterfield, attorney at law; and the inconspicuous, indeed almost invisible Archbishop John Blackwood Ryan, over the Monster's protest.

Sumner Butterfield was a tall, slender African-American gentleman, impeccably dressed in a three-piece gray suit, white shirt, and University of Chicago tie. He looked like a retired basketball star, which indeed he was.

The Monster began by warning Loretta Nolan that, while she was not under oath, nonetheless false testimony to an investigator of a major crime in the state of Michigan was subject to prosecution for perjury.

"When was the last such persecution in this jurisdiction, if I may ask?" Mr. Butterfield spoke up immediately. "I instruct you, Ms. Nolan, that you don't have to answer any of the sergeant's questions. Moreover, I urge you as your lawyer of record in this matter, to heed any warnings with which I may advise you."

"Have you ever tried any cases in this jurisdiction, sir?" Sergeant Munster sneered.

"A great many, Sergeant. I am a member of the Michigan bar. I wager I know a good deal more about the law in the state than you do."

"We'll see about that, sir."

The Monster clearly did not like any pushy African-American lawyers.

"Now, Mrs. Nolan, I believe in an interview with the corporal here you expressed the belief that your daughter Margaret Anne introduced the hornets into Archbishop Nolan's room as a practical joke, the sort of thing she has always done in her life to gain attention from the rest of her family."

"Yes, sir. I am only telling the truth about what I know, Mr. Butterfield, and I don't really need or want your advice. Margaret was the youngest in our family and she was always concerned about getting more attention than any of the others. She's a great lover of practical jokes and spectacular stunts that embarrassed the rest of us. She often swims nude in Lake Michigan at night. She owns and flies her own airplane. She uses it to fly her friends at Notre Dame to football and basketball games, even two years ago landing in a storm at the Baltimore airport. She intends to teach in a New Orleans slum for the next two years even though we have warned her about the risks. She seems to forget that one of her aunts died a rape victim with a slit throat in a back alley in Nepal. She doesn't care a bit about how that worries us or how such a scandal could ruin our family. Her whole life is dedicated to frustrating and embarrassing us."

"Because of my duty to Mr. Spike Nolan," Sumner Butterfield spoke up, "I must warn you, madam, that all this is hearsay evidence and that nonetheless it could contribute to an indictment of your daughter."

"I think an indictment would be just the thing to wake her up to her stubborn irresponsibility."

"Twenty years in prison, madam? You'd be willing to accept that kind of disgrace to your family?"

"Of course that won't happen. And, Mr. Butterfield, I hereby dismiss you as my attorney and ask you leave this room."

"Very well, madam. I will report to Mr. Spike Nolan that you have dismissed me. Sergeant, please note that I'm leaving the room."

He passed his recorder over to me as he left, just in case mine didn't work, always a possibility with one who is premodern in matters of technology.

"Now will you tell me, Mrs. Nolan, about the events that transpired at the dinner table on the night of the assault on Mr. Howard-Nolan."

"Well, we had a big argument at the table because Margaret insisted that she was going to go to New Orleans to teach no matter what we would say. She was abusive, disrespectful, and utterly unresponsive to our pleas. After all, we were only thinking about her own good. When the Archbishop said to her that she should consider carefully the feelings of her family she became very angry and insulted him. Often when she was growing up and someone crossed her she would play a practical joke on them. I am absolutely convinced that after she went out for her swim, in the nude, she came into the house, found a key to the door of Malachi's bedroom, obtained a nest of hornets, and threw it into his room. Then, to gain all of our attention, she ran and got the hornet spray, woke up my husband and son to push in the door, and became a heroine by killing all the hornets. When the ambulance came she jumped into it along with poor Malachi to prove how much he cared about him. That was a lie like so many other things in her life. She doesn't know the difference between lie and truth."

Loretta was breathing heavily, her face was red, she looked like she was about to explode. A skilled detective would have sensed that the defense attorney might destroy her on the witness stand and proceed more cautiously. But Sergeant Munster wanted to wrap it all up.

"You perfectly sure of this, Mrs. Nolan?"

"Of course, I'm always perfectly sure when Margaret is involved. It is the way she is. It is a pattern of her life. Mark my words, you will find out she's the criminal."

"And you are her mother?"

"Yes, I'm her mother and I feel responsible for what she does and so that's why I have to be open and tell you everything about her even if it pains me to do so."

I wondered, as I listened with an open mouth to this outpouring of maternal hate, did she really know what she was doing? Did she imagine that her father-in-law or even her husband could abide such charges? Was she aware that they could tear the family apart? Or had her hatred for an unwanted daughter deprived her of all ability to foresee the consequences?

"Have there been other 'practical jokes' like the one which happened here?"

"All kinds of them. She wrote so-called funny articles for the Notre Dame newspaper about us. I have copies of them I can give you. She's scheming to take over my husband's company. He's the CEO and his father is the Chairman of the Board. She wants a place on the board instead of me or my son. Her grandfather is a senile old fool. She's wrapping him around her little finger. The practical 'jokes' aren't really funny. They're part of her grab for power. I'm sure she was afraid Archbishop Howard-Nolan would oppose her plans to seize power."

Outside on the deck overlooking the swimming pool Margaret Anne and my nephew were chatting cheerfully. She was in for a rough afternoon, but she could take care of herself as she had proven by living in a house with this crazy woman. A Magic Child indeed and arguably a miracle of grace.

Loretta went on and on, one mad allegation after another. None provable, of course, none which would stand up in a court of law, but a lot which might appeal to a media-hungry Berrien County prosecuting attorney.

At the end of the "interview," the Monster praised her honesty and integrity.

"I thank you for your contributions to a quick solution to this case. As I've said before, I'm sure we'll have it all wrapped up in the prosecuting attorney's office at St. Joseph, Michigan."

Over Blackie Ryan's dead body.

The Monster announced that there would be an hour before the next interview, "and I presume the final interview with Ms. Margaret Anne Nolan."

Loretta Nolan glared at me triumphantly as she left the library.

I walked out on the deck in front of the drawing room and pushed the button on my magic mobile phone which should connect me with the personal line of Captain Arne Svensson.

"Svensson."

"Arne, son of Sven," I said.

"Blackie Ryan! What are you doing mucking around again in my jurisdiction?"

"Arne, son of Sven, you guys are out of your frigging minds! You know how much trouble you have over here at Nolan's Landing?"

"I didn't send them over there, Blackie. His nephew is my second in command. While I was away, he took the risk of giving his uncle a juicy case with which he could go gracefully into retirement. I wouldn't have done it."

"You heard from Lansing?"

"I have three messages here on my desk. Blackie, I've been away on vacation and I come home to this mess."

"You should never have left that nephew in charge."

"Tell me about it."

"If you have any sense and want to avoid tons of trouble, take the Monster off the case and come over here yourself."

"He claims he'll have it all wrapped up by tonight."

"Then he will have the Michigan State Police wrapped up in all kinds of trouble. Do me a favor and listen to the tapes he brings back tonight and then decide whether you really want him at Nolan's Landing."

"I'll certainly do that."

"On your desk you also have complaints from the good nuns at St. Vincent's Hospital in Michigan City, from the Michigan City Police Department and from Mike Casey. My sister, Dr. Mary Kathleen Ryan, will file assault and battery charges against him in Laporte County, Indiana, when she returns, after medevacing her patient to Northwestern Hospital. Hopefully he will be safe there from such of your colleagues as the worthy Sergeant Munster."

"Let me look over this stuff . . . I see your point, Blackie, the Monster has really fucked up this time."

"He is a Nazi, son of Sven. He is engaging in a reign of terror against rich people. And he is pushing the Michigan State Police deeper and deeper into quicksand. Spike Nolan has a group of very high-priced lawyers in this house and they'll be drawing up motions all afternoon. You'd better be over here bright and early tomorrow morning or the roof is going to fall in."

"I hear you, Blackie."

"One last point. The Monster is too dumb to realize that this is a locked-room mystery. Who do you know that solves locked-room mysteries?"

"I've been thinking the same thing all morning."

I thereupon entered the dining room, which was part law office, part wake. Spike Nolan, pale and taut with rage, was on the edge of eruption. His wife was weeping

softly. Phil Nolan was weeping too, a confused and be-
trayed man.

Arrayed around the tape were typists, paralegals, and
interns from the office of Triple S and S. Sumner Butterfield huddled with three of his partners, Simon Strauss, the
senior partner of the firm; Jill Marie Aherne O'Shea, a
member of my parish; and Emmanuel Rodriguez, reputed
to be one of the top five defense attorneys in the city.

No one was aware of my entry into the room because
I am almost never noticed entering a room. I could get
on an elevator and ride down fifty floors with you and
you'd never notice me. I am so innocuous and diffident
seeming that I'm the little man who wasn't there again
today. Very useful trait.

"I will say two things at this time. The first thing is that
the Monster will not prevail. In fact, already he is toast,
history, irrelevant. He will not be back tomorrow morning. The second thing is that all of you legal folk should
devote intense efforts this afternoon to creating the sorts
of material you create—writs, petitions, demands, pleas,
and any other such dangerous scripts. They must all be
directed at the Michigan State Police and other guilty
parties. They must be filed in Berrien County Courthouse
by close of business today, with copies thoughtfully delivered to the State Police headquarters in Stevensville,
attention to Captain Arne Svensson. Then all manner of
things will be well and we can get on with the solving of
this problem."

I had, incidentally, not the slightest insight into the
central issue—how could a swarm of hornets pass through
a locked door?

"We can't," Lady Anne protested, "let little Margaret
Anne go through one of those insane interrogations."

"Quite the contrary, milady, the odds against Sergeant
Munster in such a confrontation are of the dimension
of light-years. She will of course cream him, like Notre

Dame running over Leland Stanford. It is important that the aforementioned Captain Svensson hear the demolition this afternoon. I will assure that a recording of the encounter will be in his hands, not forty minutes after the session ends."

I noted that poor little Margaret was on the deck conversing with my nephew over a copy of Jimmy Joyce's *Ulysses*. Both of them wearing T-shirts and shorts. What was the world coming to?

"Ever since they made Blackie an Archbishop," said Jill Marie, "he talks like he is the Pope."

Everyone laughed.

"Not quite yet," I said modestly. "I enjoy a record of infallibility only on locked-room mysteries and only so far."

For an instant I saw how it had been done, a quick glimpse inside an elevator door before it closes. Then it vanished. If the past were any indication it would come back again. Nonetheless if I blew this one my credibility would suffer badly. Especially with my family.

I observed that on the deck Peggy Anne had produced a bowl of pasta. They were not sitting close to one another, but the scene was very domestic. I would not report it to my sister. Let her find out for herself.

"I can't act for your granddaughter. It would be unethical since I acted for her mother."

"Despite her intolerable lack of respect for her tottering old pastor, I think the valiant Jill Marie would make an excellent contribution to our project."

Jill Marie had long blond hair (natural), a crooked grin, and a razor-sharp mind. That's why someone arranged to have her elected to the Parish Council at the Cathedral.

"Fun!" that worthy agreed, her eyes dancing with mischief.

"If I may, Counselor, I would like it observed that Margaret's mother just now is in the manic phase of a serious bipolar problem. She has made some fairly serious allegations, which our mutual friend Sumner might detail."

"We'll cream her."

Of this I had no doubt at all.

Matters having thus happily arranged themselves, I ambled out on the deck and asked Ms. Nolan where my pasta was.

She dashed off and returned almost immediately with a generous helping of fettuccine Bolognese.

"Joseph said you were here," she informed me, "so I had to make you a bowl of pasta. . . . What's happening in there? When do I get my shot at the poor Monster?"

White flame indeed.

"The first thing you must know is that when they barged into your uncle's sickroom, they demanded to know whether you had been in his room after he had retired for the night. He flatly denied that you had visited him that night, under some considerable pressure from them to assert that he had. . . ."

"Poor Uncle Bishop . . ."

"The Monster, who has seen too many episodes of *Law & Order,* will try to persuade you of the opposite."

"I'll tell him that I'm shocked that a cop would tell such a big fib."

Her eyes shone at the prospect of combat. I hoped that Joseph realized that he was falling in love with a shite-kicker, just as his father had before him.

"Moreover, he will endeavor to persuade you that he is about to close the case with the finding that fits the pattern of your lifetime behavior as reported in some detail by your mother."

"Poor Mom. When she goes postal, she's like totally off the wall."

"He will attempt to intimidate you with threats of arrest, indictment, trial, and imprisonment. . . ."

"I don't intimidate, Bishop Blackie. It's in my genes . . . This should be fun."

My poor nephew almost opened his mouth with a masculine warning about caution. Fortunately for his future he decided against such comments.

"Your lawyer, the valiant Jill Marie O'Shea, a parishioner of mine, has been assigned to protect your rights. You would do well to heed her advice at least occasionally."

"Is she cool?"

"Totally."

"Fabulous."

"Can I sit in?" Joseph asked.

"Alas, no . . . both the worthy Jill Marie and I will be there. I don't want this young woman performing for a grandstand."

"I'll be good, Blackie, I promise."

"I doubt that, but what I don't doubt, young woman, is your ability to take care of yourself."

"Me too," Joseph prudently agreed.

I discovered that my attendant leprechaun had made off with most of my bowl of pasta.

"I now must make another phone call concerning our anti-Monster project."

I retired to a quiet corner of Nolan's Landing and pushed the button that would connect me with the son of Sven.

"Arne. One small issue. The good Bishop of Laramie was accompanied by a certain Father Gomez of the Companions of Jesus, a new and reactionary religious order of Mexican origin. Father Gomez's soul I believe was occupied by the ghost of an Aztec priest who specialized in cutting out human hearts and other forms of delicate surgery. Father Gomez departed shortly after the arrival of your sturdy colleagues. However, one of my observers noted a description of his car, complete with a New Mexico license plate, which I handed over promptly to your representative with the suggestion that he issue an all-points bulletin like they do in the cop movies. I wonder if he bothered. Could you check . . . ?"

"Just a minute while I check my computer. . . . That was two nights ago."

"Indeed."

He was silent for a moment.

"There's no record of such a bulletin, Blackie," he said evenly.

"I will say nothing further, save that if a rookie cop did that, you'd fire him on the spot."

10

Before I could rejoin the brain trust in the dining room, my cell phone played its usual signal of "The Minstrel Boy."

"Father Ryan."

"Your sister. Poor Malachi has had a major cardiac arrest. Sean and Joe and I are with him along with our best team of cardiac people. Eddie Morrissey's group. Touch and go."

"A triumph for the Michigan State Police."

"I'd leave such a judgment to the lawyers. They didn't help."

"I should tell his family."

She hesitated.

"Yeah, I'll call you later."

In the dining room, I signaled Spike Nolan. . . .

He nodded and his wife joined me in the corridor. Phil Nolan trailed after them.

"Malachi?"

"Touch and go."

The two of them sank into an available couch and wept bitterly.

"What did we do wrong?" Lady Anne begged.

"We certainly failed him," Spike, head in hands, murmured. "I don't know when or where or how."

Parents are that way. They delight in blaming themselves for what their kids do, sometimes perhaps with reason, more often not.

"God gives us our kids for a few years, maybe twelve or thirteen at the most. . . . Even when we do our best, we often seem to fail. We must credit our children with their own agency. For many reasons they seem to choose the opposite route than we would wish. We may have failed them in many ways, yet we must leave them free to work out their own destiny. Johnny and Elizabeth were caught up in dangerous times. They strove for maturity just at the time that it was most difficult. I don't think you can blame yourselves for Malachi. Other routes were available to him, which for reasons we cannot understand, he did not choose. Phil is a brilliant administrator who had the misfortune to marry a deeply troubled spouse, a mistake that many of both genders make. However, you must not think that God loves them any less than he loves anyone else. We must recognize the freedom of all our children and also God's freedom to work out his own plans. Besides you still have Margaret Anne, a wonder child that recalls Biggin Hill in August 1940."

It was longer than my usual exhortations, but we were treading on thin ice over the deep lake of mystery.

"Then we must fly to Chicago," Lady Anne said, rising from the sofa, "to assure Malachi that we love him and so does God."

Spike rose with her.

"You take good care of the wonder child while we are at the hospital."

"This is Mary Kathleen's card with her cell phone number. Call her. She has more than enough clout to permit you to land at their heliport."

"Good."

"Two questions before you leave. Is it true there is no master key for the rooms in the house?"

"We tell ourselves every summer we should change the locks and have new keys made and a master key," Annie explained. "Then we forget. We'll commission Michael to do it immediately after we leave. He is very efficient."

"And who then is Michael?"

"A victim of Vietnam," Spike said. "Prison camp, terrible emotional problems when he returned. Alchololism, drugs. Years in VA hospitals. Then he straightened himself out. He moved to New Buffalo and organized a group of servants, mostly Latino, not unlike Mr. Casey's security agency. He lives in the gatehouse and reads and writes, I think a book about the Vietnam years, but I'm not sure. We find him a little odd, but completely trustworthy. . . . Now if you don't mind, Blackie, we must snag a passing helicopter."

As they left, I tried to digest this information. I could not exclude the possibility that there was still a master key. That would explain the locked-room mystery in short order. Then all we had to do was to find who had the key.

Except that that person (or perhaps persons) would have to slip into Malachi's room when he was asleep and Malachi has no memory of anyone entering.

Spike Nolan, according to the feature articles, had an almost preternatural ability to pick colleagues and subordinates. His son Philip was CEO because he was good at the job. He was unfortunate in the choice of his wife. Spike's grandson and Philip's son Ignatius was a lightweight who would probably never move to the top echelons of Aviation Electronics. Margaret Anne was a Magic Child or, if one wished, a white flame. So much against the conventional wisdom he was moving her into a position in which she would become his successor. If he felt that Michael was the kind of man whom he could trust to preside over Nolan's Landing eleven months of the year, so be it.

Yet Michael was a mystery which might or might not have any import for the mystery of the hornets in the bedroom.

I encountered Margaret Anne, dressed for her confrontation with the Monster—beige summer suit, with a green scarf at her neck, nylons, a touch of makeup, and hair done up as a bun in the back of her head. The only sign of the Dome was her class ring.

"I think I'm going to enjoy this, Blackie," she said with a wicked laugh. "Do you think I ought to be scared?"

"With you and the good Jill O'Shea combined, it would be difficult not to be overconfident."

"Totally cool!"

The worthy Ms. O'Shea appeared similarly clad—a gray summer pants suit, and dark blue scarf, and blond hair restrained by a matching blue barrette.

"You two look like summer interns after the first year of law school, easy targets for a crude country cop!"

We ambled into the library, which Michigan State Police had left in something of a shambles. Paper was strewn around the room, several ashtrays were filled, furniture was rearranged, and the room smelled of cigarettes.

"It smells like a cheap bar," Margaret protested, "not that I frequent cheap bars!"

She opened the windows and the clear fresh breeze off Lake Michigan poured into the library. Then she scurried around the room, picking up pieces of paper and overcoming the mess.

"I am noting on my tape recorder," Jill said, "that my client Margaret Anne Nolan and I arrived at the scheduled time of one-thirty. There is no sign of the Michigan State Police."

"Let's sing!" Margaret suggested. "I've been working

on Stephen Collins Foster the last couple of months. Let's begin with 'Swanee River.' "

So we sang, Jill in the clear soprano voice and Margaret in a rich contralto and I adding the occasional chorus, mostly by humming mentally. Next we went on to "Camptown Races," in which I contributed the do-dah part. Then we sang "Beautiful Dreamer" and "Jeanie With the Light Brown Hair." Margaret, as was to be expected, had her own particular interpretation of the songs—they were melancholy reflections of old people in a lost era and lost loves, all very sad.

We cycled through them again and I was caught singing "do-dah, do-dah" by the upright Sergeant Munster.

"This is a very serious matter," he growled. "We are about to solve a case of attempted murder."

"We were just singing to keep morale up while we waited for you, Sergeant Munster," Jill replied. "You are twenty minutes late and I'm noting for the record that you left this library in pigsty condition, which we have cleaned up and aired out the cigarette smoke. We will add that fact to the charges we are preparing against you."

Her voice was innocent, her tone apologetic. But she was already in her shite-kicking mode.

"Who the fuck are you?"

"I'm Jill Marie Aherne O'Shea, Officer. I am appearing for Ms. Nolan. I note that I deem your foul language to be a form of sexual harassment."

"You a lawyer?"

"I am a senior partner at the firm of Schwarz, Sullivan, Solare, and San Martino. Also known as Triple S and S."

"Never heard of them."

"I hardly would have expected that you would have heard of them, Officer."

"Sergeant."

The valiant Jill persisted for the rest of the interview in not calling him by his proper title.

The sergeant sat heavily behind the table he had commandeered as a desk and sighed. Corporal Prybl set the legal stage.

"The time is one-fifty-nine p.m. We are recording the interrogation of Miss Margaret Anne Nolan in the case of the assault on her uncle Mr. Malachi Nolan. Present in the room are Sergeant Munster; Corporal Prybl; Miss O'Shea, attorney at law; and Mr. Ryan, observing for Miss Nolan's grandfather."

"Let the record show, that both Margaret Nolan and her legal counsel should properly be addressed as 'Ms.,' that Malachi Nolan should properly be described as 'Archbishop,' and that John Blackwood Ryan should properly be addressed as 'Archbishop Ryan' or 'Dr. Ryan' or even simply as 'his Excellency' or 'his Grace.' It is the belief of counsel that these inaccuracies are deliberate."

Munster ignored her.

"I should begin, Miss Nolan, by saying that I have done during my long career as a state police officer a lot of work with young people. Everyone who knows me will tell you that I understand the adolescent mind, I know how to be firm and yet sympathetic. I am not eager to bring criminal charges against any young person. However, I am prepared to do so. I am also prepared when I bring charges against you to certify to the prosecuting attorney that you have been cooperative in this interview."

Jill O'Shea leaped from her chair figuratively and almost literally hit the ceiling.

"Officer, your remarks are offensive, improper, and in violation of every rule for questioning a witness! You are trying to intimidate her at the very beginning of the interview with threats of indictment and prosecution, threats for which you have so far introduced no evidence. I am fully prepared to go into the court of Berrien County and seek relief from this unethical behavior and also to notice you to the police review board in Lansing. I hope that fact is clear to you and to the corporal at the beginning of this conversation. I will tolerate no further attempt at intimidating my witness. If there is a repetition of that intimidation I will withdraw from the interview and promptly cite you before the court."

"And I'm not an adolescent," Margaret Anne observed mildly.

The sergeant's face turned an unhealthy color of purple.

"You're not in Cook County now, counselor."

"I am, however, in the United States of America and I warn you, officer, that I will not tolerate any further threats. I hope that is clear."

I hoped that the righteous O'Shea didn't end the "interrogation" too soon. We must give the poor Monster enough rope so he could hang himself.

"Tell us in your own words," Corporal Prybl intervened, "about the argument at dinner the night of the attack on Archbishop Nolan."

"Some members of my family decided it was time to argue once more against my career decision. I had volunteered for the Alliance for Catholic Education in New Orleans, Louisiana. These members of my family disapproved of my decision and not for the first time tried to change my mind."

Patient, matter-of-fact, and in a tone of voice that was casual, almost light.

"Did not all the members of your family disagree?"

"No."

Sergeant Munster weighed in again. "Which ones took your side?"

"My grandparents, Group Captain Spike Nolan and Lady Anne Howard Nolan."

"And your uncle, Mr. Malachi Nolan?"

"I'm afraid that Uncle Bishop had gone sound asleep, bored I suppose by the argument. He didn't say anything until my mother woke him up."

"And then, isn't it true that he denounced your selfishness and irresponsibility in no uncertain terms?"

"No, that's not true at all. He said that I should pay more attention to my family. Then he went back to sleep."

"We heard a very different version of that conversation."

"I'm sorry, Sergeant, but that version is inaccurate. I'm sure that my grandparents and his Excellency Archbishop Ryan will testify that my story is accurate."

"And then what did you do?"

"I went back to my room and worked on an essay I was writing."

"What is that essay about?"

"It is a personal reflection about my hopes and expectations in my forthcoming service in ACE."

"I want to see that essay NOW."

Another opportunity for Jill.

"You'll only see it, Sergeant, when you subpoena it. We will resist such a subpoena and we will prevail."

"What did you do next?" Corporal Prybl asked, once more covering for her boss's fury.

"I went swimming."

"In your swimming pool?"

"No, ma'am. In Lake Michigan."

"Why?"

"Corporal," Jill said, "I'm going to instruct my client not to answer that question. I would suggest it is none of your business why she chose to swim in Lake Michigan."

"She swims naked every night in the Lake!" the Monster shouted, emerging once more from his Grendel's cave.

"That's none of your business, either, officer. I'll direct my client not to respond.

"It's a criminal offense to appear naked in public!"

"A misdemeanor, Sergeant, and one for which charges are rarely brought."

"I'm sorry, Jill, but I think I want to go on the record about that. I never tried to swim naked, though I often thought it would be an interesting experience. Under the proper circumstances I don't believe it would be immodest."

"Your mother testified that you swim in the nude every night!"

"Sergeant, my mother tells lots of fibs about me. To paraphrase the immortal Yogi Berra, most of the fibs are not true. I don't drink, I don't smoke, I don't do drugs, I try to be chaste."

"We hear just the opposite about it."

"If all the fibs Mom tells about me were true, I'd probably be a much more interesting human being. But I'm afraid I'm just a dull boring Catholic virgin."

"And then what happened?" The corporal was once again intervening to protect her boss from a temper tantrum.

"I climbed up the dune, still wearing my swimsuit with the robe over it, and walked into the house drying my hair. I passed Uncle Bishop's room and heard him crying and moaning. I knew he was allergic to hornet venom, so I rushed downstairs and grabbed a spray can that we use against wasps and hornets. The door to his room was locked. So I woke up my dad and my brother Ignatius and called Michael the caretaker on an extension phone and they pushed the door open."

"And then?"

"Then I killed all the hornets with spray. I was afraid that Uncle Bishop would die. So I rushed back to my room—only two doors away—and called the Murphy house over in Grand Beach. I knew there was a doctor there and a priest."

"So you became the brave little hero? And then you tried to fool everyone by jumping into the ambulance to accompany your uncle to the hospital, a brave little hero once again?"

"He was going off to the hospital and no one in the family was going with him. I didn't want him to die without somebody from the family at his bedside."

"So you had your little practical joke and also a chance to call attention to yourself?"

"I don't do practical jokes, Sergeant. They are cruel and vicious. I've suffered from enough of them in my life. I would not make others suffer."

"That's not what I'm told."

"Another one of my mother's little fibs."

I began to understand what Joseph meant when he spoke of Margaret Anne's vulnerability. Beneath the radiance and the energy, or rather mixed in with it, was the sadness of the youngest and unwanted child defending herself from the taunts of her sisters and the palpable hatred of her mother. Margaret had paid a heavy price to become white fire. So it is with the Magic Child.

"Officer, you have nothing but hearsay evidence. You are building your whole case against my client on the basis of what other people have said about her."

The Monster ignored Jill.

"Where was the master key?"

"There may be a master key in the house, though everyone says there isn't. You might ask Michael the caretaker if he can remember there ever having been such a key. I had never seen it and I don't know where it is."

"You're lying, Miss Nolan."

"No, I am not lying."

Margaret's responses were cautious and patient, grace under pressure.

"Prove to me that you're not lying."

"I thought the rules were that you had to prove that I am lying."

"If you don't have the master key, how did you get into Mr. Nolan's bedroom?"

"I've already told you I entered the room with my hornet spray after my father and my brother had shoved the door open."

"I meant how did you get into it the first time when you left the hornets' nest there?"

"I didn't leave a hornets' nest in Uncle Bishop's room."

"You had better start telling the truth, young woman! Your repeated lies will only get you into worse trouble than you are already in."

"I don't think I'm in any trouble, Sergeant."

The Monster threw up his hands in frustration and rage. It was time to take the gloves off. His tone grew ominous.

"Tomorrow morning, Miss Nolan, I will come here with the prosecuting attorney. In her presence I will charge you with attempted murder. At that point you will be out of my hands and in her hands. She will be much less sympathetic and patient with you than I am willing to be if only you would cooperate with me. Your high-priced Chicago lawyers will not keep you out of prison over here in Michigan. You wouldn't last long in the woman's correctional institution."

"That's quite enough, Sergeant." Jill's tone was equally ominous. "You've been bluffing through this whole conversation. You have no evidence on which to suggest that my client should be indicted, only supposition and hearsay. You're trying to frighten her into a confession. I will not tolerate any more of this nonsense. These kind of cheap police tactics might work with a frightened sixteen-year-old, but they will not work with my client. And I will not permit you to continue your attempts to intimidate her."

"You don't understand how things work in this jurisdiction, young woman," he shouted. "We would have no trouble obtaining a conviction in Berrien County on the basis of my evidence."

For just a moment the mask of tough cop had slipped away from Sergeant Munster's face. He had become an angry old man. Spittle was forming on his tongue. His fingers were shaking nervously, his eyes blinking uncontrollably.

"I suppose, officer," Jill asked, "you are counting on a generous pension when you retire. Since we are trading warnings, I tell you that you are running serious risk of losing some or all of your pension by your behavior this afternoon."

"Don't you dare threaten me, you fucking bitch!" he shouted, rising from his chair and overturning the table which he was using for a desk. "I'm going to put this fucking rich brat into jail for a long time if it's the last thing I do! Her own fucking airplane won't be any use there!"

Corporal Prybl, cool as ever, shut her eyes and gritted her teeth. She stood up and began to collect the papers that had scattered about the floor. Outside a procession of cumulus clouds moved majestically across the sky.

"I'll see you in jail by tomorrow evening." The sergeant gasped and collapsed back on his chair which groaned under his weight. I feared that he might be having a heart attack, one to match the attack he had caused in the Bishop of Laramie.

"Thank you very much, Sergeant," Jill said with only the slightest touch of irony in her voice. "This will prove to be a very interesting tape. Come, Margaret, we would not try your patience anymore."

We marched out of the library in solemn procession, Ms. O'Shea, Miss Nolan, and the barely visible little Bishop bringing up the rear.

"Did I do okay?

"You crushed him, kid! You made a great professional witness!"

"I kind of felt sorry for the poor man."

"Don't feel sorry for him. He probably sent a lot of confused kids to reform school by the same tactics. He's your classic abusive cop."

"Oh . . . You didn't happen to bring a swimsuit with you, did you?"

"As a matter of fact I did."

"Let's take over our pool. My mother and my sisters are out there, soaking up sun. Let's disturb them just a little."

I left them to their amusements, consoled by the thought that Loretta and her crew of vultures would be disturbed by the apparent confidence of their designated criminal. Instead I entered the dining room where the legal teams were grinding out writs, orders, petitions, and other weapons of mass destruction. I played the last recording on my tape to make sure the machine had functioned, rejoiced that the Angels in charge of my efforts at technology had protected me from disaster, and rewound the tapes from both the interviews.

I put the tapes in a letterhead envelope with its return address of Nolan's Landing and added one of my two personal business cards, both designed by my ingenious cousin Catherine Collins Curran. Inside the envelope I placed the card which simply announced my identity, "Archbishop John B. Ryan," and provided only my e-mail address. The other card was content with a single large word, *Blackie,* on an off-white background, which created the illusion that someone with a can of black paint had printed my name on a pristine white wall with such meager skill that the paint had run and smeared the wall.

I searched the room and discovered, as I thought I might, my good nephew Joseph curled up in the chair, his copy of *Ulysses* in hand and apparently untroubled by all the events going on in Nolan's Landing.

"Doubtless, Joseph, you are aware of the location of the State Police station in Stevensville?"

"Sure, Uncle Blackie. Want me to run over there?"

"It is not necessary that you run. Driving your mother's Lexus at the legal speed should suffice. This envelope should be entrusted to the hands of Captain Arne Svensson, the surname two S's please. No one else is to touch it. If anyone should obstruct your approach to the good captain, you should simply give him this card."

"Cool!"

"Should you have any trouble in this mission you may let me know immediately on the cell phone."

"I won't have any trouble, Uncle Blackie. . . . Did our mutual friend do okay?"

The good Joseph already knew the vocabulary of Chicago law and politics.

"In the words of athletic competition these days, she crushed him."

"Figured she would . . . I don't know how she puts up with her mother and sisters."

"The white fire burns strongly."

"For sure . . . Mr. Casey and his guys are out there fending off the media. They didn't have to do much fending with the cops. What do you think that awful sergeant might have said to them?"

"Arguably he promised them there would be an arrest tomorrow morning."

"Will there be?"

"Patently there will not be."

"Good deal."

I watched as the stalwart Joseph ignored the media microphones and set off on his mission to Stevensville. I expected I would get a response from the son of Sven before the close of business.

What should I do next?

When in doubt I should call Milord Cronin.

"Cronin."

"Blackie."

"What's going on over there now?"

"We are in the preliminary phase of getting rid of bad police investigation and replacing it with good."

"A long time for a preliminary phase."

"Patently . . . and what is the condition of your beloved brother from Laramie?"

"I just got back from the hospital. Eddie Morrissey says he's probably going to make it. . . . Eddie is a pretty bright guy, for South Side Irish."

"If such still remain . . . Malachi's parents?"

"They're flying back for supper this evening and will come in again tomorrow. . . . You know, Blackwood, I don't think our mutual friend from Laramie is much of a threat anymore, if he ever was. Nonetheless, I'm keeping all our friends informed."

"And the people in Laramie know nothing about the dedicated Father Gomez?"

"Only that they didn't like him and that he has retreated back into Mexico. They also expressed indirectly and cautiously a question about whether Father Gomez and the Archbishop might be lovers of one sort or another."

"And you told them?"

"I was very careful in my reply. I said that it seemed improbable, but there was still an element of scandal in their relationship. Sufficiently Italianate for you?"

"Arguably."

"Enjoying your vacation up there, Blackwood?"

"It has not been without its elements of interest."

"Well, you better solve that locked-room mystery or your perfect record will be ruined."

"Even the splendid White Sox lose a game occasionally."

Milord Cronin ended our conversation with a sardonic laugh on which he has a patent. Or maybe only a copyright.

Philip Nolan cornered me on the staircase. He reminded me of one of those Brit senior civil servants who stand behind the prime minister (doesn't matter which one) and radiate assured wisdom. However at this moment, pale and tense, he was anything but assured, a worn and exhausted man, a defeated veteran of marital wars.

"Archbishop Ryan, I owe you and your sister an abject apology. I shall write her a letter. I'll take advantage of your presence here to apologize to you personally. My behavior was execrable. I was trained at Ampleforth always to be a gentleman in Cardinal Newman's sense of the word. I fell far short of that ideal. I can offer as an excuse only that there is enormous pressure in my family. Your sister saved his life and perhaps you saved his soul."

"Apology accepted, incident erased," I said, shaking hands with him.

"Were you present for the interrogation of my youngest daughter?" he said, changing quickly to another subject.

"In the words of her lawyer, she crushed him."

Color flooded back into his face and he relaxed.

"I'm delighted to hear that, Archbishop, not surprised indeed, but delighted. Our Margaret is a very bright and very able young woman."

"I have noticed that."

"It is absurd to suspect that she, of all people, would harm my brother."

Ah, he was repudiating the family story.

"I suspect that the cloud of such an accusation will shortly be lifted."

"I am faced with a very difficult decision. It will be necessary, I very much fear, to commit my wife to a mental health center. Her bipolar disorder leaves us little choice. . . ."

"Poor, dear woman."

"When Loretta doesn't take her meds, Bishop, she's absolutely impossible. I have no choice but to institutionalize her. She will fight it every inch of the way and her daughters will scream with her even though they know that I'm right. I still love her. I don't know what went wrong. I could hardly believe what she was saying about Margaret to that creepy detective. She has the ability to make the most outrageous fantasy seem to be absolute truth. Poor Margaret, I'm afraid I've let her down."

"Margaret is a very resilient young woman," I replied.

"I guess she is. Spike doesn't want Loretta to involve herself with the firm anymore. He's absolutely correct, but I don't know how we can stop her."

"Has she ever been institutionalized before?"

"No, this is the first time, a highly recommended place outside of Kokomo, Indiana. They're sending up a car for her tomorrow. I don't think anybody can persuade her to take her meds every day."

"What do the people in Kokomo propose to do?"

"Some kind of behavior modification. It's a kind of prison where you have to earn all your privileges by accruing a certain number of points. She won't take well to that, I'm afraid. I don't know what else to do."

"Most unfortunate."

"I dread tomorrow."

"The problem for such people," I said, trying to sound sympathetic, "is their refusal to take their prescribed medications."

"This particular institution claims considerable success in such cases. I hope so. . . . I love her very much."

Poor, dear man.

11

What was I to do next? I was already hearing protests
from my stomach. Somehow, it observed, I had forgotten
about lunch. But had I not consumed a dish of pasta earlier in the day? That was not enough and it was too long
ago, came the outraged reply.

On my continued quest for the kitchen I pondered the
situation that would greet the good son of Sven when he
arrived on the morrow. Two of the more likely suspects
in the assault on the Bishop of Laramie would be irrev-
ocably gone—Father Gomez in his safe haven in Mexico and Loretta Nolan in a prisonlike mental institution
near Kokomo, Indiana, of all places. The third suspect,
perhaps, was Michael the caretaker, last name not given
or perhaps not even known. Well, that was Sven's problem; he should've come as soon as he returned from his
vacation.

As I turned into the bowels of Nolan's Landing, I observed that this was the way one progressed to the entrance to the swimming pool. I thought that the situation
there merited some investigation. Sure enough, my two
legal interns were stirring up a storm in the waters of the
pool. Loretta Nolan for her part was contemplating their

efforts with the glare that might well have turned the pool into a sheet of ice. She and her two other daughters and daughter-in-law were all garbed in garments that challenged womanly modesty, Loretta herself in a swimsuit that left no doubt about the benign effects of "healthy" eating and stern exercise. A man much younger than she would certainly find her desirable—which was the point. It was unfortunate that her demons interfered with her own enjoyment of such well-disciplined attractiveness—to say nothing of her husband's love for her.

Tomorrow would not be a good day for this branch of the Nolan family.

Finally, my now desperate search for the possible remnants of lunchtime pasta was interrupted by the always cheerful Maria Victoria—AKA Vicki—carrying a tray of drinks, which looked suspiciously like margaritas.

"The children are now safely asleep and you become a cocktail waitress?"

"The children are wonderful," she said beaming happily, "at least when their mothers are not around them. However, after their first drink the mothers are not very nice at all."

Vicki was the youngest of the staff of Garcia children. Pedro and Pablo (Petie and Paulie), the Twins, were in their early twenties, Maria Teresa (Terry) was nineteen, Maria Gloria (Glori) was twenty, and Maria Victoria (Vicki) was seventeen. Like the others, she spoke flawless English, without a trace of Latino accent, except when she wanted to. She was, as she had told me, entering her senior year in New Buffalo Township High School and then would go on to computers and technology at Lake Michigan College. Two years later she would take a deep breath and venture to Ann Arbor and the University of Michigan, home of the hated Maize and Blue. Her sisters and brothers, it seemed, were pursuing similar paths to the American dream. Barring some disasters—such as an unexpected pregnancy or arrest as illegal immigrants—their dream would come true.

"Heavy work," I observed.

She laughed as all the Garcia children laughed. "Not as heavy as working at Wal-Mart's or doing laundry or sweeping floors."

"The children are not a trial?"

"They're adorable little children, Bishop Blackie."

"Not spoiled?"

"Not spoiled enough. You gringos are afraid to love your children. There's nothing wrong with my silly little kids that a lot more love wouldn't cure."

I finally arrived at the kitchen and its blessed smell of salsa and dried beef, neither of which would be served in a home where Loretta Nolan fashioned the menus.

"Is there any possibility that a poor hungry old priest could find a bit of the luncheon pasta?"

Then I realized that I had committed an unpardonable faux pas, I had blundered into an interlude of tenderness between two lovers. Michael and Juana Maria were not making love or even embracing one another. Rather on either side of the huge worktable they were smiling tenderly at one another, with that mix of a gentle affection and deep desire that recalled previous interludes of great passion and anticipated more such interludes in the future. The electricity that surged back and forth between those two smiles could exist only in a couple that through their years together had acquired complacency, satisfaction, and delight in one another that even death could not destroy. Their tenderness was a hint, a sacrament, of the love that God has for us. Bless them both, I would later inform the Deity, and protect them and their love under the shadow of your wings. They have had to suffer and to work hard to be capable of such a transcendental moment with one another. And with You. When there is such human love, You are always present.

Were they perhaps lovers whose union was yet to be blessed by the Church? That I thought might be a misfortune for the Church. That they were blessed by Yourself and that You are very much present in their mutual delight is great fortune for those who encounter such a sacrament, however embarrassing it might be at the moment.

It was necessary that I not recognize the scene into which I had blundered, necessary for them perhaps, but certainly for me.

"I did not make the pasta. Margarita made it for her young man, a nice young man, is he not? Your nephew? Margarita has good taste in these matters as in everything, no? She teaches me how to make pasta! Interesting, no? An Irish woman teaches a Latina how to make Italian food? She left some for you because she said the poor padre worked so hard this afternoon and he will need another bowl of pasta. Is that not wonderful?"

"Margarita," I agreed, "is indeed wonderful."

"She's the best one in the family," Michael said, "except for her grandparents of course and she is so much like the two of them."

"She talks to us like we are human beings," Juana Maria said, as she put the pasta dish in the microwave. "The others all treat us like we are invisible. They talk about their problems and their plans and their loans and their marriages just like we are not present."

"The redhead and her daughters," Michael added, "discuss in our presence their plots to blame Margaret for the attempt on Malachi's life. That is absolutely absurd of course and Spike Nolan will not tolerate it. Yet it is vulgar of them discuss such matters in our presence."

"And stupid," I added.

"They think because we have dark skin we do not understand English. All of my family speaks very good English, no? We may be illegals, but if we must speak

English to be Americans, then we speak English, and very good English, no? Is that not right?"

"No, Juana Maria, it is not right. No one should be forced to speak English, so it is unreasonable that it be required for American citizenship. Indeed well into the twentieth century English was not required for citizenship."

"Padre Gomez, that pig, said you were a radical padre and I say to them how does a radical become an Archbishop? No? I am happy that Padre Gomez is gone."

"Yet he might be considered a real suspect, unlike poor Margarita."

"They will not put Margarita in prison, will they, Padre?"

"Over Blackie Ryan's dead body."

They both laughed uneasily.

"I don't know who did throw the hornets into that room, Archbishop," Michael said. "But I know it wasn't Father Gomez."

"You are sure?"

"Very sure."

The new wave of state cops which would arrive tomorrow morning, or at least I so presumed, would want to interview the servants. Arne Svensson would not give a hoot whether they were illegal. That, he would tell me with a wink of his arctic blue eyes, was none of his business. But they would want to know a bit more about Father Gomez.

"There'll be new police tomorrow. They will be much wiser and more competent. Moreover, they will not be interested in whether you have immigration papers or not. You may want to keep that in mind."

While I devoured my bowl of pasta in the library, I pondered the angry green color of the Lake. When it is truly and deeply angry, the Lake prepares for a big storm by turning green. It would not begin immediately but in a couple of hours. Already sailboats and cruisers were heading for New Buffalo. Some water-skiers ignored the color change, but at their peril.

All right, I told myself, it's time to stop attributing human emotions to the Lake and to begin to solve this mystery, a head start before the son of Sven appears. There's a dozen ways of explaining the locked room. The locked-room problems are rarely as serious as they seem to be when one begins an investigation. However, why did someone want to introduce a swarm of angry hornets into Archbishop Malachi's room knowing they might induce in him serious convulsions, even perhaps kill him. What was the motive for attacking the Angel to the church of Laramie?

I went through the list of people who were at the dinner or around the house—Michael the caretaker and the servants as well as the members of the Nolan family. It occurred to me that there was only one person present in the house who arguably had a motive. That person, alas, was John Blackwood Ryan, Coadjutor Archbishop of Chicago. He had the motive and the opportunity. He was a master at solving locked-room mysteries. He could easily set up one.

But why would the aforementioned ineffectual and harmless little Archbishop want to dispose of his brother Archbishop? The answer was easy—they had been competitors, without Archbishop Ryan's knowledge or consent, to succeed Sean Cronin as Archbishop of Chicago. Blackie Ryan won that competition without awareness of it. Yet Archbishop Nolan was still a rival, indeed a rival conspiring to reverse the decision the Vatican had originally made.

Said harmless little prelate was the only person of whom we are currently aware who had such a motive. He had left the house presumably before the hornets were introduced into poor Malachi Nolan's bedroom. He and his family could testify he was back at their house in Grand Beach but that was hardly enough to persuade an intelligent police officer to abandon his suspicion of the aforementioned Blackie Ryan. One could argue that he didn't know about the competition. Indeed he had every reason to believe that for all practical purposes the competition was over. Nonetheless it might be said that the matter was not yet fully decided in Rome because of Archbishop Nolan's rumors and gossip. A sure way to end that last-ditch campaign against said Blackie Ryan and his mentor, Sean Cronin, would be to have a swarm of hornets sting the rival.

One could make a very good case for that argument.

A very good case indeed, though of course the one making the case would have to know about the rivalry and nobody but Ryan and Cronin and Nolan knew about it.

I noted that while I had been thinking the leprechaun in charge of depriving me of food and drink had consumed all the pasta. I left the empty dish on the table that had served as the Monster's desk and ventured forth to patrol the grounds of Nolan's Landing. The only visible activity was three young men on the tennis courts— Gerry McGinity, Brendan Kelly, and Ignatius Nolan, all three dressed in the most expensive of tennis whites. They alternated between angry volleys and consumption of beer. The contest generated a steady output of obscene, scatological, and vulgar words with an occasional blasphemy thrown in for good measure.

Putting on my invisibility cloak I edged closer to the court and discovered that most of the conflict was based on charges by Iggy that Gerry was claiming false points because the ball had not fallen outside the court but in fact they had just barely hit the baseline. They both appealed to Brendan Kelly who ruled for Gerry McGinity on almost every occasion and thus caused even more obscenities from Ignatius Nolan.

Young yuppies using barroom manners on the tennis court, behavior which in their social class would be deemed utterly inappropriate and ungentlemanly.

"Loudmouths, aren't they?"

"It is the way that young males assert their masculinity," I answered, "so perhaps inappropriate for gentlemen who are not exactly teenagers."

"They fight all the time," said Michael the caretaker. "Three rivals, each one of which hopes that someday they'll be sitting in Spike Nolan's chair."

"And two of them resenting the fact that Ignatius seems to have a head start."

"He thinks he does, Archbishop, but I'm not sure that he really does. The other two are much brighter, they don't drink as much as he does, and they're not addicted gamblers."

"You have a lot of information about them, Michael."

"I can't help observing the game. None of them are bad fellows, but for intelligence and dedication and flair they trail this Margaret by several light-years."

"And are not even aware of that fact?" I suggested.

"Well, now that she's on the board of trustees and they're not, they're likely to think a little bit more about it."

"Patently."

"Let me show you something interesting," he offered.

"Like what?"

"Like a savage hornets' nest!"

"Indeed!"

He led me over to an oak tree near the northern fence of Nolan's Landing.

"See that thing up there that looks like a growth on the tree? That's a hornets' hive. The bottom part of it has been cut off. The cutter didn't get the queen so the hornets are still at work trying to replace the casualties inflicted on them."

"Indeed!"

"That's what they're programmed to do."

"What will happen to them when winter comes?" I asked.

"They fold up camp, the queen and a couple of her favorites go off in the woods someplace and find a haven where they can hide during the winter, and the others stay here and freeze to death. All their work through the summer doesn't earn them any chances at resurrection. Would you approve of that theology, Archbishop?"

"Anybody who survives the winter, Michael," I replied, "has a hint that life is stronger than death."

We were both silent for a moment and then Michael picked up the conversation.

"Whoever did the job, probably with a very sharp knife at the bottom of the hive, knew what he was doing. At the end of the day hornets sleep. It's not sleep quite like ours, more of a trance. The whole system, individual and collective, shuts down. If you want to kill them you spray them at dusk. In the day it gets more dangerous especially in the morning when they're waking up. So our friend, whoever he was, attacked them just when they were the least dangerous in the whole twenty-four-hour cycle. He cut off the bottom and placed it in some kind of container—an empty coffee can would've done—and put the cover on. Then he carried it, carefully, one must suppose, up to your brother archbishop's room."

"Without any concern about the disruption to the hive."

"I suspect, Archbishop, he or she was not much of an environmentalist."

"When would they awake?"

"When the sun comes up or they suddenly experienced a lot of light."

"Like someone turning on the lights in a room?"

"Something like that."

We both pondered for a moment the violated hornets' nest.

Why was Michael helping me? He must've known beforehand the location of the hornets' nest if only because in patrolling the grounds of Nolan's Landing he had to be aware of offending them, though in truth hornets are not particularly inclined to attack human beings unless they're attacked first.

Michael must've figured out almost as soon as he heard of the assault on Malachi where the offending hornets had originated. There was no reason for him to tell me, though he probably knew that I messed around with mysteries. He himself could easily have been the perpetrator. He had described how the deed could have been done. Michael was indeed the mystery man in this story and once again for just a moment I saw who it was and then the elevator door slammed closed and the image of Michael drifted away.

"I suppose you figured out earlier that there's something deep between me and Juana Maria."

"You give an ignorant little priest credit for greater sensitivity than we normally display."

He made that junior ratcheting noise which suggested laughter.

"I knew the second you came into the kitchen that you would catch the sexual passion. Fortunately Juana Maria was not suspicious of the poor padre, as she calls you. I hope you weren't offended?"

And why would he give a hoot whether I was offended or not?

"I certainly wasn't offended. Quite the contrary. I'm always impressed by the power of a love which is not distracted by the environmental circumstances."

"You mean disturbed when a Bishop walks into the kitchen?"

"If the Bishop believes that human passion is a sacrament of God's passion—and this Bishop believes that as well as does his colleague and brother the Bishop of Rome—of course he is not offended. Nonetheless he is reluctant to violate the privacy of such lovers."

Michael pondered that and then replied cautiously, "Even if they were not married."

"That is a private matter for you and the good Juana Maria and not for my subjective judgment."

His lonely face turned a pale shade of pink. Was it possible, after all, to embarrass Michael the caretaker?

"Well, we did exchange vows over at the church of New Buffalo by ourselves in the pews when the priest wasn't around."

"In some circumstances," I murmured, "that is all that is required."

He changed the subject.

"Do Catholics believe, Bishop, that love between me and Juana Maria is a hint of what God is like? Do you as a bishop really believe that?"

"Not only do I believe it, for whatever is the worth of the belief of an innocuous little Coadjutor Bishop, but so does my brother the Bishop of Rome and he said so in his last encyclical. Thus the electricity, the magic, the hints of transcendence I encountered in the kitchen earlier today tells us precisely that God is like that!"

"Why has the Church not taught that?"

"It's been taught often and loudly, Michael. Sometimes Catholics couldn't believe it and other times we were afraid to teach loudly for fear that people would enjoy their love too much."

"We heal one another, you see, and God knows we both need healing. . . ."

Michael walked away, even more a man of mystery. He had to be a suspect. He knew too much about hornets and he knew too much about the house, perhaps how one could move from room to room in hidden ways. He was a peculiar man with many memories that he was trying to obliterate. He knew the family too well, and nursed a deep resentment toward some of them, perhaps all of them. Yet he talked about God's love. A trick to deceive me?

Well, tomorrow we would have new detectives and a new exploration of the mystery of how death almost came for an Archbishop.

12

Back in the library the guilty pasta dish had been re-moved and replaced by a dish of chocolate malt supreme ice cream, doubtless from Oinks ice cream store in New Buffalo, and also a large glass of spiced iced tea. Both patently been borne to the room by the virtuous Margaret Anne Nolan—AKA Donna Margarita, who was grinning happily at her little surprise.

"I had every intention to bring it back to the kitchen."

"Oh, Bishop Blackie, you have too many things on your mind to worry about dirty dishes. Your nephew told me that you liked this ice cream so I bought some of it for you. We have a lot more in the freezer."

Then her lovely face turned somber.

"My dad is going to take my mother to a mental insti-tution tomorrow morning."

"What a tragedy for you and for her and for him."

"They'll settle her down and get her back on her meds and she'll be okay for another year or two and then she'll start feeling so good that she doesn't need the meds and she will go off again on one of her manic explosions."

"Your sisters and brother will resist this removal to an institution?"

"Yes, but they'll be happy to see her go. When she

gets in her supermanic phase she becomes very difficult. This time it's been about the firm. She is convinced that she and she alone can save the firm from the senility of Gramps and Gramms. Ever since we arrived here last week she's been scheming and plotting to take control of the company. She would never succeed but she is convinced that she would and that eventually everyone would be grateful to her."

"Poor woman."

"Poor everybody. Is Joseph running an errand for you?" Her face softened as light and laughter appeared once again.

"He is bringing material to a man I know at the Michigan State Police in Stevensville and he should be back soon. Do you have an errand you wish him to run for you?"

Now she was the happy joyous Margo Nolan whom everybody adored down at the Golden Dome.

"Well, I challenged my brother and Gerry McGinity to a game of doubles against me and Joseph. They won't let me play with them because they say that girls aren't as good tennis players as boys are and that I wouldn't be a challenge."

"In fact, they know that you're better than they are."

"Right! Bishop Blackie, you're a total genius!"

"Arguably. And, young woman, you are an incorrigible schemer because you know how good Joseph is but they don't."

"He is totally cool on the tennis courts," she said, clapping her hands. "He could just as well have played for the tennis team as the basketball team. We will cream them, Blackie, crush them, obliterate them, they'll be history!"

"And having humiliated them, will that force them to have any more respect for you?"

"'Course not! They're probably angry at me because Gramps is making me a member of the board of trustees.

Everybody thought that Mom would manipulate things so that Iggy would be on the board and herself too. Now she's not on the board and he has no advantage in the competition with Gerry McGinity and Brendan Kelly. They're so busy competing with my brother that they can't take anybody else seriously. Poor dear Iggy doesn't stand a ghost of a chance. Gramps would go public with all the stock rather than to give away control to Mom and Iggy."

"A conflict-ridden family?"

"It's just terrible, Blackie, like totally terrible! And their wives are part of the competition. So both Eileen and Josie, who are my sisters, hate me now even more than their husbands. Poor Consuela is incapable of any stronger emotions than wanting a new pair of shoes. Are all families messed up like this?"

"Siblings tend to compete with one another and when the stakes are as high as a Fortune 500 firm the competition can be pretty vicious."

"I don't want any part of it! That's why I'm going off to New Orleans! Well, that's one of the reasons. It's been a part of our family as long back as I can remember. I totally hate it."

"So the summer months here at Nolan's Landing are not a reward for anybody?"

"Well, Annie and Spike like it, poor dears, and so do I. For the others it's always miserable! There's always conniving and scheming and suspicion. And there's conflict between husbands and wives and viciousness and gossip and envy and any other one of the capital sins you want to mention."

"Yet summer romances are always possible."

Flushed with pleasure and pretended outrage Peggy Anne turned away from the window behind which the Lake was becoming ever greener and cried out, "Archbishop Blackie Ryan, you are totally uncool! Joseph and I are not having a summer romance! We're grown-ups! We're adults! We don't do crushes anymore."

"Don't knock summer romances, Peggy Anne Nolan. They're one of the Lord's ingenious tricks for keeping the species alive and for teaching us a little bit of what his permanent crush on the human species is like."

"I like the beach, I like swimming, I like Oinks ice cream store, I like all the good things about summer-time. I think this is a wonderful place. And I will not come back here next summer!"

"Not even to see Joseph?"

"Well, maybe for a weekend or two to see Joseph—if he will still talk to me!"

"Peggy Anne, I would venture that there's no doubt about him talking to you. Or perhaps to be true to the honor code of Irish family style, he'll spend most of his time listening to you!"

"You're absolutely wicked, Bishop Blackie, absolutely and totally wicked!"

I was saved from punishment for my wickedness by a phone call.

"Blackie?"

"Arguably."

"Svensson here. Say, isn't that nephew of yours really a first-rate human being?"

From too long association with the Irish, Sven had learned the habit of engaging in small talk before getting to the important part of the conversation at the end.

"He is not without certain minor talents," I agreed.

"It's not right for a Lutheran like me to admit that I pay any attention to what happens down at your Golden Dome. Yet I have to pay some attention to how their ath-letic teams perform, so at least I know what they're talking about on television at night on our stations around here."

"So you are not unfamiliar with the events in Baltimore at the National Invitational Tournament."

On the other side of the library desk Peggy Anne Nolan was blushing and grinning. Her grin, a mix of mischief and delight, was her trademark. White flame that's both mischief and delight? Grins like that can make one want to move mountains.

"Well, he was simply sensational. He held back until the very end when it looked like they were going to lose and then he threw in three baskets in a row and then in the overtime he took over completely and won the championship for them! He's a real class kid."

"I have heard that observation from people whose judgment I am constrained to accept."

"He brought in those two tapes and I asked him if he wanted to listen to them. He said that he didn't think you'd object if I wanted him to listen."

"An accurate reflection of my attitude."

"Anyway, when he was through listening to Munster's interview of the young woman, he laughed and said, 'Poor Sergeant Munster!' "

"An appropriate response."

"Seems like he's kind of fond of that young woman?"

"Margaret? Oh, I don't know, you can never tell about the emotions of people their age, especially during summertime!"

"Well, anyway we're putting Sergeant Munster on paid administrative leave until his retirement in three months. So he's out of the picture."

"I find that consoling news."

"Yeah, so call off your legal hounds."

"I will discuss the matter with them."

"Nine o'clock tomorrow morning I'll be there with two new detectives, all of us in civilian clothes, and the other two are first-rate professionals. Would you let them know around there that they can expect me."

"Make it ten-thirty Eastern Time. As you know in this part of the southwest corner of Michigan—in Harbor

Country, as some call it—we run unofficially on Chicago time."

"I understand, Mayor Daley time."

"I would tend to agree. . . . I will tell everyone here at the house to expect three harmless-looking Scandinavians, probably from the Upper Peninsula, tomorrow at nine-thirty Daley time. I think, son of Sven, you'll find it a very satisfying mystery. There are alternative people that one might want dead in this house but not the Archbishop."

"Then there is of course a locked-room dimension."

"Oh, I don't see any problem with that. Indeed upon your arrival tomorrow I shall show you how it all went down."

"What did he say about Joseph?" Peggy Anne demanded.

"I don't think I should answer that question," I said, trying to sound stern. "You're going to have to make up your own mind about Joseph, exercise your own judgment, as if you haven't already!"

She grinned again and then became somber.

"I'm sure enough about Joseph, Father Blackie, but I'm not sure about me. You know me pretty well by now."

"Hardly at all," I argued.

"I've come from a squirrelly family. My mother's a manic depressive who's going to be carried away from this house tomorrow. My father is a good man and a smart administrator but has never been able to control his wife or daughters. My brother drinks too much and gambles too much. We're all a mess and I'm probably a mess too. No, I'm sure! Why should I ruin poor Joseph's life?"

"I decline to answer that question on the grounds it may tend to incriminate me. But I suggest you ask Joseph's mother and she'll tell you why."

"Oh, Blackie, there's no point in that. She's already made up her mind about me."

"Not only is she Joseph's mother," I said, "she's also a

first-rate analyst of human nature. If she approves of you, you can be content that you are an approved person."

"I don't know." Her smile turned to a frown and tears began to form in her eyes. "Sometimes I think I'm just a terrible jerk."

"I will not try to argue with you on that point. I'm sure my good nephew will be much more persuasive than I."

I had been conned by this ingenious young woman into a situation in which I was being asked for my approval of the still very theoretical possibility that she and Joseph might marry. I don't enjoy that role. Young people must decide for themselves. And they do so anyway. If I should tell Peggy Anne that I thought she was a serious risk for poor Joseph then she would pursue him all the more vigorously, albeit perhaps with a guilty conscience. On the other hand if I were to tell her that I had already mentally marked out a day for approximately two years from now on the Cathedral calendar for a marriage, then she would lose her nerve and want to run. She would only talk about a wedding when she had become so much in love that she wouldn't be able to run.

That's the way God works.

13

I wondered why Margaret had set up her brother and brothers-in-law precisely at this time. What was the rush? There could be no doubt that it was a setup. Joseph Murphy no longer looked like the galoot that his mother had once called him, but he certainly didn't look like a tennis star. In jeans and running shoes he seemed awkward and uneasy, an inappropriate fourth in a match with three handsome and properly dressed competitors. Iggy, Gerry, and Brendan thought he would be a pushover because indeed he looked like a pushover.

However, my stalwart nephew was not a pushover. He had, since time immemorial, won the annual Ryan–Murphy tournament. This summer he also copped the Grand Beach tennis championship almost immediately after his return from the Peace Corps. While Margaret was unaware of these triumphs, she knew that he was good during her sophomore crush (and which now she would insist was finished). She checked him out on the ND courts. Therefore, she knew that he was anything but a setup. Moreover, she should feel reasonably confident that the two of them would cream whatever twosome the men in her family might produce. She was certainly well within the bounds of reason if she wanted to humiliate them. But why at this particular time? When there was an attempted-murder mystery at Nolan's Landing why would she distract everybody with their own little tennis coup?

Perhaps because she wanted to serve notice on the others that she had found herself a chariot driver, a knight errant, a stalwart hero. She would not be dismissed anymore as a silly little girl who because of her grandfather's favor had been elevated to the board of directors at Aviation Electronics. She was showcasing Joseph, which arguably was her right.

Or maybe in Nuala Anne's inimitable Irish English, "Sometimes, your grace, we shite-kickers kick the shite for the pure fun of it."

In any event her victory was decisive. The first match allied her and Joseph against her brother and Gerry McGinity. Joseph had adopted the mask of a smiling, gracious tennis player who was willing to concede every point the obnoxious Iggy would claim. He would only smile patiently at every outburst of obscenity from her slightly overweight and slightly breathless brother. And he could well afford to smile because it was clear from the first exchange who was going to win the match.

Margaret Anne and Joseph were leading three to zero when the helicopter swooped in and landed near the tennis court. Her grandmother and grandfather, accompanied by the ever efficient Mike Casey, stepped from the craft and glanced at the tennis court. Grandma Nolan, taking in the nature of the match, insisted that her husband join her in watching.

Michael appeared to proffer them courtside chairs.

For a moment I knew who he was and then lost him again.

Iggy, who had already consumed a good deal more than his fair share of the brew, did not moderate his language because of his grandparents' presence at courtside. Indeed he became more sullen and more obscene as Joseph and Margaret hammered them into the ground. They did not even permit them to win a single game.

"Six–zip!" Margaret announced at the end of the match. "Why did you guys even bother to come!"

The second match was quieter. Neither Gerry nor Brendan were willing to be obscene in the presence of the Chairman of the Board of their firm. But they were no match for our dynamic duo. My valiant nephew hardly had to extend himself. And while his partner rushed around the court in a frenzy, she really needn't have bothered because the outcome would have been the same six–zip if she had not acted like a dervish. However, Margaret Anne was not the kind of young woman who could be gracious in victory, not against young men who had ridiculed her as a tennis player.

She awarded her partner with a quick peck on his cheek when he had won set point with a fearsome serve.

"Anyone else want to play us?" she demanded. "How about you, Gramps, do you want to take a chance?"

Spike Nolan beamed proudly.

"Sixty years too late, granddaughter, but back in those days we probably could've beaten you. After the Luftwaffe you guys would've been pushovers!"

Gerry and Brendan shook hands with Joseph. Margaret's good manners returned and she pecked at their cheeks, in the midst of general smiles and laughter.

I decided it was time that I rematerialize and talk with Spike and Annie.

"Isn't she a fearsome warrior?" Annie asked me.

"And she found an equally fearsome wingman," Spike said with a huge grin. "I think if they let women fly Spitfires in those days and Margaret was around she would have been a great pilot."

"The Luftwaffe," I observed, "wouldn't have lasted beyond the first week!"

The victorious queen of the court swarmed over and embraced her grandmother and grandfather.

"Well, dear, the boys have been teasing you for years and they deserve a good lesson. I'm proud of you, dear, keep it up!"

"We like totally crushed them!"

I accompanied the eldest Nolans back in to the big house.

"How is Archbishop Malachi doing?" I asked.

"Much better this afternoon," his mother replied. "He is, poor dear man, so terribly discouraged. He tells us he's thinking of retiring as Bishop. He is too young to retire, isn't he, Blackie?"

"Patently," I said with little enthusiasm.

"What will he do if he retires?" I asked, wondering if perhaps he would go back to Rome and gossip all the more.

"He spoke of retiring to Ampleforth Abbey," Spike said, "and becoming a Benedictine for the rest of his life."

Such a vocational change seemed to me highly improbable.

"I suspect that Ampleforth would be considerably more lively than Laramie."

I noticed that Spike and Anne looked tired. No, *exhausted* would be a better word. They were worn out, their energy sapped by the crises in their family life. They deserved better from their children and grandchildren. Moreover they were probably blaming themselves for the problems.

I told them the good news about the advent on the morrow of Captain Svensson and his aides.

"Well, I certainly hope they can get to the bottom of this crazy mess," Spike said, with a sigh of relief. "I tell myself that this is a nightmare and I will wake up and none of it ever happened."

"Why would anyone want to kill poor Malachi?" Anne wondered. "I keep asking that question and can find no answers. He may not be everybody's idea of a Bishop but he certainly is harmless."

Not actually so harmless. But to do truly great harm one required more energy than Malachi possessed or perhaps ever possessed.

"With a new wave of cops," Spike said, "I will have to suggest to Phil that he get his crazy wife out of here before they come. It's less likely to be a spectacular show and the cops will wonder when the rest of us are going to the loony bin."

"Don't call it that!" Annie pleaded, taking her husband's arm in hers. "We're trying get poor Loretta back on a regular course of medication. She's not crazy, she just has the occasional manic interlude."

"Very manic," Spike sighed, "very very manic!"

I did not look forward to the morrow with much enthusiasm. The son of Sven would need the whole day to sort out their predecessor's mess and even when that was done we would be not one step closer to a solution. However, I would explain the locked-room part of the mystery and that might give them some hints where to look further. They would also want to find out more, I was sure, about Michael the caretaker who, for my money, was in too many places and knew too much—despite his patent good taste in women.

"So what did you think of your opposition on the court this afternoon?" I asked the redoubtable Joseph as he bore me home to Grand Beach in the family Lexus.

"Shirtsleeves law."

"Ah!"

"You know what that means, Uncle Blackie?"

"Rags to riches and back again in three generations,

though in some families it requires four. . . . You are suggesting that Ignatius Nolan is the third generation in the family which has risen to great success and now plummets toward failure?"

"You think it's genetic?"

"Arguably. Yet if your fair Margaret who represents similar genes were a male you would scarcely invoke the shirtsleeves law."

"I'm glad she's not a male," he said evenly.

"A wise choice."

"The other two guys are okay, yuppies out for the main chance."

"So?"

"Probably gifted enough in what they do, they know that their careers depend on family decisions in which they don't have much part. So they have to be careful how they treat that asshole Ignatius since he could conceivably control their futures. Not a good scene."

"Indeed."

The impending storm, which seemed a little earlier to have decided to move on, suddenly erupted. Once more we were struggling along Grand Beach Road amidst lightning and thunder and a fierce torrent of hail. Nonetheless Joseph John Murphy continued to be his cool dispassionate self.

"The Luftwaffe is out to get us, Uncle Blackie!"

"You would have been too old for the Royal Air Force in 1940," I pointed out. "All they wanted were teenagers."

"No difference between a juvenile delinquent and a hero?"

"And you and your age cohort should be thankful that you're not battling Me-109s with Spitfires, not that the world is all that much a better place today."

"Uhm . . ."

"You and the fair Margaret," I continued, "certainly did in those punks this afternoon."

"She asked afterwards if I minded her little scheme and I said I didn't mind but I would now be wary of all her little schemes."

"If a superannuated celibate may venture an opinion that was not the swiftest possible remark."

"I'm learning, Uncle Blackie, I'm learning. She is a handful!"

"Patently."

"Makes her more interesting."

"And much more vulnerable."

He thought about that for a moment.

"Arguably, Uncle Blackie."

"Maybe I shouldn't make an appearance tomorrow?" Joseph suggested after some thought. "Maybe I shouldn't come around too often?"

"Maybe you should come when your presence is necessary or someone thinks it's necessary."

"That someone would be you?"

"Not always."

"Cool!"

There would be, I thought, no useful purpose served in watching the Nolan family crack apart as Loretta Nolan was carried off to, as her father-in-law was pleased to describe it, a loony bin.

Back in my snug and dry apartment it was necessary to pour myself an extra large "jar" of Bushmills Green to settle my nerves and my stomach from the difficulties of the day. I warned the leprechaun that he could not have a single sip of it. But leprechauns are always hard to control especially when they have become resident wherever you happen to be.

"Cronin! What the hell's going on down there!"

The implication of that question was always that something wrong was going on and that I was responsible for it.

I explained to him the developments of the day and

the likelihood of a further crackup in the Nolan family on the morrow, hopefully before the new detachment of Michigan State Police arrived at Nolan's Landing.

"Is there any reason for you to be involved in such madness?"

"Insofar as my assignment is to solve the mystery of how a horde of hornets was introduced into Archbishop Malachi Nolan's room without the necessity of the door being opened, I suppose I have to be here."

"Hell of a vacation seems to me."

"Arguably."

"Well nothing much is happening around here in town. Cathedral staff functions pretty well in your absence. Though those little witches down in the office delight in pestering me."

"It is in their nature to do so."

"I suppose. Anyway Malachi seems to be out of danger. He talks all kinds of nonsense about retiring as Archbishop and transferring himself to Ampleforth, the Abbey over in England where he went to school, not so much to join the order—holy poverty would be far too much for Malachi to sustain—but for the peace and quiet and the local civil celebrity of being resident at the legendary Benedictine monastery."

"A harsh judgment on Malachi's motives, but I suspect accurate."

"Do we care that he goes to Ampleforth?"

"I do not believe so. If he announces that he is retiring as Archbishop *ad personam* in Laramie for health reasons and then announces he wants to spend the rest of his life praying in the monastic environment, those who know Malachi might find it hard to believe. Yet such a decision might contribute notably both to the length of his life and the salvation of his soul."

"Since I believe all the things you say about God

I would assume that he will be patient with Malachi as he must be with all of us. . . . But, Blackwood, why would anybody want to kill Malachi?"

"He would seem to be the last one in the family that would offend anyone and I'm sure the killing somehow is in the family."

"Who would be the most likely target for the family's wrath?"

"The fair Margaret Anne, beyond a doubt."

"Why would anyone want to harm that lovely young woman?"

"Because they see her as a future chairman of the board of trustees at Aviation Electronics and thus holding their fate in her own hands."

"They would suffer greatly under such a regime?"

"Not in the least, and they probably know that. She is resented especially, I suspect, because they know that she is the only one that will be able to replace the personality and flare of Spike Nolan."

"Well, if I were on the board of directors I'd vote for her."

"I'm sure you would."

"Hey, why doesn't she put you on the board of directors?"

"You gotta be kidding!"

"I suppose so. Well, Blackwood, solve the mystery and take a vacation and come back here because there's lots of work to do here in the archdiocese."

"Patently."

14

"*Don't you dare* weep, you filthy little whore-bitch!" Loretta Nolan tore herself away from her husband's grasp and slapped Margaret. The latter recoiled from the blow, the mark of her mother's hand red on her face.

"While I'm gone you're going to destroy the firm and disgrace us all. I hope somebody slits your throat in a back alley in New Orleans after they've gang-raped you."

"Loretta!" Spike Nolan's voice sounded like a pistol shot.

"I'm sorry that I didn't abort you like I wanted to! I'm sorry that I let your cunt of a father stop me!"

Her departure from Nolan's Landing was grand drama, appropriately hysterical. It began with high-pitched, wordless screams that grew louder and louder as she progressed from an argument in their bedroom down the corridor around the spiral staircase to the first floor and into the vestibule. It then transmuted itself into sobbing, screaming, and cursing that pushed Josie and Eileen to hysterics which, while mild compared to Loretta, were nonetheless a high-decibel protest against the evil which was being worked on their poor mother.

I suspected they would be happy to see her leave and

ready to renew their relationships with their husbands
when she was gone.

"I hope you crash that funky airplane of yours and burn
to death, slowly, painfully, a horrible death! When I finally get to heaven part of my joy will be looking down
in hell and seeing you suffering for all eternity in a burn-
ing airplane! You deserve every ounce of suffering for the
rest of your life! God damn you to hell for all eternity,
you ungrateful bitch! And I blame your father because he
wouldn't let me abort though I knew what kind of a child
you'd be—harsh and cruel and ungrateful and mean and
vicious. I should have insisted on abortion! Rot in hell!"

"Phil! Get her out of here!" Spike ordered.

Though tears poured down her cheeks and her head
was downcast, Margaret did not respond to this outpouring of raw hatred. She would never forget a word of it.
While her mother's outburst could be excused as a mani-
festation of mania, the substance of it was the way she
felt about this unwanted child of her life.

"Please stop it," Philip Nolan urged his wife. "When
you calm down and are yourself again and have forgotten all the horrid things you've said, they'll remember.
I'm not sure the family can survive much longer."

"You fucking son of a bitch! You always were a weak-
kneed husband and father! How could you choose your
senile parents over me! I hope you rot in hell with your
daughter! God damn you all to hell!"

Philip Nolan tried to ease her toward the doorway as
did the doctor and nurse from Happydale Institute in
Kokomo (that really was the name!). They had already
given her a shot to calm her down but it wasn't doing any
good. In the limousine they would administer another shot
and she would fall off the cliff of mania into the valley of
deep despair. They probably would get her to start taking
her meds again and in a month or maybe two months, she
would return to her normal self—whatever that was.

But they would have to develop an efficient means by which her husband could check whether she took the meds every day. That wouldn't be easy ~~because~~ when she began to emerge from depression to mania she would feel so wonderful that she wouldn't want to come down. Such is the cross of bipolar disorder. In the absence of a break in that cycle the rest of her life will alternate between highs and lows, between exuberance and pain, between fury and despair.

Finally Philip got her into a limousine and the attendants closed the door. The limo rolled down the tree-lined parkway of Nolan's Landing and off to the relative peace of Happydale in Kokomo.

Her daughters had to close the drama. They pushed their way to Margaret and both of them slapped her.

"Bitch!" they screamed at her.

Margaret bowed her head and did not reply. Had I been wise to ban Joseph from the scene? Perhaps not. Nonetheless, it might not have been advisable for him to be swept up in the hysteria. He would certainly have defended his fair princess but he might also begin to think that for all her beauty and wisdom and intelligence, for all the white fire he claimed she was, she might be too risky a chance. I thought not. But then what did I know? I would, however, this evening take counsel with the good Mary Kathleen and report as best I could the paroxysms of fury that began Saturday morning at Nolan's Landing.

A half hour later the new detachment of Michigan State Police appeared, dressed in conservative professional clothes—Captain Arne Svensson, a dapper little man with black hair graying at the temples, shrewd frosty blue eyes, and a smile which would light the Arctic Circle in the depths of winter. His assistant was Lieutenant Olaf Jacobsson, a hulking giant with long blond hair, a red Viking face, and everything but the horned helmet on his head to make him a berserker charging ashore at some

Irish monastery a thousand years ago. Speaking of Irish, the third cop was Sergeant Patricia Anne Elizabeth Marie Muldoon with pale blond hair that might be Norge, but twinkling West of Ireland eyes.

"You're not an Upper," I said, referring to an inhabitant of the Upper Peninsula of Michigan, where the ice melted in late May.

"Detroit Irish," she said with a grin.

I introduced them to Spike Nolan, the only one who had not retreated to the silence of his room. Spike welcomed them, assured them of the cooperation of everyone in the household, and admitted that two of those who were present on the night of the assault were no longer present. Then he led us up to his own office at the very top of the house, which overlooked the Lake, now resilient after last night's apocalyptic storm. The office spread the full width of the house and included a mahogany conference table with chairs around it, a computer workstation, a fireplace, a wet bar, and a gracious English wife, the sort one needs in an English country-house mystery. Maria Teresa brought coffee, tea, and cookies, donuts, and coffee cake. For Archbishop Blackie she also had managed to scare up some oatmeal raisin cookies.

"I don't know what to tell you to set the stage for your work," Spike began. "We will cooperate with you in every way possible. I will urge my family and the staff here to answer all your questions fully. We have two lawyers in residence in case anyone feels the need for one, but I won't intrude them into your conversations unless someone feels it necessary—as we felt with your predecessors."

Annie, now the relaxed, graceful English woman of the house, took up the formal introduction.

"I can't imagine why anybody would want to harm Malachi, at least anybody outside of the Roman Catholic hierarchy"—she flushed as she realized what she was saying—"present company excepted of course, Milord. Malachi is not a vindictive or a hypocritical man. You will have to judge for yourself if you find it necessary to go to Chicago and interview him at Northwestern University Hospital. Of all our children, alive and dead, he was the one who was the least driven, least ambitious, least difficult. Sometimes I wish he were more difficult because it was hard for my husband to enchant him into an argument. There are others in the family who are cordially disliked by some of their relatives as you no doubt heard in the tapes your predecessors made. But Malachi? No, I just don't understand it."

"And the girl Margaret?" Patricia Muldoon asked her.

"If you'd been here earlier," Spike responded, "you would have seen that Margaret was the target of much of this hysteria marking her mother's departure for Happydale—I can't believe that even in Indiana such a place actually exists—yet Anne and I are very proud of her, possibly because of what we see in her, some of the same attitudes and experiences we had back in 1940. It is as though we three are in the same generation. Still, for all the envy that she seems to attract, I can't imagine anybody would want to kill her. . . . You must forgive these ramblings of a disappointed and tired old man. Annie dear, do you have something to add?"

Anne Nolan smiled.

"When have I not had something to add? This lovely young woman who is serving the refreshments is Maria Teresa, sometimes called by her siblings Terri, and she's a very intelligent and perceptive young woman. I think you can expect her and the others to be cooperative."

Maria Teresa's face blossomed into a broad smile.

"Si, señora!"

"I'm sure the people who take care of us here probably have better insight into what we need and who we are than we do ourselves. I've already told them that I want

them to tell the truth because as St. James says in his epis-
tle only the truth will make us free."

"Sí, señora."

Maria Teresa winked at me and gave me three more
raisin cookies.

Spike passed out lists of the guests and the employees.
The cops sorted out their work. The dining room, the
drawing room, and this office would be available. Patti
Muldoon was fascinated at the opportunity to talk to Margaret. I would escort Captain Svensson to the crime room.

"If I may," I said, secreting my cookies in the pocket
of my Chicago Bears Windbreaker, "I want to specify a
time factor that might be important. It is very likely for
reasons I can detail later to Captain Svensson that the
plot against the Bishop of Laramie was already in motion before the discussion at the dinner table of Ms. Margaret Nolan's plans to teach in New Orleans, which led
to some ill feelings."

Each of the cops noted this fact in their book.

I sensed that this information was extremely important.
I also sensed that I had missed something critical in our
conversation, a mistake I would later have much cause to
regret.

I escorted Arne down to the crime room, observing as I
went by the door to the tiny chapel, just below the suite of
Spike and Anne, that Margaret, her face glowing again,
was inside lost in prayer. . . . She was, I know of no other
way to put it, drawing, perhaps even draining, more of her
white fire from the love of the Almighty.

Oh, that was what she was! Well, there'd be no fear of
what might happen to Joseph, should he risk loving her.

Or as one of my seminary classmates said of another
classmate, "He is one of your goddamn mystics."

"Nice place," Svensson said as he glanced around the
room where Malachi Nolan had been assaulted by a
swarm of hornets.

"Spike Nolan decided years ago when he was planning to build an English country house here in the dunes for his bride that he would spare no expense. Fortunately he could afford not to spare expense. Moreover he rehabilitates and modernizes the house every couple of years. It's always brand-new."

"Plenty of room, expensive furniture, comfortable bed, view of the Lake. Big bathroom, I suppose."

"With a whirlpool as well as a shower," I continued. "The rooms were designed for couples, not for celibates like Archbishop Nolan and myself. At some point Spike will have to cope with the fact that his great-grandchildren will need rooms of their own. Now the next generation is limited to three infants so they can live in the rooms with their parents, something which I think upsets his granddaughters."

"I have the reports from our forensic team," Captain Svensson said as he walked around the room, "and they all seem accurate enough. Is there something more I should know, Blackie?"

"As I said, I can explain how the locked-room mystery was accomplished. The essence of a general solution to such problems is that the murder weapon and/or the would-be killer be in the room before it is locked. So therefore sometime between the end of supper and the retirement of the guests to their rooms the hornets were introduced into Malachi's room. Malachi returned and closed the door. It locked automatically, as all the bedroom doors in the house apparently do when they're closed, unless one pushes the button in the door to keep it open."

"I understand."

"So, how did the perpetrator keep the hornets in the room until Archbishop Nolan fell asleep? Then how did he activate them from outside the locked door?"

"You tell me, Blackie."

"Our friend knew something about the habits of hornets, a knowledge he may have acquired on the Internet when he determined that he would exploit the Archbishop's allergy. He obtained the hornets outside where the nest is located, as I will show you shortly. He approached the nest at twilight when the hornets become very sleepy as their intense workday ends. He was therefore able with a sharp instrument to cut a segment of the nest off the tree where it was located and drop it in some kind of container, put the cover on the container, and bring it into the house."

"He must have gathered the hornets after supper," Arne observed.

"I doubt that. He would have had to escape too early from the after-dinner conversation to capture the hornets at twilight, brought them into the house, and then secrete them somewhere so he could bring them to the Archbishop's bedroom. I think it more likely that he had been planning this effort for some time. He had collected his hornets, hid them perhaps in his own room, and periodically lifted the cover off the can to make sure they were still active. The cover on the can is the equivalent of night for the hornets."

"So he left early from the conversation in the drawing room, came up here, found the door of the Archbishop's room unlocked, and then brought in the hornets. . . ."

"How did he know the door would be open?"

"I believe it is the custom of the service staff after they clean the room to leave the door ajar so that even if the occupant has forgotten her key she can get inside the room and then lock it. The married couples in this corridor or the other corridor down the stairs, would remember to lock the door because they would want privacy for their marital intimacy such as that may have been. In fact the walls are thick enough to guarantee privacy from the loudest noises. You may want to turn on the television full blast and see if you can hear it in the next room. I very much doubt it."

"So the killer came upstairs and activated his hornets but they apparently did not greet Archbishop Nolan when he returned to the room."

"Here he exhibited remarkable ingenuity. If you follow me I think I can show you where the hornet container was hidden and may still be."

We walked into the bathroom.

"I suggest to you," I said, "that the perpetrator entered the bathroom and placed the container in some relatively hidden spot. Then he turned off the lights, removed the cover of the container and then quickly exited the bathroom and departed the bedroom. He was careful of course to lock the door as he left."

I turned off the lights.

"I see."

Arne, son of Sven, had been watching me with the same suspicion his Lutheran ancestors might have viewed a captive Druid several centuries ago.

"Thus when Malachi Nolan came into his bedroom, having a considerable amount of the drink taken, he headed straight for the bed, quickly discarded his clothes, which you see piled up in that chair there, put on his somewhat outlandish pajamas, and collapsed into bed. Subsequently after a period of sleep, he realized that it would be necessary to relieve himself. He rose and stumbled into the bathroom here and turned on the lights."

I flipped on the light. It shattered the darkness immediately. Spike Nolan's contractors had decided that there was no reason why bathrooms should be dimly illuminated.

"The light was like a rising sun for the hornets. They stirred around in the unfamiliar place they found themselves and after some period, enough for the Archbishop to get out of the bathroom and totter back toward his bed, they emerged from their prison in the bathroom and pursued him. They were still buzzing around angrily when the valorous Margaret and her father and brother and the caretaker forced their way into the room. Margaret thereupon destroyed the hornets with the spray can that she had prudently brought along."

"I see."

"Now if my surmise is correct, the hornet container is still somewhere in this bathroom, arguably here behind the shower curtains."

The shower in the bathroom was equipped with transparent curtains rather than glass doors. However there was plenty of light to illumine the shower stall even with the curtains drawn. With perhaps too much of a drama I swept the curtains open and there are on the floor was a Folgers coffee can with the plastic lid removed.

I lifted it off the floor and displayed hornet corpses on the bottom.

"These hornets died during their imprisonment, perhaps in frustration that they couldn't do their daily work about which I gather hornets are obsessed."

"You would have expected," Captain Svensson murmured, "that the perpetrator would have returned to remove the clues."

"The only clues to what we might have found would have been his fingerprints and I suspect he wore gloves whenever he touched the coffee can. However it was a blunder not to eliminate this confirmation of my little theory."

"Who did you say opened the door?"

"The valiant Margaret with her spray can, her father, her brother Ignatius, and Michael Winter who is the caretaker. She summoned her father and brothers from their beds by pounding on the door and called Mr. Winter from his lair at the gate by house phone. With some effort the three males managed to push the door open and witnessed the Archbishop convulsing on the floor and the hornets, now furious from their long incarceration, buzzing around dangerously. Margaret was ready for them."

"So, the crime was planned and partially executed before the supper-table controversy over Margaret's New Orleans plans and the hornets attacked after supper. . . . What was the supper conversation about, Blackie?"

"It was a combined assault on Margaret for her decision to join ACE in New Orleans. I suspect that Loretta had briefed her daughters and son on the strategy earlier in the day. I should add however that, though it was a nasty attack, there were those that held their peace, the young woman's grandparents, Archbishop Nolan, her father, and a certain other and generally invisible little Archbishop. Loretta Nolan awakened her brother-in-law and demanded his opinion. He contented himself with hoping that Margaret would consider her family's wishes. Then, with little concern for the normal rules of hospitality, she demanded the aforementioned innocuous little bishop's opinion."

"And he said?"

"He observed that it was useless to try to persuade young people to withdraw some activity about which they had made up their mind and indeed family pressures would only lead to greater resistance. He neglected to apply this dictum to the matter at hand though his intent was, I suspect, clear."

"Then what happened?"

"Then Loretta Nolan, perhaps infuriated by the simplicity of the little bishop's words, became somewhat hysterical. It might have been said that she went over the top. She expressed a fear that a scandal in New Orleans involving her daughter would destroy Aviation Electronics and the family's prospects for the future."

"And then?"

"Spike Nolan said that Archbishop Ryan was right. This patently correct judgment on the situation infuriated Loretta Nolan so much that she told her father-in-law that he was a senile old fool."

"She was already over the wall by then?"

"At least on her way over the wall."

"So sometime after supper, perhaps while the main conversation was going on in the drawing room, the perpetrator slipped away and brought the coffee can filled with hornets into the Archbishop's room and positioned it where we found it in the shower behind the curtain."

"After the dust up at the table," I agreed, "but not because of it he carried out the plot he had prepared before supper and perhaps during the day."

"One cannot say that the supper argument was a cause?"

"One might say that it confirmed the perpetrator's plans."

"But if Archbishop Nolan was not a major participant in the argument, why was he the target?"

"I would assume because the perpetrator had already developed his own motive for inducing a dangerous reaction to hornet venom in a man who was known to be susceptible to such a reaction. I'm not suggesting that the attempted murder—and I think we can call it that for the sake of the argument—was independent of the tensions and constraints in the Nolan family. Archbishop Nolan was a target of these for some other reason. As I've suggested he simply was not part of the violent discussion."

"Then knowing how the criminal accomplished his assault on the Archbishop does not give us much of a hint of who he or she is?"

"I put it to you, Arne Svensson, that the attack was quite independent of the supper-table conversation but not necessarily independent of the stresses and strains in the Nolan family."

"I hear you, Blackie. In our interviews we should try to probe at those conflicts."

"Precisely. Conflicts aggravated by Loretta Nolan's desire to intervene in the affairs of the firm and consolidate her own family's grip on the firm by forcing herself and her son Ignatius on the board of directors. One effect of the table conflict was that Spike Nolan told his son Philip that he was going to appoint their daughter Margaret to the board despite her youth. We don't know how Philip reacted to that plan. However, unwisely, it would seem, he shared that information with his wife, who then seems to have been swept away completely by her mania."

"This goal is unrelated to any attempt to kill Malachi Nolan because his niece had already been appointed to the board?"

"Therein lies the mystery. It may well be that the perpetrator did not intend that Malachi Nolan die. He might not have realized that hornet venom can be fatal for someone who was sufficiently allergic to it. He might only have been trying to make Malachi Nolan ill and thus get him out of the house. Or arguably he was simply engaging in malicious mischief."

"Again you say he?" Arne asked.

"The would-be killer could have been of either gender or may have been more than one individual."

"Even if we are able to discover the identity of the perpetrator, we certainly will not be able to bring an attempted-murder charge against that person unless we can discover a motive a prosecuting attorney would find plausible to bring before a jury."

"Surely that could turn out to be true," I agreed.

The son of Sven walked slowly about the room, examining Malachi's garments, the furniture, the papers on his desk, the view from the window, his briefcase and toiletries, his purple robes in the closet.

"I don't know why I'm doing this, Blackie. I'm sure our crime scene men did a good job."

"It is most unfortunate that the Bishop's assistant departed so quickly and is now, I am told, in one of his order's priories in Mexico. . . . He would be an obvious suspect because of his flight. . . ."

"Homosexual lover?"

"No evidence of that either here or in Laramie."

"We could go down there and attempt to question him."

"They are a very secret bunch. He would disappear again."

He closed his leather-bound notebook and with a deft movement slipped it back into the inside pocket of his flawlessly tailored dark blue suit.

"I think I had better instruct my colleagues to begin the interviews. I had chosen the cook for the first one, even though I had never seen her. Yet in my experience in those few homes where there still are cooks they know everything that is going on."

"I think, Arne Svensson, you'll find the cook a very interesting and intelligent woman."

As we walked past the library on our return to the drawing room, I noted that Margaret was talking on her cell phone. She was smiling and laughing, a conversation with someone who mattered.

Well, I hadn't told him not to talk to her on the phone.

"Consider the facts," I told Arne's team. "A very rich family whose wealth has been based on the genius of the de facto founder of Aviation Electronics, a war hero who is still active and intelligent in his eighties. Who will succeed him in power? His first son was shot down over Hanoi. His daughter who had thrown herself into the drug culture suffered gang rape and murder in a back street in Katmandu. The second son removed himself from the contest when he decided to become a priest. That left the third son, Philip Nolan, as the heir presumptive. And after him? The next in line may well have been Ignatius though he did not seem to be the CEO type. Therefore it was necessary for Spike Nolan to elevate his young granddaughter, Margaret Nolan, to the board of directors of the firm and probably his eventual replacement as chairman of the board. In the midst of this atmosphere of conflict his second son, a priest, barely escapes what seems to be an attempt at murder. Your task of course is to find who brought the hornets to the Archbishop's room, who caused death to come for the Archbishop. You must not let the family conflict obscure this search, but you can hardly afford to ignore it."

"Do you have any instincts, Archbishop Blackie?" Olaf Jacobsson asked respectfully.

"None on which I would care to invest any of my commodity futures, if I had any such. However, there are some interesting people. Most notably young Margaret Nolan, a recent graduate of the Golden Dome, who admits that a couple of years ago she had a 'sophomore crush' on my promising nephew, but is also determined to do her volunteer time in New Orleans. She owns her own airplane and is presumably the real heiress to this house and Aviation Electronics.

"Then there is Mr. Michael Winter, a man with a haunted look and an air of mystery which suggest a past that may not be discussable. But he knows a lot and seems to be everywhere, watching and judging.

"We must not forget the absent Loretta Nolan, a beautiful woman with unfortunate bipolar propensities who wants to preside over Aviation Electronics and whose mania has driven the family to its present crisis, her husband Philip Nolan who is a brilliant scientist and the effective CEO of AVEL, as it is called on the NYSE, and their son Ignatius who thinks that he is capable of replacing his father as CEO of the company and drinks and gambles."

"I'll see if I can defrost Mr. Winter," Olaf said in his deep baritone.

"I'll hunt out the cook," the son of Sven said with a dubious smile. "Archbishop Ryan tells me that I'll find her interesting."

"And I'll see if this pilot, heiress, and Domer is all she is cracked up to be. . . . Will you introduce her to me, Father Blackie?"

"I will, Ms. Muldoon, but I think before her you might talk to the outsider in the family, Ignatius's wife, Consuela."

15

"I better hang up, Joseph, the Church and State are here to interrogate me!"

She favored me with her most impish grin.

"I didn't call him, he called me to see how I had done in the Götterdämmerung this morning. I told him I was breathing in and out, most of my vital signs were normal, and I was taking nourishment."

I introduced her to Sergeant Patti Muldoon, bid them both a good day, and asked that God have mercy on their souls.

They scoffed at me, as young women do when they encounter a pathetic elder clergyman.

Each of the investigators made an immediate summary of each interview that would be available to the others before the transcripts arrived from Stevensville next week.

"You'll find some of this stuff like listening to a confession in your church," Sven warned me. "We find that when we're just exploring, we don't probe so much as let people talk. If they're troubled they tell us a lot of private stuff, maybe just a little bit too much. It's from that 'too much' we get our best clues."

A summary of an interview with Ms. Margaret Anne Nolan

Saturday Afternoon

After some banter about Notre Dame and the University of Michigan we settled down to an interview which was interesting though I'm not sure how useful for the problem at hand. Ms. Nolan insisted on her deep affection for her uncle Archbishop Malachi Nolan. He was a little lazy, she admitted, and perhaps drank a little bit too much but he was a nice, gentle man and she was sure that the children in Laramie loved him. She couldn't imagine why anybody would want to poison him—poison was her word and is not inappropriate because the venom of a hornet is, like the venom of many other bites, poisonous. She didn't like Father Gomez the priest secretary who traveled with the Archbishop, more or less she thought to prevent them from getting lost. Uncle Malachi apparently has little skills in organizing his life. She absolutely did not think there was any sexual relationship between her uncle and the priest. He was not a particularly attractive man, mostly because he couldn't smile. Some of the young service people in the house like Terri and Glori complained that they did not like the way he looked at them. I doubt that he would try anything, not in our house. I suspect he panicked when the police arrived and was afraid that he might have to reveal some of the secrets of his very secret order. I'm not sure what Uncle Bishop would say about that however.

Yes, there is conflict in our family and that's understandable given the stakes at issue. The conflict is made worse by her mother's need to dominate and control the future, probably because her mother's father lost all his investments when she was a child. Mom would say "get everything organized." It is true that there is a succession crisis in the company, but it won't happen for a long time. His doctor says Grandpa Nolan could easily live 10 more years. Her father will continue as CEO because he is very good at it and also a first-rate metallurgical sci-

entist. He developed the formula for the composite that Boeing is putting on the 787. The question of who will succeed her father when he retires to be just Chairman of the Board and the company needs a new CEO is at least 10 to 15 years in the future. It caused trouble now because her brother Ignatius didn't have the personality or the talent to be CEO. He would make a good criminal trial lawyer, something which the company doesn't need. My mother is determined nonetheless Ignatius will succeed his father, and my grandfather is just as determined that it is unthinkable. Mom wants them both to be on the board of directors so they can take control of the company and so Ignatius will be the next CEO whatever his qualifications. Grandpa will not stand for that and neither will Grandma and I don't think Daddy will either. Mom unfortunately doesn't have the ability to be patient and see what happens. She has to plan and scheme and control everything long in advance. Grandpa tells me that some Irish mothers are that way because there's a memory of the famine. Mom becomes even worse when the bipolar disorder begins to kick up. Like many other folks with the same problem she won't take her meds and then she goes quite manic and does and says crazy things which hurt her and the rest of us. Dad tries his best and he still loves her very much and will stand by her. However Grandpa will not tolerate my mother's constant interference in the company. He has banned her from the headquarters in New York and all the plants around the world. There is going to be lots of conflict, a tug-of-war for the soul of the company between Mom and Grandpa. Mom will lose. Even if she were a lot more self-possessed than she is, she would still lose. Everyone will be hurt in the battle and I will become an outcast of the family. So be it I guess. No, I won't become CEO. I want to be a writer, a comic writer, if you can imagine that. I may be Chairman of the Board eventually and the conflicts with

my sisters and my brother will go on. They will never for-
give me. So be it.

The interviewer feels that the respondent understands
the risks ahead and will deal with them. Nonetheless,
since there is perhaps a need to murder in her family, she
will need good security in the years to come.

Patricia Muldoon

I put aside Patti Anne's notes, clear and objective,
though like most people, she liked the subject. The Magic
Child was clear-eyed and objective about herself and her
family, though not yet capable of believing that someone
might try to kill her.

The next set of notes summarized the interview between Lieutenant Jacobsson and the cook—the Upper
Peninsula meets Mexico.

16

A precis of an interview with Señora Juana Maria Garcia

Saturday Morning

Interviewer Lt. Olaf Thor Jacobsson MSP

I met with Ms. Garcia in her "office" next to the kitchen in Nolan's Landing. She is a gorgeous woman in her late thirties or early forties and in a black dress (with black nylons and silver jewelry) she looks like a Spanish contessa, with castanets somewhere on her person waiting for the dance to begin. She insisted bluntly that she could not violate her professional confidence about the Nolan family. She showed me her social security card as proof of her right to be in the United States. I did not ask her for a green card and she did not offer one. The month at Nolan's Landing was not her only source of employment. Her company (hers and as it would develop Mr. Winter's) had more than enough of the services they could provide in the Harbor Country. She was, after all, the best Mexican-American chef in the state of Michigan and she also was the best caterer in Western Michigan, though she made no claim to excellence in the rest of the state. Her children would all graduate from high school and college. They did not feel inferior because they were servants. They were as good as, if not better than, the people they served. They especially liked their August month at Nolan's Landing. Capitan Nolan and Donna Anna were adorable and the sainted Margarita was the good friend of all of her little family. The less she had to do with the Philip Nolan family, the happier she was. Loretta Nolan assumed that it was her right and duty to fashion the menu for every evening meal. Cook would not miss her while she was away because she was loco. Archbishop Nolan was not a simple padre of the land, like the funny little Archbishop Ryan who was muy sympatico and saw right through everyone, herself included. Her relationship with Mr. Winter, who was a good and respectful man, was not any business of the police. She had no idea of why anyone would try to murder Don Malachi and such a horrible way to kill him. The killer was also loco, no?

It was no secret that Ignatius Nolan was loco too. He drank too much, he gambled too much, he was cruel to his pregnant wife, he tried to flirt with her daughters. She warned him that if it did not stop, she would report him to his grandmother. He knew she meant it. But he was not evil, just a little boy who had yet to grow up. His sisters did not want to come to Nolan's Landing every summer because their mother interfered in their marriages and their husbands were most unhappy. Young people should be left alone, no?

Don Felipe could not control his wife. She would not obey him. Sometimes wives should obey their husbands, yes. And also and more often husbands should obey their wives. But when your husband tells you to stay out of conflicts with his company, he should be obeyed, no? Don Felipe a weak man? No, but what was he to do? In Mexico of such a woman it would be said that she needs to be spanked often. But here in gringo land I am a feminist and I will not say that, no? Who tried to kill Don Malachio?

I am sure it was that horrible Father Gomez who devoured me with his hungry eyes.

It was, as Father Blackie predicted, an interesting interview, one I will not soon forget.

Olaf Thor Jacobsson, Lieutenant MSP

Olaf had captured the personality of Cook and, being a male member of our species, had been captivated. Interesting but nothing much new. She could tell us a lot more about the Nolan family, but perhaps I would have to interview her. I didn't want to do that.

17

A precis of an interview with Michael Winter
Saturday Morning
Interviewer Captain Arne Luther Svensson
*After one quick glance at Mr. Michael Winter, I knew
that he'd once been part of operational intelligence—
CIA most likely, but possibly the FBI or some military intelligence outfit. Such professional spies give themselves
away by their eyes and the cautious duplicitous stare of
a man who long ago learned that he can trust no one.*

*I introduced myself and he responded by telling me his
assumed name and inviting me to sit down. His office
and bedroom in the gatehouse in Nolan's Landing were
neat and impersonal despite the stacks of books around
the walls and computer output on his desk. Winter was a
great reader and apparently a great writer. What he was
reading about and what he was writing I could not tell.*

"I did some time at Quantico," *I began.*

*Without blinking or changing his facial expression he
replied that he did his boot camp at Pendleton.*

"I meant with the CIA, I was in one of their special
training programs for local cops."

"Sorry," *he said with a tiny smile, the most he seemed
capable of,* "I never been to that place."

"You're in some sort of witness protection program," I said. "You folks are always waiting for the protection to break down."

"Sorry, Lieutenant, wrong number."

"Okay, I guess that's none of my business. It does make me suspicious."

He passed me a thin manila folder across his steel desk and said here's the story of my life—Vietnam, First Marines, prison camp, rehab, different hospitals, an honorable discharge, what we now call posttraumatic stress syndrome, an alcohol problem, more time in VA hospitals, AA, and now off the sauce for seven years—and never worry about tomorrow morning.

The asshole had all the right answers. There was no point in my trying to get his fingerprints or his DNA. Those who prepare phony identities for spies who come in from the cold were good at what they did. I glanced at the small file of papers and then returned it to him. Everything would be confirmed by the federal records but the records for such men lied. My instincts are pretty good. I know a CIA man on the run when I encounter one. I asked where he served, what he had done, and what was so important to hide. "Okay, Colonel," I said, "at least you can tell me what countries you worked in."

His tired eyes darted anxiously. I'd perhaps found a weakness in his disguise.

"Thanks for the promotion, officer," he said with a small movement of his lips that might have been considered a smile. "I was never more than a sergeant and I was only in Vietnam and for a while in a Taiwanese hospital. Nice try, though!"

The same thin smile. He was enjoying the combat.

"Does Spike Nolan know your background?"

"Spike knows everything about me. He wouldn't have hired me if he didn't know."

It was a flat statement of fact that indicated that this

conversation was over. I think we should be wary about
Michael Winter. No matter how many people he may have
killed in Vietnam and perhaps in his subsequent work,
once a hit man, always a hit man. He won't tell us the
whole truth about his present involvement in Nolan's
Landing. Perhaps he can't tell us the whole truth. I had
made a fool of myself by thinking I could break his mask.

He presumed Archbishop Ryan had told us about the
hornets' nest. He also presumed that the Archbishop,
who was a very clever little fellow, figured out how it
passed through the locked door into Archbishop Nolan's
room. He wasn't sure this would enable him to say who
had cut the hornets' nest, and then attempted to kill
Malachi with hornet venom.

That's your problem, Captain, not mine. I don't know
why anybody would want to kill Malachi. He isn't much.
He's harmless. All his years of gossiping and politicking
and paying bribes to people in Rome didn't get him anything more than Laramie. Or is it Laredo? It doesn't
matter, they're both nowhere and that's where Malachi
Nolan belongs. There is little to admire in him other
than a shallow grace and charm. He's really not involved in the context of the Nolan family war save as an
outside observer who dimly perceives what is happening
but can't be bothered by it. He finds Loretta's single-
mindedness boring and the intensity she has instilled in
her children disturbing—disturbing his afternoon naps. I
suppose he likes young Margaret, who doesn't like her?
Except Eileen McGinity and her other siblings. Perhaps
one of the reasons he decided to become a priest was he
wanted no part of the demands of AVEL. Can't say I
blame him. There never was a master key which would
open the doors to their rooms. Malachi can't understand
Spike's concern about keeping his creature alive after he
dies. Probably he was right in his judgment that Loretta
would destroy it and Margaret might save it for a while.

Philip Nolan is a weakling still besotted by his wife's sexual charms and incapable of imposing any kind of discipline on her. She must be spectacular in bed. He won't run the firm into the ground, though if Loretta has her way and Ignatius succeeds eventually to become the CEO, she will certainly ruin it. Here in the dune forest with sand on the beach and the sound of waves at night and with the deer and raccoons and woodchucks and skunks and the feral cats and the birds singing in the morning, it doesn't much matter so long as you have an air-conditioned room in the summertime and a cozy fireplace in the winter.

He seemed weary of it all, contented but weary.

And a woman in your bed at night?

He nodded his head.

I asked him if he earned a good living from his service of the superrich in Harbor Country. He replied that it was a respectable way to provide employment and education for the cook and her kids. Was he sleeping with the señora? He said, "I should be so lucky."

I doubted that evasion but did not think it worthwhile to push it. Michael would not tell us anything about his past or about his present. He knows what is going on in the big house at Nolan's Landing but is not about to intervene in these rich people's lives. They would have to work out their destiny by themselves. Who do you think is going to win? He thought that Margaret held all the cards, if she wanted to play them.

Loretta would eventually come back from the asylum and renew her campaign. It might tear the family apart but it wasn't any of his business. When he was much younger, he wouldn't have minded a tumble in bed with Loretta. In those days he liked dangerous women. No longer.

Did he know about the verbal assault on Margaret before Malachi was murdered? Yes, he shrugged, he had

heard about it. Didn't sound like all that much of a bat-
tle. It would take a while longer for Loretta to get up a
full head of steam. He wasn't surprised by Spike's return
gambit. He moved a new queen on the chessboard, a very
dangerous one, especially teamed with that Notre Dame
giant. Would he have made a good Marine?

Murphy was too smart to be a Marine.

Had Loretta ever come on to him?

He was too old for that kind of stuff.

The conversation was going nowhere and would not
no matter how much I probed. I did not believe that
Michael Winter was neutral in the Nolan family conflict,
as he pretended to be. He must've known that, if Loretta
should take control, he and his lover and her children
would be swept away from Nolan's Landing. He did have
some vested interest in the outcome, but it was not clear
to me how much he would be willing to exert himself in
the battle. In a way he was too lazy to fight, just like
Malachi but with perhaps better reasons.

I studied him carefully during our conversation and
concluded that he was indeed a government gumshoe
and probably a hit man. He also had done time in prison.
Occasionally an expression crossed his face, however
briefly, that you see often in ex-cons, as they glance to
see if the guards are still watching. In the possibility that
it might have some bearing on the attempted murder of
Malachi Nolan. I'm going to check with my friends at
Quantico and see if they can tell me anything. It will be a
waste of time. I'm sure they will never have heard of
Michael Winter. They would pass the word that I had
asked about him up the network to those who did know
the name, but they would never tell.

A.L. Svensson MSP

Ah, the good son of Sven had sensed the mystery and
indeed the danger that permeated that little room. Yet, I

thought to myself, he's wrong. Winter is involved with the struggle in the Nolan family and almost certainly on Margaret's side. But Arne had not seen the quick opening and quick closing elevator door that told me who Michael was. Much good that quick image did me. I still could not figure out who he was.

Now for the intriguing interaction between the giggly Consuela and Patricia Detroit.

18

A synopsis of an interview with Consuela Reynolds Nolan

Saturday Morning

Interviewer PAM

Consuela, in the early stages of her first pregnancy, is jumpy, and does not want to carry her child in a corridor where a serious crime occurred. She wants to go back home to her apartment in New York and settle down and relax and enjoy her pregnancy. It's not a difficult pregnancy, not as difficult as the one Mom suffered with Margaret—I always call my mother-in-law "Mom" because she seems to like it and I want to please her—I've been sick a couple times and I don't have any particular unusual aches and pains. I think I look happy as you should look in the first months of the first pregnancy. But I'm not happy at all. This house makes me unhappy. There's a conflict here. So many people watching us—the servants and now the security people and the lawyers and just everybody is spying on us. I can't go out for a walk in the beautiful park behind us because there are television people out there taking my picture. I wish we could go home tomorrow. Ignatius says we have to stick it out. Margaret is the problem. My other sisters-in-law say she is a spiteful, evil woman. She's been that way all of her life. The family wishes she'd never been born. She does outrageous things. She stirs up conflict between various members of the family. You can see evil in her eyes. Maybe she's put curses on me and my child. Spike Nolan is in her power. She can destroy poor Ignatius's future at AVEL. And she is truly obsessed with her little airplane. I couldn't believe the size of it when my mom showed it to me at the Michigan City municipal airport. We were driving into the Marquette Mall to shop and we passed the airport. It didn't look like an airport at all just a lot of garages. Mom asked me if wanted to see the plane. Margaret had talked about it so much I thought it might be a great big twin-engine jet like the company's Gulfstream 4. But it is a little plane painted red; it looks like a ramshackle automobile from 25 years ago might look. I can't imagine why she flies it every day. Maybe I think it's a substitute for a boyfriend. Mom said to me, that's Margaret for you—if it wasn't dangerous, if it didn't get attention, she wouldn't do it. Just like everything else in her life. She was water-skiing on the Lake today. That's a terribly dangerous sport especially for women and especially on unpredictable Lake Michigan. She has hooked up with a terrible boy from down the beach who Mom said was nothing but an Irish bum pursuing manic Margaret for her money and power.

Mom has her moods. The things that happened in the family the last couple of days put her into a bad mood. It was not right, however, to send her off to an insane asylum especially in Indiana. She ought to take her medicine more often and this wouldn't happen. Still my father-in-law got rid of her because Mr. Nolan couldn't stand her around the house. She should not have called him a senile old fool. He does not seem senile except that he seems to like Margaret. I don't think he's a fool either. He's nice to me, always friendly and respectful, asking me how I feel. His wife Lady Anne is just as kind. But I don't trust either of them because they are trying to squeeze Mom and the rest of our family out of the firm, Ignatius included.

Only someone who was unbalanced could have tried to kill Father Malachi with hornet stings. I don't know why anybody would want to kill him. He was a nice sweet old man who liked to tell stories about Rome which sometimes were very interesting and occasionally very funny. The worst part of the attack on him as Mom said was that Margaret jumped into the ambulance with him and rode to the hospital. That was an example of her narcissistic behavior. She was grabbing attention for herself because the Archbishop might've been dying. What good would she have been in the hospital?

I'll tell you the truth about my marriage. It has not been especially happy. Before we were married he seemed very eager to have me. Then in a few months he lost interest. I think he may be seeing other women. Don't get pregnant right away, he said. We should wait a while to have children, get to know each other better. I was in a hurry and we got pregnant anyhow and Mom supported me. But he is more interested in that gambling casino in Michigan City. I hate that place. He comes back every night bragging about how much money he has won and smelling of a lot of drinking. Then he falls asleep and ignores me. Mom says that's because he's so concerned about what Margaret is doing to the family. She said that when I had the baby he'd settle down and love me the way he did when we were courting. Josie, who was a classmate of mine at school, says the same thing. She says Ignatius is all right, just needs a good wife to settle him down. I've tried to settle him down. I must not know how because he's wilder than he was before. He will certainly be the next CEO in the corporation. He deserves it and it would be only fair, but Margaret is in the way. Mom thought that she herself and Ignatius would join the board of directors at their next meeting but now it looks like Margaret's going to be

*the member of the board. That's a terrible setback for Ig-
natius. They don't get along at all. I don't blame him for
not liking her. If she can block his promotion, that's the
end for Ignatius. He will have to leave the company and
go into the practice of law. He tells me he wouldn't mind
that. It's a lot more fun in the courtrooms than in the AVEL
offices. They are certainly exciting on television, I replied
to him. He says courts in New York are much more exciting. It's like a National Football League team on Sunday
night. I hope he's happy whatever he does and when our
baby is born as happy as I am and everything will be fine
again. Mom says it will. Mom is such a reassuring person.*

*The argument at dinner that night was awful. Without
any warning Mom brought up her opposition to Margaret's teaching school. Her point was very reasonable.
If Margaret is killed down there that'll embarrass us all
and weaken the firm. Like Ignatius says we'd be well rid
of her but still it would be embarrassing. Almost everybody supported Mom but she wasn't getting what she
needed. I could see she was becoming angry. I know
what happens when that starts. She goes into one of her
wild fits. When she found out the next day that Margaret
was going to be elected to the board of trustees instead
of her she became more crazy. Still she doesn't belong in
that insane asylum. Phil should have brought in a nurse
and a doctor to take care of her until she calms down.
She didn't seem deeply angry at Archbishop Nolan because his support for her argument against Margaret
was kind of weak. But she was furious at the other little
priest who said that Margaret would probably do what
she made up her mind to do and trying to prevent her
would just make her determination stronger. That's no
way for a priest to talk. It just encourages young people
to be disrespectful with their parents. I thought as usual
Phil equivocated trying to please his own father and
please his wife and taking care of his children all at the*

same time. He's a very difficult man to understand. Ignatius claims to admire him but he doesn't seem to have respect for Ignatius.

I suppose I'll have to combat this terrible place every year because it's what Grandpa likes. Mom says that when Grandpa dies everything will change. We won't have to come here anymore. It's a terrible lonesome place when you're pregnant and don't have your friends to talk to and the family is in open conflict with one another. I hate it! Mom says I must hang in there and be patient. When the baby comes things will be a lot better. At least I'll have someone to take care of and something to do besides reading magazines and watching television—and playing the occasional card games. Ignatius gets very angry at me for playing cards because I usually win. He claims I couldn't possibly beat him unless I cheat and I never cheat. Ignatius is a smart man, but he is not a very good card player.

I still have nightmares about Archbishop Nolan. His room is just across the corridor from ours. I didn't hear him screaming until Margaret had to wake us all up so we can help the Archbishop—and she could show off how smart she was by killing hornets with a spray can, always thinking of new ways to showcase herself. So I put on a robe and followed Ignatius over to the Archbishop's room and took one look and rushed back to my own room to vomit. I was sick for the rest of the night. I don't know how long I can stand being here. My Mom and Josie and especially Eileen are very nice to me. But they don't understand everything that's happening to me and they don't understand that Ignatius pays no attention to me. Eileen said I should try to be more intelligent. I should read so I can talk intelligently to my husband.

I read much more than Ignatius reads. He glances at The Wall Street Journal *and then picks up* USA Today. *I read* The New York Times *every day and I know a lot*

more about what is happening in the world than he does.
Yet whenever I try to express my opinion, Ignatius tells
me to be quiet, I don't know what I'm talking about.

(This interviewer suspects that there are rumbles of
rage inside this shallow and passive-aggressive young
woman. For her own good I hope she blows up at all of
them. "Settling down" her husband might require a two-
by-four—preferably verbal.)

PAM

Ah, the insightful Ms. Muldoon sees hope in the
matter of Consuela Reynolds Nolan, a quality which is
invisible to me. My only conclusion from the memo
is that Consuela knows more than she is telling us.

19

A summary of an interview with Eileen Nolan McGinity
Sunday Afternoon
Interviewer P.A. Muldoon
*Ms. McGinity is a well-preserved woman in her early
thirties, with flaming red hair and an overt sexuality she
may have learned from her mother, whom I have yet
to meet. She was openly hostile. Her mother's testimony
to Sergeant Munster explained the whole case. The attempted murder of the Archbishop was one more opportunity for her sister Margaret to call attention to herself. To
upstage the rest of the family. Obviously Grandmother
and Grandfather had intervened to protect Margaret and
the present investigation was a charade. They would go
back to Stevensville with an open case. And nothing more
would be heard, especially since Malachi was apparently
recovering. Margaret had been that way all her life. She
was an obstreperous baby who wailed and cried and mis-
behaved all the time. She refused to learn to walk, she
didn't want to talk, she resisted toilet training. She is a terrible brat, always has been. If her mother, poor woman,
had an emotional problem, you didn't have to look far to
see who was responsible for it. A fourth child like Margaret would drive any mother crazy.*

Eileen has two children and she certainly loves them both though they have to learn how to accept discipline and behave. She wants no more children because a fourth or even a third might deprive her of her sanity. We have done our duty to the continuation of the human race, she said curtly. That's enough.

There is no real conflict in the family. Her father, after all, still is the CEO of AVEL and will also become the next Chairman of the Board when Grandfather dies. She doubted that Ignatius would succeed him. He didn't have the taste or the discipline for that sort of work. It probably would be smart to get out of the firm while he still could—make a ton of money perhaps defending the New York Mafia.

The promotion of Margaret to the board of directors surprised no one. Her senile grandfather is like everyone else in the family except us. He makes her his favorite. However she is too scatterbrained, too narcissistic, too unstable to be an effective chairman. Poor father would have a hard time especially being torn between Margaret and his wife. Under such circumstances he might end up in a mental institution too. He had been very cruel to ship her mother off to Kokomo. It did take some pressure off him for the moment because Spike Nolan hated her so much. I told her a couple of times that the only way to win Spike over was to sleep with him a couple of times. And she just laughed at that and said it might be worth a try. I'm convinced she didn't try it. Next summer she and Gerry would simply decline to spend the month of August at Nolan's Landing. It is a hellish experience. It destroyed all the romance of being away from home on the shore of the Michigan dunes. Her own kids go crazy and the little Mexican bitch who was supposed to take care of them was too busy flirting with the younger men to do her job. Moreover she and Gerry thought it was the right of the husband and wife to have a bedroom for *themselves. If your children slept in the same room with you, it was very hard on intimate relationships. She herself would be very happy if the whole escapade was over. Perhaps Spike would take the hint and not invite people to come back next summer.*

She also detested the reversion to adolescence of her husband and her brother and her brother-in-law as soon as they got to Nolan's Landing. They spent most of their time playing golf or tennis and drinking and gambling over at that horrid casino boat in Michigan City. That was always a setback for her own family during the next couple of months because men, after a month away from the civilized influence of New York and their friends, have become uncivilized. It would require some major effort on her part to settle Gerry down. And she didn't want to have to go through that again.

Ms. McGinity shares her mother's low opinion of her sister Margaret. I'm not sure that Margaret will stay on the board of directors for a long time. My mother is right when she says that Margaret is a lot like Aunt Elizabeth and will die the same way in a back alley somewhere or maybe in the plane crash. She's too reckless to be useful.

Patricia Anne Muldoon, Sergeant MSP

Note: This is one very nasty woman.

Right on, PAM, right on. Also just a little crazy. These acute summaries of the various members of the third generation of Clan Nolan merely confirmed that they were a dysfunctional family, most of the problem traceable to their bipolar mother and vacillating father. But would any of them try to murder their Uncle Bishop?

20

A summary of an interview with Ignatius T. Nolan
Saturday Afternoon
Interviewer Lt. Olaf Thor Jacobsson, MSP
Ignatius Nolan is a superannuated juvenile delinquent.
We should have brought Sergeant Munster back here.
Munster knows how to treat people who have the bodies
of adults along with the personality and the desires of a
16-year-old. From beginning to end of the interview, Ig-
natius was unnecessarily offensive, apparently for the pure
hell of it.

I work in the courts in New York, he told me. I know
what cops are like and you guys don't frighten me one
bit. You're not going to intimidate me. Forget about it
and leave me alone.

I didn't try to kill that asshole Malachi. Is that clear?
I can't stand faggots. I never could. My blood turns cold
every time I see one of them. I'd like to punch their fag-
gotty jaw.

I'm not dumb enough to try to kill my faggot uncle.

Don't bother asking me where I was at the time when
somebody must have planted the hornets in his room. Af-
ter supper and the battle royal my crazy mother created,
we all went into the drawing room and watched a little

baseball. Nobody said much of anything. We're all as-
tonished at how my crazy mother blurts out that Spike is
a senile fool. She's the one who's a fool. Nothing is
wrong with Spike—he's a genius and a nice guy too. He
shouldn't have to put up with my mother and my father
and my crazy sisters. Mom is okay some of the time, but
she'd never leave me alone about getting married. So fi-
nally she talked me into marrying Consuela and that has
been fun. I can do anything I want to her when we're in
bed. She's just plain dumb. All she wants out of marriage
is babies. I'll let her have one, maybe two, and that'll
keep her busy. She won't be hanging on me all the time.
And that will keep my mother off my back. Yeah, I'm go-
ing to be president and CEO of this company sometime.
I'm next in line, the last of the male Nolans. My mother
is a little crazy, no, a lot crazy. But she'll fight for what
she wants and she wants me to be CEO. I'm in line for
the job and nothing is going to stop us. That little bitch
Margaret is an airhead.

Gerry and Brendan and I agreed that night we'd go to
the casino again. The night before I had a great run of
luck. After a big killing I wanted to see if my good luck
was continuing.

So we slipped away from the crowd in the drawing
room and left at quarter to nine for the casino boat on
Trail Creek, pretty much a dreary casino compared to
what we have on the East Coast and California. Still it
was a place where we could win a lot of money from
rubes. There were plenty of rubes there . . . people just
asking to be taken. Also some pretty good-looking women
but I know better than to try something like that in this
part of the country. I filled my pot again and came back
with a lot more gold than I had begun with and the guys
said they thought they better get back to their wives. I was
in no hurry to do that because my wife cries all the time
and is frightened of her pregnancy but maybe she'd be

asleep by the time we got home. So I just got into my bedroom and was taking off my clothes. Then crazy Margaret is running around screaming that Uncle Malachi has convulsions.

I wanted to stay in bed. I was tired. I had a couple extra drops of booze to celebrate my victories. Margaret keeps pounding on the door. I had to stagger out just to shut her up. I almost vomited at what I saw in the room. Malachi, a gross guy, is screaming and shouting and foaming at the mouth and pissing himself all over. Man, it was ugly!

Yet it was pretty funny once I got over how awful it was. Malachi, so prim and proper in those grotesque pajamas and covered with piss, begging us to save his life. I didn't think his life was worth saving and I still don't. Margaret got us a doctor and that weird little priest from Grand Beach and they saved Malachi's body and soul. I don't know whether it was worth it but they did.

Why would anybody want to kill him? Why would anybody want to kill any queer? Queers are disgusting. There was no real reason why he should live. He was a total human waste. But why should I kill him? It was no skin off my ass. Malachi disgusted me but not nearly enough that I wanted to kill him. There are guys I know that would want to kill him, kill any queer they can.

I don't worry about Gerry McGinity. Brendan Kelly wants my job as CEO at AVEL and he thinks he's smart enough and clever enough to get it. Maybe he is and maybe he'd do it okay but he hasn't got any right to it. It's my job.

My father? He's an elegant cover picture CEO for Time *magazine. He doesn't know how to have any fun. He doesn't enjoy life like someone in his position could. He doesn't understand how many women would like to sleep with him. Instead he worries about what to do with his wife.*

I have nothing against him. He's been good to me. He would have supported me if I refused to marry Consuela. But I figured it would be better to get my mom off my back and marry the little bitch. Like I say, I have a lot of fun with her. She doesn't enjoy it much, but that's her problem.

Would I ever kill Brendan Kelly? I'm not that stupid. I might put a contract out on him some day. I reserve the right to do it if he tries to take away from me something that's mine. But it would be so smoothly done that nobody would ever catch me.

I disgust you, don't I, officer? I don't give a damn what you think about me because you disgust me. I like nothing better in court than to get a cop on the witness stand and make him seem like the asshole he is. You guys are so confident and so professional. It's great fun to chew you up and spit you out. Makes me feel good like when I win $20,000 at the casino.

Margaret? I don't give a fuck about fucking Margaret. She's a stupid bitch but she's not going to keep me from exercising my right to the company. She can go off on her do-good trips and get herself killed like my aunt Elizabeth did. Margaret isn't strong enough or smart enough to stand in my way. If she does try to interfere with me she'll regret it. Michael Winter? He probably belongs in some VA hospital for the rest of his life. If you asked me who I think might have tried to get rid of Uncle Malachi, it could've been him. Those twin sons of the cook? It is easy to see they're both faggots.

The daughters are another matter. I wouldn't mind having a romp with any of them.

Their mother? Wow! Would she be something to feast on! I would eat her teats all night long!

Write all this stuff down, show it to people, and have a good time with it. Just know I'm laughing at what a stupid asshole you are.

(My conclusion at the end of the interview is that Ignatius Nolan is not a sociopath. He is a fool. His comments were deliberately intended to offend me just for the pure hell of it. Did he try to kill his uncle? He might have. But beneath his sniggering bravado, I don't believe he's capable of anything that would get him in serious trouble. Still, he bears close watching. Most of the nonsense he was talking was an act. Some of it might be more.)

Olaf Thor Jacobsson, MSP

The wise Thursday man had read Ignatius correctly—a nasty, inadequate little man, not entirely certain about his masculinity and for that reason perhaps dangerous. However, he had no particular motive for going after the Angel to the church of Laramie. A sick, sick family, save for the Magic Child—if that was what she is.

21

I shoved the summaries into my now-bulging briefcase. They told me a lot about people whom the state troopers had interviewed, but provided few new clues, if any. I had the uneasy feeling that I had missed a clue, or maybe an important fact somewhere.

What was it?

No way could I pull it out.

Michael Winter was a very smart man who might easily have been a professional killer for the CIA. Spike Nolan was something of a genius but there was little he could do to control his family or to get over the pain of family losses. And Margaret Nolan continued to be herself—a dangerous white flame, according to my valiant nephew. But still something of a mystery. How did she survive the verbal abuse that seemed to mark most of her life? She turned, it would seem, to deep prayer when the family assaulted her. She was not unlike Chantal, the hero of Georges Bernanos's novel *Joy,* also an unappreciated Magic Child.

The comparison troubled me, and not because of the surprising mystical side of the fair Margaret. She had apparently established a boundary between herself and the rest of her family. I worried because Chantal in the novel was an extraordinary young woman deep in joyous mystical union with the transcendent and yet would die a horrible death at the hands of a brutal killer. Because someone reminded me of a fictional character it did not follow that such a one would die the same way the character died. Did it?

However, one could certainly feel secure in the thought that should there be a World-to-Come—and of course I am biased in favor of that belief—Chantel would flourish just as she had in the world she left behind. So too would Margaret. Yet we should protect her from Chantal's fate lest we face stern questioning from the One-in-Charge.

Juana Maria was a survivor. She had survived whatever problems had driven her from Mexico. She had survived an apparently callous husband. She had survived as the mother of a brood of attractive, ambitious, and charming kids. She even survived an intense love affair with Michael Winter, who might at times in his life turn dangerously melancholy. Was she not sleeping with a volcano? Did she know it? Was she afraid of him? Or did she perhaps enjoy and love the furies that bubbled within him?

Again what did the One-in-Charge expect of me?

Most likely that I solve the mystery and mind my own business.

Would Juana Maria kill someone whom she perceived to be a threat to her family and her lover? No doubt about it! But was Malachi Nolan such a threat?

Eileen McGinity was a surrogate for her mother. In the absence of Loretta she kept alive the theme of a struggle to wrestle AVEL away from the hands of her senile, as she saw it, grandfather and keep it under the control of her own branch of the family. Her sister Margaret was, as always, the enemy within who thwarted the good work of the family and now threatened to destroy their campaign to save the firm. Eileen was probably not bright enough— or twisted enough—to try to kill through hornet venom.

Was she?

Her brother Ignatius assumed that ultimate control of AVEL was his right and he would triumph. Lieutenant Jacobsson was doubtless correct in his conclusion that Iggy was all talk, a hollow man reveling in the pose of a brutal psychopath, a barroom braggart who boasted of his many sexual conquests to hide his many failures in the sexual arena. Yet he might work up enough whiskey courage to commission a hit on someone who threatened this ascent to power. But in what way was Malachi a threat to Iggy?

Who wanted to kill Malachi? How was he involved in the family power struggle?

Much later it would dawn on me that, while the Bishop of Laramie might be part of the struggle, that was the wrong perspective from which to begin the investigation. Why should those who experienced a threat to their right of succession want to kill him, if they were to kill anyone?

As I drove back to Grand Beach, under a procession of cumulus clouds that paraded solemnly along the shore but delicately avoided the Lake, I pondered the story I would tell at the Saturday afternoon Eucharist. We had a custom of long standing at the Ryan–Murphy compound that we celebrate the Eucharist on the tree-shaded lawn at the top of a dune overlooking the Lake. Father Johnny Curran, a young pastor in Chicago, and I alternated driving out from our respective parishes on Saturday and then driving back. In my case I would forsake the Cathedral precincts on Saturday afternoon and then drive back to the Cathedral to say the ten o'clock mass in Spanish and the twelve in English for the tourists and then the six o'clock mass in the evening for yuppies and youth and other assorted members of the people of God. Each Eucharist had to be drastically different from the others because they were drastically different congregations. The same story, however, would suffice for all of them. That's the advantage of stories and that's why Jesus told parables.

At Grand Beach the custom has emerged that one of the various matriarchs of the Ryan clan would organize a barbecue on the deck down at the beach when the Eucharist was over. The Eucharist is a somewhat tailored version because you really can't keep a crowd of people on a hot summer day on the lawn underneath the bright sun and expect to hold their attention.

I always tell stories because, as Jesus knew, people remember and love stories. Generally the stories should not be biographical and, like the parables of the founder, they have to be paradoxical and challenging. You aim the story at the kids and you've got the adults in the congregation sewed up. I have to be careful not to repeat stories, at least not for five years. The Gospel of the day was the one about Jesus on the Sea of Galilee. The apostles, according to the one version, put out at sea after he'd spent a day feeding the hungry folk with the loaves and fishes, and Jesus remained on the shore. In another story, which was probably a version of the same story, Jesus went out on the boat with them but then fell asleep. Then a big storm swept down on the lake from Mount Lebanon and there was lightning and thunder and waves and the apostles were terrified. Jesus had to settle them down and bring them safely to shore. The story has undergone many permutations through the years but there was no doubt about the basic fact that Jesus had taken care of them on the Sea of Galilee either by waking up or by actually walking out on the water.

The point of the story is that we who are people of faith must trust in God and Jesus and the Blessed Mother

to take care of us when things go wrong or even when
our expectations are wiped out. All fairly simple stuff,
but nonetheless at the core of our faith. So I would tell
the story of a boy and a girl and a daddy who went out on
a little lake, not one like Michigan on a perfect day and a
storm came and capsized their boat. I could imagine little kids with eyes bulging if I made the storm scary
enough.

The boat literally was the bark of Peter, which was in
deep trouble then (second half of the first century) and
still in deep trouble two thousand years later. Even today
those of us on the boat really don't believe Jesus will
take care of the bark of Peter. Or to put it precisely, we
don't really believe that the bark will continue to sail
more or less in the proper direction despite we idiots
who are in charge of the bark. It was Peter in one version
of the story who cries out, "Save us, Lord! We perish!"

Those of us aboard the bark today don't seem to realize that maybe every day we should echo the words of
the first Pope. "Save us, Lord! We perish!" The bark
seems to be sinking and the waves are pounding and the
skies are dark and the lake is filled with terror.

The story might apply also to the story I was engaging
in now back at Nolan's Landing, a story of fear and hor-
ror and hatred and destruction and the end of innocence.
My job was to help navigate the innocent people caught
up in that story to a safe shore so that we could all enjoy
a gorgeous August Saturday afternoon. And thus to
experience a gratitude for the grace that summer is—a
light breeze from the Lake, the sailboats and the catama-
rans drifting by, water-skiers and noise of kids on the
beach and all the other things that make summer so powerful a story of hope.

I arrived about thirty seconds before the Eucharist was
supposed to begin. If I had arrived any earlier there
would have been consternation among the congregation—

is the Bishop sick? Bishop Blackie is never late but he's never early either, the crowd would have muttered anxiously. They were already gathered, chatting merrily about the sorts of things people chat about before church—politics, business, sports, the White Sox, the Cubs, the Bears, and of course the Golden Dome and the fate of the Fighting Irish. I attempted to don my vestments and generally made a mess of them, as is my custom. My three sisters swarmed around straightening things out and making me look presentable, something they had dedicated their lives to since my arrival on this earth. Among their other dedications to husband and family and career, keeping the punk (that's me) looking presentable may have been their most difficult.

As I appeared behind the altar the conversation stopped or at least ebbed and little kids all swarmed up in front because it was their right to sit down on the grass and watch the Eucharist up close. If there is any disturbance or noise or disorder among at them, I stare at them and they are supposed to wither. Unfortunately I'm quite incapable of scaring dogs or the children, or even, as far as that goes, cats.

My threats go unnoticed because they don't take me seriously. However, their parents take me seriously. If I make a face of disapproval and the parent knows his child is being disapproved of (usually for purposes of fun and laughter), that kid is in real trouble. Generally they are well behaved until story time comes, and if I don't captivate them with a story then I have completely failed my mission as a Sunday morning/Saturday afternoon storyteller.

Just as I began mass I noticed a new member join the congregation—Margaret Nolan, and herself attired for church in garb that was less informal than that of most of the young women in the congregation, jeans and T-shirts. Margaret, wearing dark blue slacks and a light blue blouse with a red and white scarf, looked distinctly out of place among the more ruffian-like people around the altar. Moreover because she came in late she was in the back of the crowd and scarcely visible. I kept an eye on her because as the women of the Ryan–Murphy clan could observe, her presence could say many things and also it could say nothing.

Arguably both.

I explained before I read the Gospel that the bark of Peter represented the Church and all of us who are its members, an acceptable prelude to begin my story. I observed that somehow my stalwart and valiant nephew had slipped all away across the back of the dune so he was standing next to her. Love can persuade us to do incredible things, can it not?

So I told the story about the boat.

Once upon a time two kids, a boy, eight, and a girl, ten, went out on the tiny lake where their family had a small summer home, for a boat ride with their dad. There's supposed to be a storm, their mother said, be careful. But moms always worry and there wasn't a cloud in the sky. No one put on life jackets because it was not a dangerous lake. Right? Well, they had a nice ride from one end to the other while their dad told them about some of the silly things he had done when he was a kid and then when he was an officer in the Navy flying off an aircraft carrier. They hardly noticed that the sky was filling up with clouds and the wind was picking up. Put on your life jackets, said the daddy. Daddy! said the kids! That's an order, he said. He never talked that way so they put on their life jackets. They rowed across the lake toward their cottage, but it started to rain, and they couldn't see the shore. Next a big storm hit them and the waves banged against the boat. The kids were scared; the little girl began to cry. Don't worry, said the daddy. Then a great big wave rolled the boat over. Hang on to the sides, were the last words they heard their daddy say. The kids sunk deep into the lake and sucked in a lot of water before they bounded to the surface. They both screamed for their daddy (well, wouldn't you?) and hung on to the boat for dear life. Then they cried a lot. They were in the water for a long time. Then suddenly the storm stopped and the sun came out. They saw their daddy at the stern of the boat, pushing it. Put your feet down, he shouted. They did and you know what? They touched bottom. They looked around and saw they were right in front of their cottage. We were never afraid, they told their mommy, because we knew daddy was with us all the time. Mommy seemed skeptical, but that's the way mommies are.

I then went on with the Eucharist and distributed communion. I said to her, "the body of Christ, Peggy Anne." She dutifully and reverently responded, "Amen," and with Joseph trailing behind her, retreated once more to the back of the congregation.

Joseph's presence signaled to all oglers present that he was claiming right of first refusal. I didn't need to see my sister's face to know that it bore a complacent smile.

The singing at the Grand Beach Eucharist is erratic. On those days in June and July when Nuala Anne and her brood are around we have some of the best congregational singing in North America. During August when they are in Ireland, we revert to typical Irish singing patterns. We do the first stanza with some vigor, not always on key, then sing the chorus and add a forceful and confident "amen." It doesn't sound like much and in fact it isn't much but then one must consider that it's been perhaps a millennium and a half since the Irish sang at the liturgy. We've just begun it again. It will take a couple generations before we can do it with the enthusiasm the Methodists, the Episcopalians, or the Baptists or other such congregations bring to their singing. I often think we should hire Southern Baptists to teach us how to sing gospel music in church.

The last hymn is always "Lord of the Dance" because it may be the most suitable hymn in the popular Catholic repertory and because it is a hymn of joy and hope during which little kids, and even high school girl kids, can clap in tune with the music. The rhythm necessary for such behavior seems to have escaped the male of the species, the priest alas included.

Like most Saturdays the hymn was not what one might call glorious. Indeed, quite the contrary, it was slightly off key and then gradually faded out to an anticlimax. I am useless in such circumstances because I am a mental hummer. However another voice joined in, a powerful and confident contralto which demanded response not only because the woman knew the notes but because she knew all the stanzas!

I was distracted by the thought that it would be an interesting day when Nuala Anne and Margaret Nolan sing together. Arguably they might hate each other on sight or perhaps more arguably would bond together against the rest of us.

As she sang and led us in singing, she drifted up to the crowd of little girl kids at the altar who were clapping enthusiastically. She took the hands of two very enthusiastic clappers and danced around with them, the two being my grand nieces Katiesue Murphy and Catieanne Maher, both matriarchs in the making. Then all the other little girl kids joined the dance as did a couple of boy kids and two teenage girl kids. It was a transforming experience for the Ryan clan liturgy.

The congregation applauded and modest tinges of pink appeared on Margaret Nolan's lovely face. People swarmed around her, some of whom had been contemporaries of her at the Golden Dome (and called her "Margot"). No one seemed to notice (though everyone did) that Joseph Murphy, who had indeed sung but neither clapped nor danced, followed after her. Joseph was definitely in charge of this beautiful and seemingly fragile young woman.

Maybe he realized as I did that she was Chantal.

She and the good Mary Kathleen embraced like old friends, or maybe, I thought inappropriately, like mother and daughter.

The crowd descended to our spacious deck just a couple of feet above the sand—where you have all the advantages of a beach in such circumstances, without actually getting your feet dirty. Kids do not accept this. Unless they have covered their feet and indeed their whole bodies with wet sand, it just wasn't a good day to be at Grand Beach.

Normally I would've grabbed a quick hamburger and diet cola, climbed into my retro cruiser, and sped back to the Cathedral eating my dinner on the way, in some violation of the traffic laws of the states of Michigan and Indiana and Illinois.

However, this particular day, since I was under stern orders from his gracious lordship Cardinal Sean Cronin not to return to the Cathedral until I solved the mystery at Nolan's Landing, I was constrained to accept the ongoing hospitality of my family. Therefore I descended the steps to the deck and began to collect enough food to see me safely through the night and the next day no matter what happened. The reader may have noted that Irish womenfolk still fear the Great Famine is going to return or arguably the Great Depression. In either case, when they're preparing a meal, they prepare far more than mortal humankind can be expected to consume. The half which is left over is thereupon delivered to friends, neighbors, the poor, and, as a matter of last resort to the Cathedral rectory. One must understand that the need not to run out of food and the need to see that none of it is wasted can easily coexist because we Irish and Irish-Americans, especially the women members of the group, repealed the principle of contradiction long ago.

I adjusted to the situation by gathering up enough food to sustain me against the rigors of the following day—in which the state troopers would spend the morning reviewing the forensic data and consulting with various national and international agencies and then return to investigations at Nolan's Landing. Moderation, I felt, dictated no more than two small slabs of barbecued ribs, two Chicago style hot dogs, fish salad, and a Dove chocolate-on-chocolate ice cream bar. As I polished off the latter, Joseph Murphy and his older brother Peter approached my private corner in which my invisibility cloak had apparently not operated. They were accompanied by their womenfolk, Lieutenant Commander Cindasue L. McLeod of the Yewnited States Coast Guard (permanent womanfolk) and Margaret Nolan (undeclared and perhaps only transient womanfolk).

"I'm sorry I took over your liturgy, Archbishop Blackie," the latter said, with not the slightest trace of regret.

"Young woman, you are not sorry at all! Moreover you shouldn't be. You were, as we might have expected, most effective."

"I won't ever try to sing when Nuala Anne is here."

"Yes, you will. And you will love it, and so will she."

"Well, maybe . . ."

There was no maybe about it.

Margaret had not worked the congregation after mass but had retreated into a corner on the deck under the protection of her Joseph and his relatives.

Cindasue took over the conversation.

"Happen you feel like a-driven the boat, we'uns might hanker a-going along wid you down to that thar harbor, maybe do a li'l water-skiiin'."

Cindasue spoke three variants of English—Bureaucratic when she was playing Coast Guard Officer, Standard American when she was with ordinary Americans, and her own brand of mountain talk when she was with "just plain folks." She claimed that she thought in mountain talk.

"I suppose our watercraft will have to submit to safety inspection."

"We uns always concern about water safety, Mr. Priest. We don't approve of shanty Irish boats."

"The *Mary Kathleen* is always *semper paratus*."

"My ma always a sayin' never trust the word of a Catlick priest."

Irish Protestant that she was, Cindasue always insisted that she was a one of them "Hard Shell Baptist" critters. She had however drifted into the Church of Rome, kind of by default, and referred now to herself as Hard Shell Catholic.

"We should leave the harbor at eight hundred hours," I insisted, "before the waves pick up and the power boats spoil the skiing."

They all groaned.

"I'll get the boat and then come by here to get the Murphys and pick up Margaret at the Nolan's Landing beach."

They agreed that it was a good idea.

"Eight-fifteen and eight-twenty," I insisted.

They groaned but agreed.

I then slipped away to seek my firstborn niece, the ingenious Caitlin Murphy Maher. Kevin Maher, her husband, owned a farm in Indiana some twenty miles south of LaPorte. They made a lot of money on the farm and traded it for a horse farm in the horse country between La-Porte and South Bend on Old Chicago Road. I have never been able to figure out whether it was an old road to Chicago or a road to old Chicago. However it has been replaced by U.S. 20 and I-94. Caitlin, a photographer from the days she first borrowed her mother's old Kodak, has won prizes for her shots of children, dogs, and horses.

"Do you remember that program you installed on my computer which enables one to age or unage individuals of whom one might have a picture?"

"You've forgotten how to work it, Uncle Blackie?" she laughed, as matriarchs laugh at little boy kids.

"I think I know how to turn it on."

That was not altogether true, as I demonstrated after I had turned on the computer.

Caitlin chuckled complacently as she clicked on the proper icon.

"Where is the picture?"

"I did take the precaution of placing it in the scanner."

"But not right side up!" she said as she lifted the cover and turned the picture over.

"Umm, cute kid! What do you want me to do to him?"

"Add thirty years to his life."

She clicked a few icons on the task bar and the subject matured.

"Too bad we have to age," Caitlin said with the required West-of-Ireland sigh. "Now what?"

"Make him look like he's had a lot of suffering in his life."

"Pain, disappointment, failure?"

"That would do nicely . . . Now remove his hair."

The result was what I had expected.

"Bad news?" she asked me.

"I'm not sure. Arguably . . . Thank you, Caitlin—nice photo of me in my full robes."

"I was glad we could find Catherine Curran's pectoral cross."

"Otherwise we would have never dared to take the picture."

"I look forward to you in crimson!"

"I don't," I said fervently.

The next morning the Murphys were waiting for me on their beach, laden with thermos jugs of coffee and tea. I had obtained the expected coffee cake, donuts, and sweet rolls (called Danish in Michigan, but *always* sweet rolls in Chicago).

Perhaps I should note that I fast during Lent and don't lose weight and eat whatever I want the rest of the year and don't put weight on. My siblings despair of this behavior.

I had devised a plan for responding to the challenge that Caitlin had created with her computer black magic. The whole matter must be handled delicately—if one can delicately throw a grenade into a crowded room.

Margaret was sitting on a rock, bundled up in a large blue and gold Notre Dame jacket. She apparently owned nothing that was kelly green of the sort that the South Side Irish seem to prefer. Her eyes were closed, not in sleep I imagined but in prayer. I permitted the *Mary Kathleen* to drift toward the edges of the sand bar.

"Margaret," Joseph shouted.

She did not stir.

"Li'l polecat asleep."

Polecat is Cindasue's favorite word, even in Standard American.

Margaret did not stir.

I beeped the horn.

Margaret appeared to wake up. She waved enthusiastically and waded into the water between the shore and the sandbar. Proving me wrong, she removed her Notre Dame jacket, revealing a kelly green Notre Dame bikini which caused the lay members of our band to gasp.

"Shunuff," Cindasue murmured.

Margaret tossed her jacket, towel, shoulder bag, and sunscreen tube into the *Mary Kathleen*.

"Since I'm already wet, I'd better make a fool out of myself first."

"You a-wearin' this hyar official life jacket thing," Commander McLeod ordered, tossing the jacket to her.

"Shunuff," Margaret replied, stepping off the sandbar into the cold Lake.

Joseph threw her the slalom ski. She slipped into it quickly.

"Hurry up, Joseph. It's cold!"

"You a'takin up that thar slack, priest man."

"Yassum."

I straightened out the line.

"Go!" the faithful Joseph ordered.

I jammed the throttle forward. No need to look back. The tug on the boat indicated that Margaret was already up and leaping over wakes.

"You shunuff lucky polecat a-bein' jularker to that tasty li'l chil, Mista Joe Murphy."

In mountain talk a "jularker" is a swain. The origins of the word are obscure.

"I'm not her jularker," Joseph said firmly.

"A-fixin' to be."

"She's teaching in New Orleans for two years."

"Happen thar be e-mail down thar."

"Katiesue," Peter Murphy said, "already calls her 'Aunt Peggy.'"

I glanced back. Margaret was spinning and cavorting and jumping over the wakes with reckless ease. I turned the watercraft toward Michigan City. Give her the full run thar, uh, there and back.

"Shunuff that li'l polecat a-havin' a cute figure."

"I've noticed," Joseph admitted.

Margaret finally cut way over to the side of the boat, waved, and then jauntily cast the ski rope into the air and sunk into the water.

"First time in Lake Michigan," she admitted as she swam to the side of the boat and tossed her life jacket up to Joseph. "A lot colder than the Mediterranean."

She clung to the side of the boat, catching her breath. Joseph simply lifted her over the gunwale and wrapped her in the towel (it said Notre Dame too) she'd brought. There was a brief moment of sexual tension between them.

"High-quality attendants you have, Bishop Blackie," she said, breaking the tension.

"You've been coming here every year and you have never skied?" Joseph asked in astonishment.

"We have a big boat in the marina, but no one in my family wants to use it. . . . I came to the Eucharist last night looking for skiers."

There was a moment of embarrassed silence.

"Perfectly virtuous action," the resident Coadjutor Archbishop pronounced his solemn approval, "just like scanning the beach every morning for the possible appearance of a fellow Domer."

We all laughed, Margaret with guilty pleasure and Joseph with a crimson face.

"Domer fella," she corrected me.

Despite denials they were caught up in a summer crush. Indeed the most poignant of all summer crushes, a late summer crush.

I gave up skiing, a sport at which, like all others, I did not excel, a couple of years previously when I discovered that after a morning's ski I needed a long nap and then, after lunch, yet another long nap. I figured that the One-in-Charge was sending me a signal.

So the younger generations, with much laughter, skied till exhaustion and perhaps beyond. I dropped them at the Murphy house and drove the *Mary Kathleen* back to New Buffalo.

22

I had orchestrated in my mind how we would deal with the pictures. It would be necessary that Joseph be present. August would end soon and both would move on to the next phase of their lives. There was no useful purpose to be served by pretending that their summer crush did not exist. Whether it would survive the long, cold winter (in Chicago at any rate) remained to be seen. That would depend on God's plans—and their own. I would not bet a contribution for a votive candle against it. Just the same, there would be a lot of angst as there must be in our times when a couple like them wrestles with the issue of whether it would be intolerable for them not to spend the rest of their lives together.

The four young people were spread out on the Ryan–Murphy deck, reading *The New York Times* and finishing the last of the sweet rolls—Margaret stubbornly called them Danish. I remonstrated with them for falling out of condition at their age in life.

"Hesh you mouth, priest man . . ."

Katiesue and Peteyjack arrived with their beach impedimenta and begged their parents to come play with them.

"Don't anyone bother me," Joseph sighed. "I'm tired."

"It's all so peaceful and beautiful," Margaret murmured, eyes closed and smile beatific. "I wish it could last forever."

"It rarely does . . . Would you two be good enough to accompany me to my computer?"

"No . . ." Margaret insisted. "You have secret information that we are related within the degree of kindred that we shouldn't associate with one another anymore. . . . I don't want to see it. Not today."

However, she struggled to her feet, wearing the expected Notre Dame shorts and T-shirt.

"You went to the Dome, didn't you, kid?" her jularker asked.

"Solves a lot of my fashion decisions," she fired back.

They both laughed, as humans do when they are in their late-summer crushes. A shame, I thought, that they can't last forever. Except some of them do.

At my computer workstation I invited them to sit down and then turned on the system. After booting up I tried at first unsuccessfully to access the computer program Caitlin had installed. Then I clicked on the file icon and clicked again on one that I had labeled "1970."

"Uncle Johnny," Margaret said. "He was only a year older than you at that time Joseph."

"And already a Marine aviator," I added.

"I'm glad I'm not a Marine aviator."

"I am too."

"But you are an aviator, Margaret," he said.

"With a certificate for a single engine aircraft . . . like Grandpa Spike's Spitfire. Next year I'll upgrade to multiple engine and maybe eventually a jet. No rush . . . Does that bother you, Joseph?"

"Not all," he laughed. "If I need a ride, I'll know where I can find an air taxi."

They laughed together, one minor obstacle swept aside.

"Someone who has flight in her bloodstream like you do, Margaret, should be a flier."

"Eventually I want to fly one of those 787 Dreamliners my dad made. No rush."

We all laughed.

I pushed a key for the next option. Uncle Johnny aged thirty-five years.

"What have you done to him!"

"Let him age thirty-five years. It's how he would look today."

"Good God in heaven," she said sadly.

"Then we add a difficult life with suffering and sadness, maybe a lot of pain, physical and emotional."

Margaret began to weep, quietly and slowly.

"Finish it please."

I pushed the last option.

"Michael Winter! He's Uncle Johnny! But how can he be! He's been dead since 1970!"

"Officially, Margaret, but not really."

"Michael Winter, our caretaker, is really Johnny Nolan, Spike's oldest son, my dad's brother, and my uncle! Out of sight!

"What was he doing all those years?" Joseph Murphy asked. "Where was he hiding?"

"We don't know, Joseph. He was working somewhere for the government, where and doing what we may never know."

"His wife and son . . . ?"

"We don't know, Margaret, again we may never know. It's safe to assume that he's had no contact with them. They have rejected all attempts by Spike and Margaret to relate to them. Maybe that's part of the deal with the G. He wanted to be a hero like his father. He knew he wasn't quite the fighter pilot, though the situation was so different. Vietnam was not the Battle of Britain. So he had to take another path to heroism. Maybe he figured that his marriage was already in trouble."

"From which he could never return? Never be known as a hero?"

I shrugged.

"What could he have been doing?" Joseph wondered.

"The American military has done many crazy things, run many crazy experiments on innocent people. This was probably some Pentagon genius's idea of a brilliant scheme."

"And it ruined Uncle Johnny's life!"

"Caused him a lot of suffering anyway."

"Mike Winter is Uncle Johnny," she said as the truth began slowly to intrude on her consciousness. "Where does that leave our family?"

"I'm not sure, Margaret, that it leaves it anywhere that it is not already. But on the other hand it might change the whole picture. I presume that Spike and Anne know. How could they not? Your father and Malachi? Probably not. Does it have any connection with the assault on Malachi? I'm not sure. I don't think Michael has any great grudge against his brother."

"He seems kind of happy," Joseph suggested.

"He earns a decent living. I assume the G provides him with all the money he needs. He's close to the rest of the family in some strange kind of way. He's in love with Juana Maria and adores her children. He likes living in the dunes. There are worse lifestyles. . . ."

"We don't want to spoil it for him . . . and for Gramms and Gramps either."

"No way," Joseph agreed.

The two young people sat in chairs in front of my computer, playing the program over and over again. They pondered the pictures obsessively, as though the story would eventually go away, the bad dream eventually end.

"I wonder if those twins are my half brothers," Margaret said, her face suddenly glowing. "They're such adorable little guys."

"I wonder the same thing," Joseph agreed.

"Cousins," I corrected her.

That thought had not occurred to me. They would be far better siblings than the present bunch.

"Don't you have some contacts at the CIA, Uncle Blackie?"

"A few, but I would not try to make an issue of this matter until we know more about it. We don't want to put him in any danger. I would be inclined to follow his judgment, even if he refuses to talk to us."

Margaret shook her head grimly.

"He wouldn't do that, would he? I'm his niece, after all."

"Surely his favorite niece," I said, "though the competition is not all that strong."

They both laughed. Would they laugh their way through life together?

Arguably.

"We must tread lightly," I suggested. "Let the truth emerge under its own momentum."

"We should say nothing that we don't have to say," Joseph insisted, as though it was now a family matter for him too. That was fine with me, as I had said, the fair Margaret was not the worst possibility.

"Exactly," I agreed.

"My notion, subject to review, is that we go over there now and show him the pictures."

"Right now?" she asked cautiously.

"Any reason why not?

"Can't think of any . . . Joseph?"

"I have a hunch, Margaret, that he'd like to have you as a niece."

That was not impossible, but then my galoot of a nephew was in his heart of hearts a total romantic.

"Joseph, you're so sweet. . . . All right, John Blackwood Ryan, Coadjutor Archbishop of Chicago with Right to Succession, let's do it!"

23

"*You went to* Notre Dame, didn't you, Margaret?" Michael Winter said with a quick upturn of his lips, his usual touch of a smile.

"You noticed that."

"I did, not that I have anything against them," he said.

Unasked, we sat down across his desk. He had swiveled around from his computer when we entered. He did not at first seem happy to see us. Then Margaret melted him with her smile. *Of course* he was proud of his niece. What else would he be.

She began our confrontation.

"We know who you are, Uncle Johnny."

"What do you mean?!" His face contorted in fury.

"You may be Michael Winter who is a nice man and a powerful lover," she said softly, "but you're also my Uncle Johnny Nolan whose jet disappeared over Hanoi in 1970. I don't care what happened between then and now. You're still my Uncle Johnny and I love you."

Well, that was magical.

"We don't intend to interfere," Joseph added. "We want you to know that we know and want to help if we can."

The anger faded from John Nolan's eyes.

"That's very nice, Margaret. I'd like to be your uncle, but I'm not John Nolan."

Margaret placed the folder with the pictures in front of him. He glanced at the pictures. Color drained from his face.

He closed his eyes, his jaw tightened, his hands clenched.

"I suppose this is your doing," he snapped at me.

"We don't intend to do or say anything," I said. "I've known who you were since almost the beginning, though it was only yesterday at mass I knew that I knew. We have to solve this mystery before someone else is killed."

He nodded his head.

"I don't want to embarrass Juana Maria or the children," he said slowly.

"Are any of them my cousins?"

He laughed, his usual croaking laugh, but now with a little more mirth.

"No, Margaret, dear. They're not. But they all love you more than your real relatives."

"Spike knows," I said.

"I didn't fool him for more than five minutes. He agreed with the arrangement. So did Annie. They realized that it was the only way to go. Malachi doesn't know, self-centered as he always was, he couldn't care less. Your dad, Margaret? I don't think so. You can't tell with Philip. He has enough family troubles as it is. I'm sure he's never discussed it with Spike, much less with your mother."

"What happened, Uncle Johnny? Can you tell us where you were all the years?"

"I suppose I can give you a rough outline of the story, Margaret. I didn't fly to Hanoi that day. I disappeared rather into the secret world of spies and clandestine operations. They came and picked me up in a jeep at the airfield and took me to one of their safe houses in

Saigon. Then they transferred me to another place and I began my life in the world of shadows, a world that I will always be part of. They sent me to several other countries and taught me various things. I was sworn to absolute secrecy about what I would do. I was told I could never see anyone in my family or anyone I knew ever again. I was dead and I had better stay dead or they would find a way to make me so. Those were different years. The appeal of spook work for the good of the country was powerful for some. I wasn't the only one that was sucked into it.

"On the *Kittyhawk* we were not fighting in the jungles. We weren't taking heavy causalities. We weren't suffering from the heat and humidity and the stench and the ever present enemy lurking in the jungles. Life in a carrier was pretty comfortable—good food, lots of ice cream, no drinks, of course, although we smuggled them on. Yet it was a frustrating business. We dropped bombs on the enemy and strafed them and shot up their trucks. None of this was going to accomplish anything because the war would end in a couple more years after I had left when Nixon and Kissinger stopped messing around. We'd already lost it.

"It was not England in 1940. I would not be a hero like my father. My marriage was finished. My wife was sleeping around before I left San Diego. I figured, why not?

"I was warned that this mission was not only secret but, as my instructor said, it was terminally secret. Johnny Nolan would disappear from the face of the earth. Later a new person would emerge that would have nothing to do with Johnny Nolan's past. They sent me out to a camp in the jungle for training, they told me as thorough a training as I would've received at Quantico—the CIA academy in Virginia. Then I was sent to other countries to learn some particular secrets—how to sabotage a particular target or how to eliminate a particular subject. I handled these assignments neatly. They were pleased with me. Then they gave me what they called my final assignment. When it was finished my job would be over. I thought it might be something that would run a couple days, a couple weeks, a couple months at the most like the other assignments.

"This one was much different. I was to become a traitor and be absorbed into the shadow world of this other country. They would think I was a traitor, an American informing on our plans and weapons, our difficulties and our weaknesses. I would have to be a very good actor, they said. Only after I got into it did I realize that when they said 'last' assignment, they meant a terminal assignment. I was not supposed to come back.

"They gave me a lot of information to pass on to the other side. They assured me that this intelligence would persuade the other side that I was a traitor. I'd be a double agent spying on the spies. I would be an invisible man in the dark world of the other country's intelligence network. They were very good at it, I was told, probably better than we are. I would be lucky if they didn't see through me. Was I willing to take the risk for the good of the United States of America? I was a good Marine and I was willing to take those risks, Yes, SIR!

"Later when I saw the movie *Rambo* I realized that the same motivations were working in me and that my superiors considered me a lethal weapon to be used against the enemy—and very little else.

"I was extremely successful at this crooked game. I supplied Washington with an enormous amount of information about the country I was watching. The people in that country treated me like I was a hero. When you live in the double world of a double agent sometimes you forget which side you're on. You have to establish friendships with your fellow agents and act your new role so persuasively that even their political commissars are convinced. In the meantime you send information back to Washington that convinces them that you are still a loyal American.

"Occasionally I would meet someone in a dilapidated apartment at night on the edge of the town or at a crossroads out in the country who would claim to represent my friends in Washington. He would pay for my work and give me my new assignments and warn me of the necessity of absolute secrecy. As long as I had these occasional contacts with my friends in Washington I could maintain some kind of sanity. I knew I really was an American named Johnny Nolan who was working successfully in this new country.

"I was given some extremely risky operational responsibilities. I was to damage some of their equipment, see to the crashing of one of their test flights, slip our monitors into their offices. I was convinced that I was really a superspy. I could do anything.

"Then the contacts with Washington ceased—to this day I don't know why. None of the people who recruited and trained me are still alive. Their names don't appear in any of the directories of the various agencies in Washington. Maybe they were the ones who were terminated with extreme prejudice. I didn't know that the messages I was sending back to Washington ever got there. I was on my own, not sure that anything I was doing mattered for the United States. Indeed when I did come back nobody seemed to know anything about me.

"So it went on for years. Johnny Nolan was dead and whoever I was didn't really exist. I became careless. They caught me and interrogated me for months. They reduced me to a vegetable and then they decided that I really didn't know anything that I hadn't already told them. I was worthless. There was no reason to hang me or shoot me. Rather they sent me to a work camp so I could contribute to the growth of their country. The work camps are everything that the books say they are. I was supposed to die. I almost died. I desperately wanted to die. But there must've been a little bit of Spike Nolan's genes in me because I didn't die. So I tried to escape and got away several times, almost froze to death once in the snow, but each time they caught me and they beat me and they put me back to work. A live worker, you see, is more useful than a dead worker.

"Then it all stopped. A big 'social transformation' had occurred. The camp closed. I was put on a train and sent back to the capital of the country. I found my way to the American embassy, stumbled in, and demanded to see the Resident. He had never heard of me. He assumed that I was some sort of double agent, which I was, but a double agent working for the United States. I told him about the jobs I had done, the various mail drops I had delivered, and how many years I had been in a work camp. I had a hard time talking English because it had been so long.

"So I was locked up in what was in effect a prison cell at the embassy and left to wait again. A couple of months later three characters arrived from Washington. They weren't the people who had recruited and trained me but they had some of the same sleek and sophisticated style. They weren't your typical FBI people barging into your house in the middle of the night. They questioned me again at great length for weeks.

"Then I was put in a Gulfstream jet in handcuffs and flown back to Washington to meet another crowd of interrogators at another one of their safe houses and told the same story I had told before. They told me I was a fool to think I could get away with such nonsense. Then finally one day an older man with white hair and terribly cold blue eyes came to see me alone.

" 'So you're Johnny Nolan?' he said.

I continued the game.

" 'Johnny Nolan is dead.'

" 'They've forgotten about you in this place. That whole operation was terminated. It was assumed here that you were terminated, perhaps you should have been. But you were still doing mail drops even then, weren't you?'

" 'Were you getting them?'

" 'We didn't believe them. Then we found out that they were true, so we weren't sure what to do. So we forgot about you and then you disappeared from the face of the earth. Now you're back here again and we don't need you, especially since you no longer exist.'

" 'You're calling the shots.'

" 'You remember the promise you made?'

" 'I remember it.'

" 'We intend to hold you to it. We are going to give you a new life, new name, new social security card, new fingerprints, new DNA. We also will reward you handsomely for your service to the United States of America. In another world and in another time we would have proclaimed you a hero. We can't afford to do that now for security reasons.'

" 'You mean because you and your predecessors would look very bad.'

" 'Yes, that's true too. When I say "reward you richly," I mean that the kind of a salary that a four-star general gets with all the perks, all the benefits, everything you need to be comfortable for the rest your life.'

" 'But only if it remains a secret. Is that clear?'

" 'I guess it is.' It didn't make much difference to me, you see, but they didn't want me to die. I don't know whether it was conscience or gratitude or what but they released me from the safe house and sent me to a hospital they ran and put me back together again. When I was pronounced cured they moved me to a luxury apartment in Washington and told me to enjoy my life. That's when I started to drink. The shadows were still all around me. I hadn't escaped the dark world. I still live in it, especially at night. The alcohol kept me going.

"They decided that I was dangerous and sent me to a rehab center. That happened a couple of times and then I decided that I didn't want to drink myself to death. So I moved to New Buffalo, Michigan, started my service company, met Juana Maria and her kids, hired them. Fell in love with her—as Archbishop Ryan rather quickly observed—and settled down for a dull and quiet life. Juana Maria is much better than whiskey. I read all these books to catch up on what I've missed in the history of the United States from the Vietnam War to the Iraqi war. ⌐"It was not reassuring reading. Our shadow world is more incompetent than that of the other side. In our shadow world ambition and bureaucratic maneuvering and pressure from higher officials corrupt the work. If they had read my drops they would have found out a lot of things to protect them from awful mistakes. But they really weren't interested in good intelligence. They were interested in giving the impression that they collected good intelligence.

"So I read and write and at some point when I'm dead what I've written will come out and I will have settled some of my score with those who live in the shadow world.

"I noticed in the New Buffalo *Times* an ad for a caretaker at Nolan's Landing. I applied for it and was hired by the lawyer that represented Spike here. I called my friend in Washington and told him what I was doing and warned him not to mess with either me or my father and mother. If they did I would kill them. The people I talked to this time had a hard time remembering who I was and what I had done but they agreed it was all right to take the job so long as I didn't disclose that I was Johnny Nolan and that I had been working for the government for the last thirty years. So I moved into the gatehouse figuring that I could watch my family, get to know them again, perhaps love them again. I didn't fool Spike. He knew who I was and even guessed what I've been doing. Spike is a very tough guy. He wanted to go after the government and blow this operation to hell.

"Part of me said that's what we should do. Yet it didn't seem fair to the love in my life or her children or fair to Spike, who had better things to do than get in new wars with dangerous people in the government. I didn't think and I still don't think they would try to terminate Spike or Annie. I warned them again that I would blow the whole thing open. We might have to terminate you too, they said. Not before I terminate some of you people, I told them. I got to be pretty good at the termination business when I was working for you.

"That's about all I can tell you, niece Margaret. It is not a history which I am proud of but I did survive and I did return to Nolan's Landing, a place I've always loved. I'm not sure whether it was a good thing or a bad thing to meet my family. Spike and Anne are wonderful human beings and so are you. In between? If I had never met them again, I don't think anything would be missing from my limited happiness—limited but still happiness."

Margaret hugged him.

"I'm so proud of you, Uncle Johnny!"

"Let me warn you," Michael Winter continued, tears streaming down his face. "I lie a lot. I lied all the time when I was in the shadows. I lie a lot here. I have to make up stories that will keep Juana Maria and the children happy. For all you know I may be lying now. The truth is hard to come by when you have avoided it for as long as I have. I keep my eyes open around here, as you've no doubt noticed. I don't trust your mother and your brother and sisters, Margaret. But I don't know why they would want to get rid of Malachi. Your mother doesn't like him very much, she never has. She considers him a parasite, which he probably is. But kill him? It makes no sense at all."

"Do you think there might be other killings?" I asked.

It was a stupid question because of course there could be other killings. For a moment I realized whom the target of such killings might be. What a fool I had been! But how could Loretta, safely incarcerated in Kokomo, Indiana, preside over other killings? Besides, Loretta was manic, but she did not seem to be schizophrenic or sociopathic.

By now the alert reader will have figured it all out. I have no excuse except for the dulling of my instincts brought on by age and related causes of deterioration.

"Does Juana Maria know that you are the son of Spike and Anne?" Margaret asked.

"I haven't told her. I don't think she understands or cares why I chose to settle in New Buffalo. She's delighted that I have. She does not like to ask herself too many deeply troubling questions because there have been many events in her life she likes to forget."

Margaret and I walked up to the house while Joseph returned to my retro cruiser and departed for Grand Beach.

"Poor Joseph looks so sad and lonely. I hated to let him go home but you know what, Bishop Blackie?"

"Yes. Margaret, as much as you hate to admit it, you're sleepy—too much partying, too much water-skiing. All you want now is to take a long afternoon nap!"

"I'm sure I'll have nice dreams about Joseph anyway."

"So long as dreams don't turn into nightmares."

"Nightmares about Joseph, don't be totally ridiculous!"

"You can always send him an e-mail!"

"*Certainly* I'll send an e-mail but only after I wake up."

I was not too proud of myself for solving the puzzle of Michael Winter. As Johnny Nolan he could have considerable interest in the future of AVEL. It might be risky for him now to claim his heritage. A lot of people would want to investigate. He didn't seem to have much affection for his brother Malachi and little respect for his brother Philip either. He was still a suspect as far as I was concerned—though one that could tell a good story.

24

My sister the good Mary Kathleen Ryan Murphy has a very enlightened attitude toward the raising of children. She vigorously supports their rights to make their own decisions so long as their decisions have been carefully considered. She almost never exercises veto power on any of their decisions about dates, courtship, or marriage. As she herself admits she wouldn't dare try because she'd lose. But every once in a while she breaks the rules and expresses caveats which she knows are foolish just because sometimes a mother has the absolute right to worry—as she always insists quite explicitly.

So it was Monday morning at the Maison Ryan–Murphy when her youngest son Joseph Murphy announced that he was going to fly up to Saugatuck that morning with Margaret Nolan for lunch.

"You're going to do *what*?"

"Margaret invited me for lunch at the best restaurant in Saugatuck. We fly up there in her plane. It takes about twenty minutes and we land at the local airport and a cab driver takes us to the town. We walk up and down the streets of Saugatuck, and look at the boats and the shops and such like—which I guess is what you're supposed to do in Saugatuck—and then we have lunch and we fly back!"

"Why?"

My silent position during this discussion was that Joseph Murphy Jr. is an adult, a veteran of two years in the Peace Corps, someone substantially beyond the age of reason, and quite capable of making his own decisions. Moreover, Margaret Anne Nolan was a licensed pilot with an impeccable record who could fly anyplace she wanted to. She kept all the FAA rules, which I assume being Spike Nolan's granddaughter she certainly would. But as I say, I held my peace.

"But that child is too young to fly an airplane!"

Her long-suffering husband, the good Dr. Joseph Murphy, also kept his own counsel.

"No, she is not, Mom," Joseph argued not unreasonably. "She has a certificate, which is what they call a license. She can fly an airplane. She can carry a passenger with her. Her airplane is fully equipped with all the things it needs to fly. She keeps it in tip-top condition. She's a very careful and responsible woman."

"She's too young" Mary Kathleen insisted, "much too young."

"She has graduated from the University of Notre Dame with high honors. She has been accepted by ACE to teach poor kids in New Orleans. She is an adult. She's probably a safer pilot than most people around here are automobile drivers. She is, after all, Spike Nolan's granddaughter. He flew Spitfires."

"Her plane is not a Spitfire, is it?"

My sister was sinking into the irrational.

She was arguing because of her maternal fear that this young woman, whom she admired greatly and would enthusiastically accept as a daughter-in-law, could make a decision about marriage, but couldn't be trusted to fly a perfectly safe airplane that, according to all judgments could practically fly itself.

"What if the plane crashes?"

"Then Margaret and I, having received holy communion at Uncle Blackie's mass yesterday, would end up very quickly in heaven and we could work out with God whether our trip was responsible."

"What if there's a storm?"

"The weather forecasts are for clear skies and light winds for the next five days. There are no other fronts anywhere near and no hurricanes coming up from the Gulf Coast, no threats of thunder, lightning, high winds, or any such hazards. It's a perfectly safe trip. You fly in airplanes all the time in bad weather. So does Dad. So does Archbishop Blackie, though he gets sick. Why are you worried about this flight?"

"Because she's too young to fly an airplane!"

My sister was now arguing from repetition, an argument against which one of our professors at the seminary so many years ago had warned us. "No matter how many times I repeat the argument or how many times I pound the table, it is not a good argument."

"Uncle Blackie, is not Margaret a responsible young woman?"

"I am not the appellate court in his family, Joseph Murphy."

"Dad?"

"If the Federal Aviation Authority gives her a certificate and she has the requisite number of hours for flying, we must assume she is a competent pilot."

"First time I've ever heard you argue from your confidence in the United States government. Are you still a Democrat?"

"Mom!" Joseph insisted. "It's only a half-hour flight along the lakeshore. The Lake is warm even if we have to ditch. . . ."

"Ditch!"

"Wrong word, Joseph," I murmured.

"You keep out of this, punk," she said, reverting to my childhood nickname.

"We will be in constant contact by my cell phone," Joseph argued. "She has a radio in the plane, and if we need the United States Coast Guard, I'm sure they'll get a helicopter out for us immediately."

"You call us every ten minutes! And be sure you fly by here on the way up so that we know you got safely off the ground!"

"Mom!" Joseph insisted. "Are you saying that you don't believe Margaret Anne will be a good pilot? How can you believe she's capable of making a good choice for a husband, supposing of course that she is in the mood to make such a choice!"

"Trapped!"

"She is still too young to fly!"

"Mom!"

"All right, I'll be saying the rosary the entire time and you call me when you take off and you call me every ten minutes."

I ferried Joseph over to Nolan's Landing whence his lady fair would translate him to MCMA in her battered Toyota.

She was waiting at the entrance of the house, wearing khaki slacks, a beige Notre Dame Windbreaker over a dark blue T-shirt, and a matching ND baseball cap—her hair trailing through its back—with "scrambled eggs" on its peak. She was clearly a professional pilot. Yet she still looked too young to fly a plane with someone else's child in it.

"I'll bring him back alive, Uncle Blackie! It's an old plane, but we have all the latest avionics inside."

"I'm sure you will," I said, I hope with confidence.

Off they went. Bound for Orly Field in Paris or some such historic destination.

Feeling even more ancient than I usually do, I entered the house and found the state troopers in the library, looking disconsolate and weary. They had besieged their DC contacts for information about Michael Winter and learned nothing.

Captain Svensson summarized the data.

"He allegedly served in Vietnam in the First Marine Regiment of the First Marine division, was captured briefly, escaped, and then was returned to the United States. He became a victim of alcoholism and drug abuse and was in and out of the VA hospitals. He finally seems to have recovered from his physical and mental ailments and then become successful as a small businessman in Southwestern Michigan."

"Remarkable."

"This information was passed on to us by contacts who were obviously reciting a line. Nolan is in some kind of witness protection program, a Marine witness protection program, which means it's very tough."

"Perhaps," I suggested, "you stirred up something among his masters in Washington. Perhaps they will be watching more closely in the days and weeks ahead. He will perhaps perceive a threat hanging over his head that if he cooperates with you, he and his loved ones might be terminated with extreme prejudice."

My three colleagues went dead silent in response.

Ominously.

"They wouldn't do that, would they?" Sergeant Muldoon broke the silence.

"If he is in some kind of witness protection program, Patti, then it dates back to the Vietnam era. And that's not the sort of thing they would do today unless you are a Muslim."

"I don't think we'll make any progress along that route," Captain Arne Svensson said. "When those guys won't cooperate, they simply won't cooperate. They couldn't care less about the attempted murder of an Archbishop in New Buffalo Township, Michigan."

"But surely you have some interview summaries from the denizens of Nolan's Landing?" ⌐

"We did these this morning, Blackie." Arne handed me a folder with a thin pile of papers. "I hope you can make something out of them because heaven knows we can't. Interesting confessional material, but no clues. Moreover at some point our own bosses are going to say that so long as the Archbishop is alive and has left our jurisdiction, then there's nothing further we can do."

"And the police south of the border?"

"They know about Father Gomez's order but they too don't seem to know much about him. However, there's apparently no permanent record on him. They go to some of his rallies to keep an eye on him because they're not sure what he might be up to. He travels around a lot. He is one of theirs and what he says and does is none of our gringo business."

The Michigan State Police were losing heart, not a good sign.

I decided on a leap in the dark.

"Might I suggest that you could spend some useful time exploring the six trash cans I note hidden carefully at the end of the garage? It could be that you might find some traces of the debris from the hornets' hive."

Captain Svensson glanced at his colleagues.

"We'd better do what the man says," he groaned. "The boss will ask if we did."

So they rose reluctantly from their chairs and shuffled down the stairs to the ground floor.

I thereupon called Malachi's room at Northwestern Hospital.

"Blackie! How good of you to call! I'm doing fine! Everyone here is doting on me. Sean has a lot of clout in this city."

"Patently."

"I think I might retire and return to Ampleforth, spend the rest of my life as a monk, well, a quasi-monk."

Remarkable.

I settled down under a yellow umbrella and began to read the summaries. As insights into human nature they were remarkable, but the sophisticated interview techniques of the Michigan State Police apparently had not generated any clues.

25

A summary of an interview with Philip Thomas Nolan
Sunday Afternoon
Interviewer Captain Arne L. Svensson

I told Mr. Philip Nolan that it was not necessary for him to endure a police interview on a day which undoubtedly had been traumatic for him. He answered that taking his manic wife to a mental institution was indeed traumatic because he loved her very much. Nonetheless it was necessary that they all get on with life and deal with problems, however painful they may be.

Mr. Nolan is a tall, broad-shouldered man with iron-gray hair, the picture of the healthy chief executive officer of a mature corporation, and one that had so far in his term been extremely successful. His responses were thoughtful and carefully phrased. But the look in his eyes was one of deep sadness, a man just returned from a wake.

He had no idea when he met his future wife at a cocktail party in New York that she would become bipolar later in life. He still would have married her because she was a wonderful woman most of the time. She was bright, sexy, and very funny. She was also charming and gentle and sensitive. Margaret is the only one of the children who had inherited these three characteristics, though the compari-

son sent Loretta into a rage once on the rare occasion when he suggested that similarity. She enjoyed her first three children—Josephine, Eileen, and Ignatius. Bright, likable kids, fun to have around the house, fun to be with. But Margaret was an unexpected pregnancy. Loretta, a devout Catholic all her life, even seriously talked about aborting the fetus because she could tell that it would be evil. Trouble the child was, especially in the later stages of an extremely difficult pregnancy. Childbirth was a painful and dangerous experience. Afterward the child's mother sank into a deep stage of what we know now as postpartum depression. That was the beginning of the bipolar cycle in which she now seems to be trapped.

During her courtship in the early years of our marriage before we started having kids, Loretta always insisted that our lives be organized and well-planned. One child was a challenge, which seemed then a minor obsession, but two and three and finally the unwanted fourth demolished it. She tried to impose order on chaos for the good of the children, she would say, and for her husband's good too.

I rose rapidly in the bureaucracy of AVEL, partly no doubt because I was the boss's son but also because I was both an able administrator, and because, as it turned out, I was something of an electronic and metallurgical genius. No one looked askance when I became vice president and president and then, when my father retired, chief executive officer of the firm. I have to say that I've done a pretty good job.

A CEO in a firm like mine must make sure that the organization hangs together in some kind of sensible way and that he does not deprive its members of their creativity. Then, if I were really my father's son, I would have to produce some of the insights and guesses and brilliant innovations that have marked his career. Again I think I've done pretty well. Moreover I enjoy the job, the challenge of the give-and-take of ideas and plans, the search, *sometimes desperate, for new ideas that will enhance our profitability and also serve the airline industry—an industry which doesn't trust me because it doesn't trust anyone, but also is only too willing to celebrate achievements we've made possible without a word of gratitude. Our firm's strength has always been its ability to innovate, but that strength is only as good as our most recent innovation. Our new ideas have to exist on the outer edge of the zany, but not quite cross that edge.*

I have, however, failed as a husband to this day. I don't know exactly how I should respond to my wife's bipolar disorder. I can sustain and support her as she comes out of depression and rejoice in her beauty and her love when she hesitates in that sometimes all-too-narrow border between depression and mania. Then, God forgive me for it, I turn away in fear and disgust when she becomes manic. Sometimes the cycles are long, sometimes short, but there doesn't seem to be any cure except the meds which she takes until she begins to feel normal. Then she announces that she's cured and doesn't need them anymore.

I have insisted in recent years that she take one every morning. At the beginning of the week I place seven sets of meds on the dresser in our bedroom. Each morning she dutifully picks up today's ration. She secretly spits them out. She's well, she doesn't need these terrible-tasting things anymore, they make her sick. She has to get on with her life.

As you've probably heard, Captain Svensson, she now feels an obsessive responsibility for the firm and a determination to intervene in its processes and relationships because she is my wife and Spike's daughter-in-law. She is not welcome in our New York offices or any of our plants around the world.

That simply increases her obsession that she and she alone can save the firm. Spike has banned her from all our properties but she still sneaks in and insults and offends people. She acts as though she is the queen of AVEL, the one who really has the power and the right to tell people what to do.

Unfortunately her mutation to the manic now comes with less warning. I can never be quite sure when it will explode. I was completely unprepared for her tantrum at supper the other night.

I don't know how long this can go on. Spike has told me that my own future as CEO is in jeopardy if I cannot control her. That's easy for him to say because he's never had control problems with my mother. They have always enjoyed an easy partnership since the days when they were lovesick teenagers at Beggin Hill with the Stukas diving down at them.

You're not interested in any of this family grief. You want to know why someone tried to murder my brother Malachi. I have no idea why that would happen. Of all of us in the family, he is, to put it in a strange way, the hardest to hate.

Why hate Malachi? What harm can he possibly do? He's a little strange, a little funny, a little, if you will, weird. Tragically so. He had great hopes for his ecclesiastical career and ends up of all places in Laramie, Wyoming, a failed candidate for the Archdiocese of Chicago. He told us several times in recent years that he's been assured on the highest authority in Rome that he would replace Sean Cronin. Cronin is still very much alive and very much the Archbishop and also a good and generous man who has treated Malachi with the greatest respect and affection since he's been hospitalized.

The churchmen I know, especially at Fordham and Notre Dame and New York archdiocese, tell me that Malachi never had a chance. He did not serve in the papal diplomatic service and he did not rise to the top of the congregation where he worked in Rome. He did not publish any books, did not distinguish himself in any particular way.

He is a good man, they say, a hardworking man within his limitations, but definitely not the sort the Church would want to make cardinal today. I've come to know a fair amount of bishops and college presidents and cardinals. I have to say that Malachi would do better in ecclesiastic office than many of them. He would foul up less than they have.

He is a lovely person, and charming, gracious, friendly, and helpful. He is certainly not caught in the American work ethic. He finds the Italian laid-back style much more appealing. I didn't like it when he showed up here with that terribly grim Mexican priest. I talked to the chancellor in Laramie. He assured me that Father Gomez's job was merely to take care of the Bishop and to make his trip easier. He doesn't travel very well, you know.

I didn't know that, because he travels very well in his trips back and forth to Rome. Apparently the trip from Laramie to Chicago to Nolan's Landing is a more complex journey. I was relieved when we got rid of Father Gomez. My wife, as you know, had begun an election campaign which would give her a major corporate position inside of our firm. She and Ignatius both would go on the board to support and help me help Spike as he grew older. In my observation Spike needs no help at all. If she ever got herself a place on the board while Spike's still alive, he would quit. Her plans to insinuate herself and Iggy into the power structure of AVEL was doomed to failure from the start. Iggy might be a good lawyer in the hurly-burly of New York courts where he did his internship, but he doesn't have what it takes to be a corporate executive or even a corporate lawyer. He tries to act like he does because that's what his mother expects, but he would much prefer spending a good part of the day in a bar somewhere, or going to the horse races or making trips to Vegas or putting on weight and having a grand

time. I was not excited about his marriage to silly little
Consuela, a pretty child who certainly could have found
a more appropriate spouse. Josie and Loretta pushed
hard for it. They both believed that Consuela would
"straighten Ignatius out." There are some women who
can straighten some men out but Consuela is too weak to
take on such a task with somebody as potentially dissolute
as Ignatius. I worry about her pregnancy. She is very eager to have a child. He couldn't care less. She can raise
a child if she wants to. He still has to go out with the
guys at night. Iggy has the emotional maturity of a 17-
year-old.

I'm reluctant, Captain, to be burdening you with our
family conflicts. Nonetheless, you have to understand
them if you're to determine why someone tried to kill
Malachi. I'm convinced it's someone in the family, perhaps someone in my immediate family. When Loretta
goes into one of her manic phases she has a terribly neg-
ative influence on my daughters. Eileen goes along with
all her mother's fantasies. Josie tries to slow her down.
The husbands of the two young women have bright
prospects in the company but they are awed by Ignatius's
presumptions and my inability to separate family matters
from the firm.

Could any of them in some kind of prank attempted to
have some fun at Malachi's expense? I don't know how
they could've entered the room. I don't know why they
would leave a swarm of hornets in his bathroom. That's a
bad practical joke. It's a sign of madness. Is there someone in this house that is mad? I mean really mad, not
manic like my wife? Is there some crazy person around,
maybe affected by the conflict in my family? Then would
he not go after Margaret? Why go after poor Malachi, who
is no threat to anyone?

Michael Winter? I don't know what to make of him. I

don't really trust him. He's a mysterious fellow, seems to know a lot more than he says. He turns up at odd times in strange places and is always watching everything very carefully. He makes me nervous. However, Spike wants him around and that's that.

I wonder what would've happened to me if Johnny had lived. I suspect there would have been conflict between us two. Johnny worshiped his father as firstborns do and also was in constant rivalry with him. I think he looked down on me as an intellectual. If he came back alive after that airplane flight over North Vietnam, we would have become intense rivals. I think you've noticed none of us Nolans are very good at coping with rivalry.

Had his wife quieted down when they reached the institution in Kokomo?

Oh yes, they gave her several injections that they said would calm her down for a while. Then she will go into depression and the whole cycle will begin again. You have no idea how much I hate all of this.

Note:

Philip Nolan is a good man who deserves better than he has received out of life. What happens when unprepared for it, you find yourself the responsible crown prince of an immensely successful corporation?

Did he try to kill his brother Malachi? I very much doubt it. Yet who knows what rivalries there may have been between the two of them as they were growing up. Or what resentments they might have for each other's lifestyle.

It is churlish of me to suspect this able and intelligent man, suffering from an acute crisis in his marital life, might turn to murder, much less to the bizarre murder with a nest of hornets. Yet it would be worth our while in this investigation to keep a very close eye on what Philip Nolan does.

Captain Arne L. Svensson, MSP

If he were to kill anyone, it seemed to me, it might have been his wife. Surely he had ample grounds for a divorce and an annulment. But he loved her still. Love does strange things.

A statement which would not win me a Nobel prize in pastoral theology, not that there was any such.

26

A summary of an interview with Ms. Josephine Nolan Kelly

Monday Morning

Interviewer Sergeant P.A. Muldoon

(Ms. Nolan, like her sister and her mother, is Junoesque, auburn hair, full figure, and maybe a bit more intelligent than either of them and certainly less manic. However, she shares their animosity for Margaret. She is sexy but in a more subtle fashion than either of the other women, which makes her less a threat to men and therefore probably more appealing.)

There is certainly a succession crisis in our family, though it is far too early to worry about it. But poor Malachi isn't part of it. The attempt on Malachi's life was all part of Margaret's scheme to take over the firm. A plot, if it were real, would far exceed Margaret's limited intelligence. Why would anyone want to kill Father Malachi? He is a harmless old fool. Nobody in the family would gain anything by getting rid of him. He's not on the board. He doesn't have any control over the corporate decision-making. He's out of the loop.

My husband, Brendan, who may well someday replace my father as the CEO of the firm, thinks it's ridiculous to *even suspect that whatever was done to Malachi is part of the struggle within the company. No, I don't think my husband's chances of succeeding are at all affected by this incident or by the scene Mom created at the supper table. Anyway it's easier for us if Mom is locked up in a funny farm. She went over the edge more quickly than usual this time, probably because Spike rebuked her in public. The story she told to Sergeant Munster and Corporal Prybl was absurd. It probably hurt her credibility with the State Police. It is true that there is a struggle on for the soul of AVEL between Mom and Spike, perhaps a struggle between two former lovers. Mom is not going to win it as long as Spike is alive. He and Grandma control the company and are not about to let her take it over. Spike is content with Dad as CEO as long as he can keep Mom quiet. If he can't, he's finished, poor man. I'm not sure whether my Brendan will become the next CEO but if there's any inclination to keep the job in the family, he's the only one available. Neither my brother nor my brother-in-law have the ability for that position. Both of them see one another as the principal rival since my Brendan is a quiet, soft-spoken man—they don't consider him a candidate.*

It's pretty obvious that before Mom married Dad, she made a play for Spike. Particularly at that age Mom must've been irresistible so I think they had a fling and both feel guilty about it, Spike more than Mom. They're fighting each other precisely because of anger over what happened maybe 30 years ago. I don't think Dad knows about the affair. It is not the kind of thing he would suspect, much less look for. His radar screen on human relations is pretty insensitive.

All the women hate this month at Nolan's Landing. It's sterile and dull. There's nobody around here at our social level. The men like it because they can play tennis and have their little golf tournaments and gamble at night.

There's nothing for us to do but sit at poolside and wish we were back in Westchester County or in our Manhattan apartment. So we sip martinis or margaritas or whatever and soak up sun, which isn't good for our skin. When Eileen and I are here Mom takes charge of our lives. So we are no longer someone's wife but her daughters. She tells us what to do and accepts no refusals and no arguments. As you can imagine, husbands don't like that, but everybody seems to feel that they have to put in a month here because Spike expects it and because they don't want to offend him lest they lose points in their struggle to be head of the firm. I don't blame anybody for wanting AVEL. That's the name of the game. If it weren't for that, Brendan and I would not be here in this godforsaken place. We'd be in New York or at our house on the Vineyard.

Who might have tried to kill Father Malachi? I would suspect some local servants because of greed. He brought all those precious rings and tools and crosses he likes to wear. I don't know where they are now. Everyone says those illegal immigrants will stop at nothing to make a few extra dollars. You folks should be cross-examining them intensely. I believe they're criminals. I don't like the way they look at us. I don't like the way the women flirt with my husband and the other men and I don't like that cook who I think must be some kind of witch. I mean that in the real sense—she's got some power to hypnotize people. And worst of them all is that Michael Winter, the caretaker, who seems to be everywhere and see everything and know everything and watch everything—he's a very dangerous fellow.

I don't expect the police to admire the way we act with one another, frankly. None of us have anything against Father Malachi. He's not a problem. Margaret is. I wouldn't approve of it if someone tried to kill Margaret. Of course I wouldn't have any part of it. But I'm saying that in the present state of our family she's the one who is causing the trouble. She has no right at her age with her history of irresponsibility to think that she can control the firm. What's really going on is a struggle between Mom and Margaret and if I have to choose I choose my mom over my bratty, bitchy sister. But that doesn't mean I approve of trying to blame her for the assault on Father Malachi. Like I said, I don't think she's smart enough to cook up an idea that vicious. Margaret's problem is not meanness. It's greed and anger. I know who's going to win. Mom even in her good moods thinks we ought to hire a lawyer to look at the functioning of the board and Spike's control of the firm. After all, our trust funds to some extent are dependent on the future of AVEL. If it's going into the tank, some of the money we're counting on would disappear.

If someone had tried to kill Margaret, I could understand that because practically all of us consider her the enemy. I mean, I think we're all reasonably good Catholics even if we don't go to church too much. The only time we go to mass is when that senile old man from Notre Dame comes over and mumbles the prayers, but we don't do murder. And even Mom when she goes off the deep end isn't that way. She's one of the most wonderful women in the world when she's between depression and mania, a wonderful mother and grandmother and good friend, but she's only that way for maybe a third of the time, maybe even less. When she's in the depressed state she's often dangerously close to suicide. I had to pull knives out of her hands several times and once we ended up in the emergency room with blood all over her dress. She can't believe her depressions are real depressions and then when she goes through the normal state, which, like I say, seems to be briefer each year, she becomes manic. She gets into fights with people, insults them, and becomes cruel.

I'm sorry I'm crying. I'm trying to talk my husband into bailing out of the firm and working for somebody else. He's got all a company would look for—a good record at AVEL, lots of friends, and plenty of contacts. He is a charming and good-looking blond Irishman. He doesn't need this fighting, I don't need it, and our children don't need it. To be caught between Spike and Mom as we have been this month is enough to make me believe again in the Catholic teaching about purgatory.

(I believe Ms. Kelly is trying to break away from her mother's control. I suspect that Spike Nolan's life may be in danger and that Reliable Security should keep close watch on him.)

P.A. Muldoon, Sergeant, Michigan State Police

The good Patti Anne may be inclined to give the women she interviews the benefit of the doubt. I saw no overt indication Josie was trying to break away from her mother, only that she wants out of the succession folly. Maybe she will sell her angelic-looking little husband on the idea that he should find another and more peaceful corporation—if such exists.

A synopsis of an interview with Brendan Kelly
Sunday Afternoon
Interviewer O.L. Jacobsson
(It was a relief to listen to Brendan Patrick Kelly. He is an intelligent, sensible young man who likes Nolan's Landing and does his best to stay out of the family battles. He's just a little below medium height [taller than Blackie!] with curly blond hair, a winning smile, and the gift of laughter, especially at himself. However, I've learned through a long life as a police officer to be suspicious of charming Irishmen, et dona ferentes.)

The fight in our family is essentially between Loretta and Margaret, though Margaret doesn't know it. I hope her mother recovers from this latest spell. I hope she doesn't end up institutionalized for the rest of her life. I have to admit, however, that I'm not sorry she won't be around the rest of these great weeks here at Nolan's Landing.

Josie's father may have to step down as CEO, which would be a terrible shame. He's still a young man, a sound executive, and a brilliant scientist. However, Spike will not put up with Josie's mother. And as far as that goes he may not put up with Josie because of her mother. I wouldn't blame him for a moment.

It will be ten years before Phil will retire. They may well go outside the firm at that time. But if they try to continue the family presence in it, I'll be the one, mostly because the competition isn't very serious. Poor Iggy is a hollow man, who covers with bluster and obscenity his essential lack of character and confidence. He is even more dominated by his mother than my wife is. Gerry is a lawyer and the company probably should have a scientist instead of a lawyer at the top anyway. I think I have the inside track but I don't much care. I like my work. I like the firm. I like the excitement that comes from being on the leading edge. Right now that is enough for me. I see no point in speculating or wasting my time or energy or diminishing my happiness by worrying about what's going to come next.

It's strange to me that someone tried to kill Malachi Nolan. He is harmless and boring and not much fun. The atmosphere there is so bad that I'm surprised that someone has not tried to kill Margaret Nolan. Margaret is the enemy. My mother-in-law is convinced that she has conspired with her grandparents to ease Loretta's branch of the family out of power in the firm. Loretta desperately wants an appointment to the board of trustees for herself and for Iggy. She drove her daughters to believe they were entitled to these positions and that only she could

*save the company from the senility of Spike Nolan. The
conflict between the two of them seems to go back a long
way, so the battle is between Spike and Loretta. Malachi
probably wasn't even aware of the battle and certainly
wasn't part of it.*

*I tell Josie that I'm proud that I'm the only one on my
side of the family that can honestly admit that I like Margaret. She's a charming and witty and perhaps even a
holy young woman. I don't understand why Josie seems
to hate her so much except that she stands in the way of
her mother's quest for power. If Loretta had kept her
mouth shut the other night instead of telling Spike to his
face that he was a senile fool, Spike would not have made
Margaret a member of the board of directors. That
should seem obvious to everyone but I'm the only one
apparently who believes Loretta brought this on herself.*

*A person who has manic phases like that can't really
count on power in a corporate bureaucracy unless she
has some sexual hold over the people on top. I don't
know why the struggle had to come out in the open during this time at Nolan's Landing, save for my mother-in-
law's mania. And that isn't going to be cured for a long
time. Why not bide your time? Why struggle at this stage
of the game for a seat on the board?*

*Margaret's plans to teach in New Orleans are a threat
to the family? That makes no sense at all. I feel sorry for
my wife. People say that Loretta is a wonderful woman
except when she's manic. But she's not wonderful when
she's depressed either and she crosses the transition between the two very rapidly. You can never be quite sure
when Loretta is going to explode. Her outburst at dinner
the other night was a surprise. She had, I gather, been
quite calm earlier that afternoon at poolside, soaking up
sun and drinking margaritas.*

Margaret is not a prankster, which my wife knows, and

she's not the kind of person who would cut off part of a hornets' nest and carry it into Malachi's room. Nor is Margaret capable of conniving to take all power away from our family.

What if I get a seat on the board? Will that threaten my marriage? Of course I've thought about that. Or what if I'm appointed executive vice president or something like that? I will make it clear to my good wife that it's either me or her mother. I will not be tolerant the way poor Phil is. Will I win?

I hope so.

Iggy? He has personal grudges against everyone. He hated Malachi, because he said Malachi was a queer. When somebody talks that much about queers, he is not completely certain of his own sexual orientation.

Michael Winter? He sees everything and seems to know everything. There's something sinister about his eyes. Yet he certainly seems to be happy in his relationship with the cook. Most men his age would be similarly delighted with such a relationship. Indeed most men of any age would be delighted with it. My wife doesn't like her but she admits that she's probably extremely good in bed and forbids me to fantasize about her. I don't think they are the villains of the piece. I'm a romantic Mick and I don't believe lovers are killers. Still, I keep running up against the question who would want to go after Malachi? Another way of asking that question is to ask if someone wanted to kill anybody, why not kill Margaret?

Margaret's a wonderful young woman and I'm proud to have her as a sister-in-law. Since the night of the attempted murder Margaret has been showing up with this young fellow from down the beach—Joseph—whose parents are psychiatrists. I like the guy and I think he and Margaret might make a wonderful couple. He would have no interest in being one of my rivals for the firm, of that

I'm sure, but still I'd like to get to know him better. This morning I watched them water-skiing on the Lake— Joseph and his brother and I guess his brother's wife. I kind of wished I could go down to the beach and swim out and join them in the boat.

You have no idea, Lieutenant, how weird this place is. There's some sort of crazy custom that we don't associate with the others from Grand Beach or Michigan City or any of those other places. Somehow we would be harming our image and hurting the firm and risking the family if we play golf or tennis or go water-skiing with the locals. It's one of the unwritten laws of Nolan's Landing, unwritten by Loretta, that we maintain our privacy. As far I can say none of the people in the other villages around here are trying to violate our privacy. So I have to play golf with Iggy and Gerry and sometimes, but not very often, my father-in-law. Golf and tennis is all there is. There's nothing else to be done. We don't let Margaret play tennis with us because Iggy doesn't think that's right. We have to let Iggy win at golf and tennis or he becomes vicious. I don't like losing just to keep the family happy, but that's the rules of the game and I don't have to play the game the other eleven months of the year. Conversation is usually pretty stupid, the others are all Republicans and very conservative Republicans. Spike is a Roosevelt/Clinton Democrat but he usually doesn't say very much. He recently asked me to go out for a walk with him on the beach. It was a lot of fun because he's really a good guy and has had a remarkable life. I hope he continues to live a long time. He represents what I think business leaders in the system should be.

So we Nolans are different from everybody else. As I suppose you've heard from others sex life just ceases here because for some reason Loretta doesn't think it's proper that husbands and wives have too much fun when living on the same corridor of bedrooms. My wife is caught up

*in this craziness but not completely. So we do have some
fun in bed though we try to be quiet. Despite the thick
walls Loretta knows what's happening. Perhaps she sees
it in her daughter's eyes in the morning.*

*I've been gabbing. I don't know who tried to kill Fa-
ther Malachi. I don't know why we're fighting a succession battle for the firm that won't come up for a while
even if Spike should not die. Phil might not continue as
CEO or become the Chairman of the Board. There's no
reason to think that can't happen. Margaret as Chairman of the Board? Say, that's a good idea! Besides she
flies airplanes, doesn't she!*

*(Brendan Kelly seems a sane and sensible man, but I've
listened to this family so much I think maybe he's after
the main chance too, but more cleverly than the others.)*

OTJ MSP

Olaf Thor had a point. In this zoo of Eugene O'Neill
characters, a relatively sane man does seem suspicious. I
had encountered a clue in all that reading. A light had
flashed, but somehow it had blinked out.

27

They searched all morning and just before it was time to eat lunch they reappeared on the deck to which I'd retreated to make a few phone calls to check on the parish. In addition to Milord Cronin's mutterings about how my detective skills were waning, the only other event worth noting was that the Megans (four high school juniors who guard the gates to the rectory fortress) reported to me that they had moved the rectory down the street a block and it looked much nicer.

"So here's your nest," Captain Svensson reported. "As you said, Blackie, the perp was careless. We also found his gloves and his knife in a nice shopping bag. Bloomingdales, you'll observe."

"Fingerprints?" I asked.

"Maybe. The knife is from this house and it might give us some clues."

My cell phone rang, innocently enough, it seemed. I searched in my pockets for it, finally found it, and flipped the lid open. "Father Ryan."

"Joseph, Uncle Blackie. We're both okay. Don't worry. We had to make a forced landing on Highway 31 a couple of miles south of Saugatuck."

"Indeed! You're both all right!"

"Unharmed. Margaret made a perfect dead-stick land-ing. No damage to either aircraft or passengers. She says that you should tell Grandpa Spike about it and tell him he's only two up on her."

Houston, we have a situation. . . .

"Indeed?" I realized that my legs were now very weak.

"We landed on the highway which we have pretty ef-fectively blocked. Not very many people using it this morning, but a local cop wants to arrest us and impound the plane, er, aircraft and insists that Margaret give him her certificate—that's her license—and she won't do it. Do you think that maybe your friends in the State Police might be able to help us?"

"Why did you have to make this dead-stake landing?"

Next to me at the table in the library, Patti Ann Mul-doon tightened up.

"Dead-stick landing," she muttered.

"The motor, uh, engine stopped. It sputtered and then died. Out over the Lake. Look, this cop is really being obnoxious. He told Margaret she's too young to fly and he's going to bust her unless she removes her ah, aircraft. How does she think emergency vehicles can get around the plane?"

"Just a minute, Joseph." I handed the phone to Captain Svensson.

"What's wrong, Joseph? You what? What happened to the aircraft? Did you have enough fuel in the tank? Al-most full? The engine sputtered, died out, started again sputtered, and then failed? Margaret tried to guide the plane to the beach and then beyond the beach toward the freeway? You could only make it to Highway 31 and she made a perfect dead-stick landing? Let me talk to that obnoxious cop!"

He put his hand over the phone and said, "Patti Anne, get up there, Highway 31 south of Saugatuck, and deal with that cop!"

"Yes, sir!" She rose from the table, car keys already in hand.

"I want the aircraft impounded and brought immediately to our aviation headquarters at Grand Rapids so we can check out whether the aircraft was sabotaged, got it?"

"We're gone!"

"Blackie, you better go with her. Heaven only knows what state those two kids are in!"

In fact, they were doubtless having the time of their lives.

So! as Seamus Heaney begins his epic. In a Michigan State Police car with siren screaming in protest and the angry light spitting out its rage, we tore down Old Grand Beach Road out into U.S. 12, through New Buffalo with the siren now at the peak of its rage. We exploded into I-94 North at speeds approaching eighty miles an hour toward Douglas and Saugatuck, Michigan, where Highway 31 struggles with I-96 for a Lake view.

"Call the boss," I asked the pilot.

"Muldoon to base, Muldoon to base, over!"

"Someone try to give you a ticket, Patti?"

"I think Father Blackie has just solved the mystery. I can tell by his smile."

She was right.

"Even though it is not exactly in your jurisdiction, you might venture over to Margaret's hangar at Michigan City Municipal and do a thorough search. You should be specially alert for brown paper bags much like the one in which you found the hornets' nest, the gloves, and the knife."

"Immediately. Stay in touch. Muldoon, sergeants with law degrees from Old Blue are rare. Take care of yourself."

"I'm the best driver in your team, sir. Over and out."

She grinned complacently.

I, on the other hand, could find no reason to be complacent. This was the worst blunder of my checkered career as a puzzle solver. The solution wasn't hiding in the usual elevator. It was out in the open, as big as day. No one could understand why Margaret had not been the target. She should have been, given the twisted dynamics of the Nolan family. We should have surrounded her with Mike Casey's Reliables. . . . More detailed gratitude later, I informed the One-in-Charge. Good of you to make up for my stupidity. Doubtless the reply was that only the Pope was infallible and that but rarely. I was suitably rebuked.

"They'll probably try to take her license away, won't they?" Sergeant Muldoon said. "Don't you think she's too young to have one?"

"The FAA has given her the certificate because she's lived up to all the requirements. Unless they can find some evidence of negligence she'll keep her certificate and probably get some extra points for having achieved a dead-stick landing on a state highway. Besides she is several years older and infinitely more mature than her grandfather was when he was flying Spitfires and saving the thousand-year empire."

Did the One-in-Charge have a special regard for Margaret Anne Nolan? I believed he did.

I was too concerned about the two young people to ask such a question. In any event the plane was well insured.

We screamed up I-94, past the State Police station in Stevensville and through the fringes of St. Joseph and across the St. Joseph River—the south bend of which gave Notre Dame's home city its name—and then left I-94 to fend for itself on its way to Ann Arbor and Detroit and turned north on I-96.

There was a fair amount of traffic on I-96, which we generally ignored. We were the cops, weren't we? Suddenly another two squad cars joined us also at full speed.

The seventh cavalry is coming, Joseph and Margaret! Fear not!

We pulled off I-96 at the Saugatuck exit and instead of going into the town turned south on 31. Shunuff, a mile down the road we beheld an ancient Red Cessna, apparently undamaged, sitting firmly in the middle of the road, already protected by two State Police cars and a large flatbed truck. Like Spitfires landing at Beggin Hill, our squadron landed, lights flashing, sirens wailing. The advance guard of Michigan State Police had arrived in time to protect the pilot and her consort from being incarcerated by the local constable, a man who looked askance at the three new State Police cars racing toward him.

The young constable, in a fancy khaki uniform with a heavy weight of gold braid that might have been appropriate somewhere in Dixie at the time before Martin Luther King arrived on the scene, was shouting at Margaret Nolan. The latter worthy, Notre Dame cap pulled down over her eyes and hands on her hips, was confronting him in front of her aircraft and shouting back. Two State Police officers stood back and watched the confrontation, as their squad cars blocked the constable's squad car. As far as I can see there was no damage to the Cessna. Then Patti Muldoon erupted from our car and with a stream of invective of which I would not have thought possible intervened between Margaret and constable. She warned him, so far as I could translate her comment, that she was placing him under arrest for interfering with the State Police in the execution of their duty. Thereupon he shouted back as a cop would when confronted by a woman that wasn't even wearing a uniform.

"Officers, take this loudmouth asshole into custody and impound his car and bring both into the station house and that's an order."

"I ain't going nowhere!" the constable replied. "It's

against the law to obstruct traffic on this highway. I've already arrested this young woman for blocking the highway. She had no right to land her vehicle on this highway. She is in violation of the law! She should have landed at the airport. You have no right to talk to a police officer like that!"

The cop pronounced the word vehicle as all police and military officers do: ve-HICKLE.

"Officers, you heard my orders!"

"Yes, ma'am, Sergeant ma'am, right away, ma'am!"

They were having the time of their lives. They didn't like local constables either. I searched for my nephew and found him where he ought to be, standing behind his lady fair.

"You should also charge him with assault on the pilot of the plane! He tried to drag her into his squad car!"

Sergeant Muldoon managed to look like an avenging angel.

"Margaret, did he hit you?"

Margaret considered this for a moment.

"He shoved me and when I shoved him back, he shoved me hard enough to knock me down and then Joseph pushed him away and I think he lost his nerve."

"That's good enough for an assault and battery. Idiot! Federal law directly instructs a pilot of the plane that's lost its power to seek out a highway to land. That law supersedes any local or state law, which this officer is apparently trying to enforce. Get him out of my way!"

"Patti," Margaret chortled, "that was wonderful. I'm going to have to try to learn how to imitate it!"

Observing that he had struggled with some success to suppress a laugh, I ambled over to my valiant nephew.

"I hope you called your mother," I said.

"I was too busy fighting that fool cop to call. Now I think I will." He opened his cell phone, pushed one of the numbers, waited a second, and then said, "Hi, Mom! I thought I'd tell you that we have made an emergency landing on Highway 31 near Saugatuck! Yeah, an emergency landing. We didn't think it was a good idea but there wasn't much choice because the motor stopped."

"Engine," his lady fair corrected him.

"Both of us are fine. Margaret's a wonderful pilot. She made a dead-stick landing, which means that she landed without the motor, uh engine, working. Her grandfather only made three of them in all the years of the Battle of Britain so Margaret's catching up. Yeah, she's a great pilot like I said she was. Uncle Blackie's here. Where else would he be? Sabotage? We wouldn't be surprised!"

Then he passed the phone over to Margaret.

"Hi, Dr. Murphy. There wasn't any problem at all. I mean there was a problem that the engine stopped working but I learned how to do dead-stick landings when I was in training. It's not so easy but it's not really difficult. The plane doesn't have a mark on it. Neither do the two flyers. . . . I was too scared to be frightened. . . . And Joseph . . . Well, you know what he's like. Always totally cool . . . Thanks, thanks very much, Mary Kate, I love you too!" Only then did she begin to cry. After the first tears, she collapsed into the embrace of her knight protector.

"Okay, guys better get pulling out of here . . . Margaret, are you sure you didn't run out of fuel?"

"Absolutely! I filled it up the last time I flew into Michigan City. It was full when I left and is practically full now."

"Officer, can you siphon off some of that fuel into a secure container for me?"

"Yes, ma'am, right away, ma'am, right away, Sergeant ma'am!"

The state troopers were having a big laugh, obviously very proud of their sergeant.

When the trooper brought the gasoline container, he shook his head.

"Some particulates in the fuel, ma'am. Looks like sabotage."

"Bring it into the lab."

Of course it was sabotage. I had been an absolute idiot not to anticipate some such event. Margaret was the target all along. I had been faked out like an over-the-hill linebacker.

The two flyers ran out of energy in the back seat of the squad car as we sped back to Nolan's Landing.

"I'm beat," Margaret admitted.

"Me too. You provide exciting trips."

"If I were a drinker, I'd need a drink."

"We should stop at Oink's for ice cream."

My cell phone buzzed.

"Blackie."

"Arne. You were right, Blackie, as always."

"Patently."

"We found a bag of sand in a trash bin at Michigan City Municipal."

"A Bloomingdale bag, I presume."

He said nothing for a moment.

"Patently," he observed, stealing my most treasured line.

"Reread your summaries."

Satisfied with my insights and with Sergeant Muldoon's driving skills and wishing to give the young couple some privacy in the back of the car, I closed my eyes to give them their usual mid-afternoon rest.

A few moments later, I felt the familiar bounce of the Michigan Central tracks beneath the car. The squad car, I assured myself, must have grown wings.

"A good nap, Uncle Blackie?" Margaret asked brightly. "It must run in the family—your nephew just woke up."

"Recovering from my traumatic experience," Joseph murmured.

Mike Casey and a couple of his Reliables stood guard

at the gate to Nolan's Landing. They were restraining a media horde. Michael Winter and his brood waited at the door of the gatehouse.

"Should I say something, Uncle Blackie?"

"It might be useful. Don't forget your line about being too frightened to be scared."

"Too scared to be frightened," she corrected me, as Irish women do when their menfolk make mistakes. . . . "Joseph, you better scrinch down so they don't ask who you are."

"Bodyguard," he said, as he tried to lower his profile.

Margaret adjusted her Notre Dame cap to the most appropriate angle and emerged from the squad car. Three cameras started to whirl. Microphones were pointed at her like dangerous weapons.

"I filed a flight plan from Michigan City Municipal Airport to Holland Saugatuck. Over the Lake the engine of my aircraft developed some problems. It stuttered, stopped, and then started again. I adjusted our course toward land. We began to lose attitude. I hoped we could make it to a highway, preferably I-96. However, we were still some distance off the beach when the engine stopped. I thought we'd have to land on the beach, which would have been difficult. The engine coughed and then started again weakly. Then it stopped. I decided to land on Michigan 31 and managed to land the plane. I have reported the incident to the Federal Aviation Administration."

"Was there gasoline in the tank, Margaret?"

Quick smile.

"There was."

"And the motor had given you no trouble recently."

"No trouble at all. We did a regular maintenance on the engine just ten days ago."

"So it was a dead man's landing?"

"Dead-stick . . . Our family folklore testifies that my

Gramps, Group Captain Nolan, did three of those during the Battle of Britain. Now he's only two up on me."

"Was your plane damaged?"

"No noticeable damage, but it was a hard landing, so we'll have to check out its structure."

"Will you lose your license?"

"The FAA will lift my certificate only if they believe that I was responsible for this incident. . . . now 'cuse me, I gotta report to Gramps."

"Do you think the plane was sabotaged, Margaret?"

"I hope not."

Applause from the Michael Winter's claque.

Margaret hopped back into the car and, having put on my invisibility cloak, I slipped out.

"Patently it was sabotage," I said to Mike Casey. "You should keep a couple of your people on her all the time. Also have someone drive over to MCMA to pick up her car. Then drive them both back to Mary Kate's house."

Mike was surprised when I appeared from within my cloak, but I've done it so often it doesn't bother him.

"I'll drive them myself. I can tell by the expression of a dozen swallowed canaries on your face that you've solved it. Who?"

I raised my hand to signal patience.

"Superintendent Casey will drive you both over to the airport," I told my young charges as they left the squad car. "You might pay your respects to Joseph's mother on the way back."

"Gotta report to Group Captain Spike and Lady Anne first."

"Keep her away from the other cops till we get out of here," I whispered to Sergeant Patti.

She nodded.

28

I ambled into the drawing room where the police had assembled.

"Herself is taking Margaret and Joseph up to report to the Group Captain. Then Mike Casey is getting them both out of here. I don't think it wise for her to be in at the next phase."

"It's a strange twist, Blackie," Olaf Jacobsson said. "Lots of evidence, but I don't know how it will play out."

He gestured toward a table on which were two small Bloomingdale shopping bags.

"Two attempted murders," the son of Sven joined our conversation, "and not enough for a conviction, not that we want a conviction exactly. . . . Get the witness, Olie."

Sumner Butterfield, in a three-piece dark-gray suit and a Harvard tie, entered the room, looking especially grim.

"Mr. Nolan has authorized me to represent the suspect in this interview," he said solemnly.

"Happy to have you." Captain Svensson shook his hand.

Outside the windows, the Lake was mirror smooth. An occasional multicolored catamaran sail drifted by and water-ski boats cut slices on the mirror.

Eventually all was ready. An anxious Consuela Nolan

sat on one side of a desk, a solemn high Sumner Butterfield next to her, Lieutenant Jacobsson across from her.
A tape recorder lay on the table between them. A civilian
stenographer and Sergeant Muldoon were taking notes.

"Mrs. Nolan, as you know this is an investigation into an
attempted murder. Mr. Spike Nolan has asked Mr. Sumner
Butterfield to appear for you. You may refuse to answer
any questions, if you wish."

"I'm not afraid to answer questions," Consuela said
with more spunk than I might have expected.

"Very well. Let the record show that Ms. Consuela
Nolan will be interviewed by Lieutenant Olaf Jacobsson. Ms. Nolan's counsel is Mr. Sumner Butterfield.
Captain Arne Svensson and Sergeant Patricia Muldoon
of the Michigan State Police are also present."

Blackie Ryan was therefore not present, as he usually
isn't. The little man who wasn't there again today.

"Now, Ms. Nolan, when we spoke the other day you
admitted that you and your mother-in-law Ms. Loretta
Nolan went shopping at the Michigan City Mall early
last week, did you not?"

"I didn't admit it, I said it. And they call it the Marquette Mall, incidentally."

"I stand corrected."

"What was the purpose of this shopping expedition?"

"Mom—as I call my mother-in-law—felt that I needed
some new maternity clothes. She wanted to advise me
about the purchase."

"Is that a frequent event?"

"That Mom and I go shopping? No, in fact it has happened only once before, when I was choosing my bridal
dress."

"I see. Were you able to find any appropriate dresses?"

"No. Mom was not impressed with the selection at the
mall."

"How long did you look?"

"About a half hour, maybe forty minutes."

"And you returned immediately to Nolan's Landing?"

"Yes."

Out on the Lake a water-skier fell trying to jump the wakes.

"I thought you told me—"

"Yes, of course. Mom wanted to show me my sister Margaret's airplane."

"And where was that airplane?"

"At the Michigan City Airport in a hangar. Mom thought it was a silly little airplane and wanted me to see how it was not worth Margaret's obsession with it."

"I see . . . Now, did you or your mother-in-law enter the hangar?"

"Yes we did."

Consuela was faltering.

"Was the hangar locked?"

"Yes, it was, but Mom had a key to it."

"Did you ask where she obtained it?"

"No, it was on her key chain."

"I see. Then what happened?"

"Mom said it was a silly old plane, not worth the family quarrels over it."

"Did you agree?"

"I thought that Margaret talked too much about it. The rest of us thought that the plane was boring."

"I see. Do you get along with Ms. Margaret Nolan?"

"I think she's okay, but she's the cause of a lot of conflict in the family. I don't understand why, but she is."

"Did you or your mother-in-law bring any packages into the hangar, which you had probably entered illegally?"

"We don't admit that it was an illegal entry," Sumner Butterfield cut in.

"I'll strike that from the question. Did you bring into the hangar any packages?"

"No, I did not."

"And your mother-in-law?"

"She was carrying a medium-sized shopping bag."

"Any identification on it?"

Consuela knew that she was in trouble, though not serious trouble. Or so she seemed to think.

"It was a Bloomingdale shopping bag."

"One like this? Sergeant, will you bring that bag over to this table, please?"

"Yes, sir."

"A bag like this, Ms. Nolan?"

"Yes, one like this."

"Was there anything in the bag?"

She sighed.

"Yes, there was."

"And what was in it?"

"Sand."

"Would you care to look inside this bag?"

"You don't have to do that, Ms. Nolan," Sumner Butterfield insisted.

"I might as well."

She looked in the bag.

"What do you see, Ms. Nolan?"

"Sand."

"I see. So this is the same bag?"

"I don't know that. It looks like it, but I don't know it's the same bag."

Sumner Butterfield grinned, proud of his client.

"Did you do anything with the bag?"

"Not at first."

"What happened?"

"Mom talked about what a disruptive force Margaret is in our family and that we should take steps to teach her a lesson. Mom often spoke of teaching Margaret a lesson."

"And this time what did she suggest?"

"She said that we ought to put sand in her gas tank so

that the next time she tried to take off the plane wouldn't start."

A pregnant—one should excuse the expression—silence descended on the room.

"Those were her exact words?"

"As close as I can remember. I do know that she said it would be a good prank on Margaret if her plane didn't start."

"Did she not say that the engine might stop after Margaret had taken off?"

Consuela leaped out of her chair!

"My God! No! I didn't think she was trying to kill her own daughter! That would have been a terrible sin!"

"Did she pour the sand into the fuel tank?"

Consuela began to sob.

"No, she had to hold the cover to the tank open so I could pour it in. . . . I didn't want to kill Margaret! I didn't!"

"Are you aware that Ms. Margaret Nolan endeavored to fly from Michigan City to Saugatuck this morning and that the engine of her plane ceased to function over the Lake?"

"No! Oh, no! Poor Margaret! I wanted so much to be her friend and now I've killed her!"

"Ms. Margaret Nolan survived, Consuela," Sumner Butterfield interjected.

"Hence the charge against you, Ms. Consuela Nolan, will only be attempted murder."

"Will my baby have to go to jail too?"

"You will find excellent maternal facilities at the Woman's State Correctional Institution, Ms. Nolan."

Not very likely to happen, I thought. Consuela might have intended malicious mischief or possibly disorderly conduct. She would have to testify against her mother-in-law.

The interrogator let her cry herself out.

"Now, Ms. Nolan, we have a few more questions before we take you into Stevensville and book you."

"Come now, officer, you really don't want to do that, do you? This young woman has been forthcoming in her testimony. It is clear that she was misled by her mother-in-law. You will need her testimony as this matter progresses. I'm sure we can work out a process that will protect her for the present time."

"What is the present time, counselor?"

"Until you are ready to bring charges against her mother-in-law?"

Olaf glanced at Arne.

"Let's finish the interrogation first?"

"Very well."

Sumner Buttersworth had made his point and was satisfied with it. So was I.

"Ms. Nolan, have you ever seen another shopping bag like this one?"

"There are thousands of them in heartened New York City."

She was dabbing at her eyes, hearted by her counsel's suggestion that she might not have to go to jail.

"I mean in this house and recently."

She took a deep breath and decided to go for it.

"Mom gave me one the day after the hornets attacked Archbishop Nolan."

Aha!

"What did she ask you to do with it?"

"To throw it in one of the trash cans at the side of the house."

"Did you look in bag?"

"No."

"Why not?"

"I did not want to find out what was in it."

"Did you have any idea as to its contents?"

"I thought I felt a knife inside. I didn't want to know anything more."

"Might it be this shopping bag?"

"It might, but I'm not sure."

"Where did you put it?"

"In the trash can nearest the road, that's the order we're supposed to follow."

"I understand . . . Would you look inside the bag?"

"All right."

"What's in it?"

"The knife I felt, a pair of gloves, some kind of paper."

"Perhaps the materials from a hornets' hive."

"It might be."

"Were you suspicious of the shopping bag?"

I signaled Patti Muldoon and gave her a slip of paper with a question that would solve the last bit of the mystery.

"I should have been. I could not imagine Mom trying to kill anyone, especially the Archbishop, who was a harmless old man. I tried not to think about it."

"I see."

"Thank you, Ms. Nolan. You have been very forthright and very helpful in your testimony. Would you be willing to sign a statement containing a summary of what you have said?"

She glanced at Butterfield.

"I would strongly advise you to do that, Ms. Nolan. I will help you prepare such a statement."

"I just want to say that I hope Margaret will find it in her heart someday to forgive me."

How about tomorrow?

Patti Anne passed my note to Lieutenant Jacobsson.

"Might I ask one more question, Ms. Nolan?"

"Why not?" she said bitterly. She thought she had lost when in fact she had won.

"When you all went into the drawing room, this room, after supper the night of the argument, did anyone leave to go upstairs before the group broke up?"

She stared at him hard. She understood why the question was asked.

"I believe Mom went upstairs right after we left the dining room. She told me she was going to the washroom. She was back almost at once, before the boys left for the casino."

Long before the young men left for the casino. The Ryan Theory of Locked Rooms—less sophisticated than the String Theory of Astro-physics—was not disconfirmed by the data: The criminal enters the locked room before it is locked. She brought the coffee can into Malachi Nolan's room long before Malachi entered it. Imagination, nerve, even courage, if you will. Madness, of course. A brilliant if berserk criminal. Guilt? Leave her to heaven, to coin a phrase.

Sergeant Patti, Sumner, and Consuela huddled over a computer, working out a statement that caught the flavor of naiveté which marked her testimony. Periodically the son of Sven came to peer over their shoulders and nod his approval. No indictment for Consuela and her child. Loretta? Would they see her as a homicidal maniac who should spend the rest of her life in a mental institution or would they plead her out on a disorderly conduct charge with an agreement that she would spend a certain amount of time in Kokomo or similar institution? It would be a spectacular trial—a crazy mom using a daughter-in-law as a tool in attempting the murder of her daughter. Probably they would send one of their psychiatrists down to Kokomo to interview her. Most likely they would decide that she wasn't capable of standing trial and settle for a plea that would wrap everything up neatly. Justice would be served, more or less. The sloppiness in hiding evidence would indicate that the potential defendant was in-capable of rational behavior. Worst still, a jury might sympathize with her.

A poor woman homicidal maniac might not get such an easy break, though she might deserve it too.

I dialed Milord Cronin's number and reported a satis-factory conclusion to the case.

"Still unbeaten, Blackwood?"

"Patently."

"Clumsy killer, not many points on winning that one."

"As we are learning with the White Sox, a game is either a 'W' or an 'L' no matter how inadequate the opposition."

"I suppose you might as well stay down there for the rest of the week. The Megans and Crystal Lane and I have the situation under control."

"Perhaps . . ."

But he had already hung up.

My next call was to Grand Beach.

"The aviators have just arrived. You know, Black-wood, she is an intolerably cute young woman."

"Arguably."

"Who tried to kill them?"

"She has probably not figured it out yet. Her mother, doubtless criminally insane, orchestrated the whole sce-nario."

"How terrible!"

"Indeed."

"The poor child . . . Fortunately she has the resistance to bounce back."

"That is your official diagnosis, Doctor?"

"Certainly."

"It would be a good work to delay her return here un-til after supper."

"I can arrange that . . . she tells me that she has a fam-ily meeting at seven o'clock. Presumably you won't be there?"

"Just now I am arguably indispensable at this house. The whole thing will go down at that meeting. She should be there."

At that moment Ignatius Nolan and his two brothers-in-law stumbled into the room, bulls looking for china to break, bulls in point of fact smelling of the drink taken.

"What the fuck is going on here?" he demanded. "What the fuck is this thing you've just signed, Connie?"

"It's a statement she agreed to make for the police," Sumner Butterfield said meekly.

"Who the fuck are you?"

"I'm Sumner Butterfield of the firm Triple S and S and I am acting as Ms. Nolan's attorney."

"The fuck, you say! Well, you're fired! I want a white lawyer for my wife!"

"She has already made her statement," Captain Svensson insisted.

"This is a lot of horseshit! . . . You ratted out my mom!"

Messrs. Kelly and McGinity tried to calm him down and lead him out of the room. He shook them off.

"Buttercup," he snarled. "You're fired! Get out of here."

He tore up the statement.

"That document is the property of the State of Michigan. You cannot destroy it."

"I'm her husband. She's not committing herself to this crap. . . . Butternut, didn't you hear me? You're fired! Disappear."

"Only Ms. Nolan can dismiss me, sir."

"I'm her husband."

"That doesn't permit you to discharge her attorney."

"I said, I'm her husband, I can fucking fire anyone I want."

"Young man," Captain Svensson said solemnly, "we already have two charges of attempted murder and aiding attempted murder against your family. I am about to add an obstruction of justice against you to the list."

"Ignatius! Stop acting like a teenager! Sit down and shut up! Mr. Butterfield has arranged to protect your wife and child from jail. Why don't you try to act like an adult for a change?"

Ah, the good Consuela had determined that it was time for there to be a shift of power in her marriage. Better late than never.

"Sumner," she continued, "naturally you're still my attorney. I apologize for my husband's racism. He's not a really bad human being until he drinks his first bottle of beer. . . . Sergeant Muldoon, will you print out another copy of my statement, please?"

Shaken—and shorn of his accustomed power—Ignatius stumbled into a couch and collapsed. His two colleagues disappeared from the scene.

As did Blackie Ryan, who hadn't been there in the first place.

Spike and Anne were waiting in their suite, both reading and enjoying the light Lake breeze which was blowing through the open glass windows, which had disappeared, doubtless at the push of a button.

"Marvelous way to enjoy a porch without any danger to Irish skin," I commented as I sank into a leather chair.

"A glass of Middleton's?" Lady Anne asked.

"A splasheen. The day may be a long one."

"You will be in attendance at the family meeting this evening?" Spike closed his book and removed his glasses.

"Inside my invisibility cloak."

They both laughed because they had become aware of my secret ability to be so unobtrusive that no one notices me.

"It will be an important gathering. Phil and I will put an end to all of this nonsense."

"Long past the proper time," I said.

"These things are like kittens." Lady Anne extended the splasheen to me with royal respect. "Before you know it they grow into monsters that destroy all the furniture."

"What happened downstairs?" Spike asked.

"Mostly what we expected. The police patently were authorized by the local prosecutor to seek amicable settlements—disorderly conduct and malicious mischief."

I recited the events which had just transpired.

"So Loretta was behind the attack on Malachi? Why am I not surprised? Who else? But why?"

I explained her scheme to demonize Margaret. And a backup plan to wreck her plane? Kill her? Just teach her a lesson?

"A crazy woman," Anne said with a shake of her head. "Beautiful but quite round the bend."

"I had a phone call from Phil. He had brought her clothes and books down to Kokomo. She has a private room without a phone, thanks be to God, and is still manic but under heavy sedation and hence not in restraints. Phil intends to leave her there until they get to the bottom of the problem, which may take a long time."

"Please God that it does," Lady Anne added. "She won't be able to run away from therapy like she always has in the past."

"Phil is not exactly a weakling with her, but he has never really been able to control her, not after that first spell when Margaret was born."

"Poor Margaret," Lady Anne sighed. "I wonder what all of this will do to her."

"It is," I admitted, "not every day that one learns that one's mother has tried to kill one."

As I was leaving, Spike asked a final question, "What do you think of young Brendan Kelly?"

"Bright and able kid," I said. "Has his head attached properly to the rest of him."

"And his wife?"

"Is not unaware of her mother's pernicious influence and would like to be friends with Margaret."

"We will have to put an end to the idea that Iggy might be the crown prince. The very possibility demoralizes a lot of our younger workers. Not right now, but perhaps soon. Would you concur?"

"In the words of the high Irish compliment, Brendan would not be the worst of them."

"Executive vice president, maybe. Give us a chance to keep an eye on him. On both of them. Young Gerry McGinity is a good kid, but he's essentially a lawyer. We need a technology man at the top."

"Margaret will be on the board," I said, turning to leave. "Her input would be crucial, I imagine."

In the drawing room the son of Sven was wrapping up his operation.

"The lab reported that it was indeed sand in the fuel tank. The plane will need a new engine. They also could find no fingerprints on the bag we pulled out of the garbage or any of the material in it. That day, at any rate, she was careful."

"Why was the prosecutor not eager to press charges?"

"No real case at all against Consuela. They had one of their psychiatrists call Kokomo. Their advice was that the woman was quite mad and the case would be a zoo. We don't need that in Berrien County. . . . Anyway there won't be any more attempted murders here at Nolan's Landing."

"Not at the moment," I said, not at all sure that Loretta's influence would not persist even in her absence, poor troubled, haunted woman.

29

The atmosphere in Spike's office for the family meeting was a mix of a wake and a trial. Moreover, from the angry looks on many faces, they had come prepared for a fight. I had crawled into my little corner and enveloped myself in my invisibility cloak. Margaret, I noted, had seated herself at the very back of the room, as though she was waiting for an assault.

"I want to know"—Eileen began that assault—"what right Margaret has to blame our poor mother, who isn't even here, for her crashing her stupid old airplane?"

"How can a woman who is in an asylum in Kokomo sabotage a plane?" Gerry McGinity asked. "And what evidence do you have for your charges, Margaret?"

"I didn't make any charges," Margaret said.

"Margaret is the one responsible for driving Mom over the deep end!" Eileen insisted, her face as red as her mother's when the latter was angry. "She is the cause of all our problems."

"I made the charges," Consuela said calmly.

"Shut up, Connie," her husband muttered. "Haven't you done enough already?"

"You shut up, you adolescent asshole!"

"How did you know that she sabotaged the plane?" Josie asked, as one seeking information.

"I was the one in the hangar with her when it happened."

"Will all of you please be quiet?" Spike interrupted the shouting. "Philip Nolan and I have some things to say. First of all, it is unlikely that anyone in this family will be indicted. However, there is not the slightest doubt that Loretta Nolan introduced the hornets into Malachi's room and the sand into Margaret's Cessna 177. Consuela knows because she was an innocent collaborator. I have every reason to believe that there will be no prosecution or at least no one will face incarceration. Fortunately for us the honesty and integrity of Consuela's statement has been of substantial help in this outcome. The details can be discussed later. . . . Phil will now make some remarks."

"I visited my wife at the hospital this afternoon. She has a comfortable private room and is quite calm now and not in restraints. However, this has been accomplished because of powerful medications. She is still in a manic phase, during which psychotherapy is impossible. The medical and nursing staff seem to be excellent. They specialize in bipolar disorders and understand the problem of patients not taking their meds. They made no promises other than that it is much more likely your mother will be able to avoid that problem in the future. I anticipate hers will be a long stay. If we had been able to persuade her years ago to accept hospitalization we might not face the present problem."

"She would not have the problem if it were not for Margaret," Eileen insisted.

"That is one of the two illusions I wish to discuss this evening, Eileen. The first illusion, however, is the more important of the two. It is the illusion that there is a succession crisis in AVEL. There is not and there won't be one for some considerable time. Your mother, as long as

I have known her, has been involved passionately in causes to which she has given herself with all the energy and fire and commitment of her passionate nature. Unfortunately those commitments have often been misguided and then blighted by unrealistic enthusiasm at the manic end of her bipolar disorder. The current commitment is to AVEL and is based on her conviction that the present staff are ruining the company, a conviction that is so evident in her view that it does not require evidence other than her strong feeling that it is true.

"In fact, it is not true, as all the research on the company establishes. The solution, she believes with all her heart and soul, is for her to take charge of the company and save it from the maladministration of my father and myself. She assumes that she will be named to the board of directors and that Ignatius will be confirmed as the heir to my position. I told her often that for all his ownership of much of the company your grandfather does not have that power. The other directors would veto her appointment and resign if he and I should insist on the appointment. The same would apply, Ignatius, to your being named as my successor. Unfortunately you do not have the technical background that the directors would insist on and the employees would expect for such a person. I told your mother that too, but she dismissed it. We had the power to make such appointments and therefore we should do it."

"Thanks a lot, Dad, for screwing me!"

"Shut up, you fool," Consuela barked. "If you wanted the job, you should have gone to MIT."

Ignatius shut up.

"I tried to explain to her the constraints within which the leaders of corporations must work—the media, the markets, the regular customers. I don't think AVEL needs salvation just now, but despite the passion of your mother's enthusiasm, she would have destroyed the firm if she were given influence in it."

"So you locked her up because you loved the firm more than you loved her?"

"That is unfair, Eileen. I will not respond to your accusation."

"Maybe you should shut up too, Eileen," Josie said.

"You just want your moron Brendan to get Iggy's job. . . . Why did Spike have to give Mom's job to Margaret?"

"I must repeat, Eileen, that it was never Mom's job. She had no right to it, no matter how strongly she believed that she did."

"How long are you going to keep her locked up?"

"The hospital will release her when they think they've done all they can. It won't be too soon for me."

"Spike, why did you give her job to Margaret? She's been nothing but trouble. She doesn't deserve it. Mom does."

"We needed another member on the board, Eileen. The rumor that your mother was to be the new director had swept the company. There were already some resignations. I had to put the rumor to rest."

"That is the final illusion I want to dismantle." Phil resumed his presentation. "I realize it will be impossible at first. Your mother believed with all her heart and soul that Margaret was a problem child. She was not. She was lively and exuberant. However, she never knowingly made trouble for anyone. You have been, I hate to use the word, brainwashed with the conviction that Margaret was the cause of conflict in the family. She was only the innocent youngest child. I tried to defend her, to argue with your mother that she was not being fair. Again she would listen to me but not hear what I said. I now fear that I didn't try hard enough. I'm sorry, Margaret."

"It's okay, Dad. I understand."

"I have one more announcement and this meeting will stand adjourned. . . . Anne and I have come to understand that Nolan's Landing is not the fun place it used to be for your families. We'll be here next summer for anyone who wants to come. However, if there is a sense of obligation that you have to come, I want to assure you that you don't."

Consuela embraced Margaret as she left. Then, after hesitating, so did Josie. The two siblings wept together.

Well, a couple of reconciliations, however tentative, were on the whole more than one might have expected.

Margaret drifted by my secret corner where I was not invisible to her.

"Ice cream at Oinks?"

"Done."

30

She was already waiting for me, surrounded by the swarms of adorable rug rats who gather at the ice cream store on every summer night. A black Reliable sedan lurked around the corner. The kids around her were devouring ice cream cones with which they had smeared their faces—clowns on the Red Arrow Highway.

"Go 'way, kids," she asked politely. "I have to talk to the priest."

The kids complied promptly. Great primary schoolteacher, among other things.

"Chocolate malt supreme." She offered me my reward. "If it's melted, I'll get another."

My ice cream was in a dish. Hers was in a cone, just like all the other kids. Thoughtful.

"That may be necessary eventually. My resident leprechaun usually eats most of my treats."

She blinked, frowned, then grinned, understanding almost at once the critical role the leprechaun plays in my life.

"Uncle Blackie, will you be my spiritual adviser?"

"Would that not involve a certain conflict of interest?"

Again she was momentarily puzzled.

"Oh, you mean Joseph? I'm not asking you to be my romantic adviser, only my spiritual director. Besides Joseph right now seems to be the only available boy."

"Ah."

"That means, like you say, he's totally not the worst of them."

"Indeed . . . Well, until informed otherwise I am available for nonromantic spiritual direction."

"Mostly by e-mail?"

"That's acceptable."

"Good." She settled down. "I'm worried because I find it too easy to forgive all those idiots in my family. Forgiveness should be difficult and so I don't think I'm really forgiving them."

"What do you think God would say about that scruple?"

"She'd say, 'Chill out, Margo!' "

"She elects to use that name?"

"Till I tell Her that my official name now is Peggy Anne."

"It has been a difficult day, Peggy Anne. You and your not-the-worst-of-them-boyfriend almost died in a plane crash, one orchestrated by your mother whose delusions in your regard have not been fended off by the rest your family. Moreover it is revealed that she also orchestrated an attack on your harmless uncle so that you would be blamed for it. . . . Are those not horrible deeds worthy of anger?"

"I feel so sorry for them," she said, lowering her head in dejection. "They have messed up their lives so badly. They're my family and I want to love them. They'll feel so guilty they probably won't let me."

"Josie and Consuela seem open to rapprochement."

"It will be hard?"

"For them or for you?"

"For me. I can't make it look too easy for them."

"I see . . . Who was your therapist in Switzerland?"

"Good guess! Madam Lange-Kellerman. She had some kind of contract with the school. She was very good too!"

"I should think so."

"Big help and then at the Dome I had an elderly Holy Cross Nun who was a Freudian. Madam was Jungian. . . ."

"I believe that's all they do in Switzerland."

"And I'll find one as soon as I arrive in New Orleans, but not before I make arrangements for flying. . . ."

"A shrink for the rest of your life?"

"Why not? I suppose it wouldn't be right to try to sign up Mary Kate, would it?"

"Not if you will have another relationship with her."

"I think I'll know that by next summer."

"Arguably."

"You think I've already made up my mind?"

"I'll plead immunity on that one."

"He is a *very* nice boy," she said, pondering the thought carefully. "He did tell me that he loved me today, just before we didn't crash."

"Simultaneously with a similar assertion from you."

"Dead even."

A frown appeared on her forehead.

"I'm terrified about ACE."

"Why?" I asked gently.

"I'm afraid of everything and everyone—the students, the other teachers, the parents of the students."

"But you will have the cachet of being the teacher from Notre Dame, will you not?"

"The spoiled rich kid from Notre. Some of the other ACErs might hold that against me too."

"You seemed to have overcome such prejudice when you first appeared at the fabled Golden Dome."

"It wasn't easy and this is a lot different. . . . It's not fair.'

"I had it on the authority of a certain young man that day when we were walking down the beach that you'd cream such problems."

"Probably . . . But let me be scared for a while."

"You wouldn't be mostly Irish if you were denied that right."

We both laughed. Joseph had been correct. She was a very vulnerable young woman.

"So what did your previous spiritual directors have to say?"

"The Dominican in Lucerne was terribly afraid I was deceiving myself. So was I. Finally he said that it appeared to him that I was greatly blessed—that was exactly what he said."

"And at the Golden Dome?"

"He was a Jesuit graduate student, like totally concerned that I wasn't doing enough for social justice."

"And you told him what you were doing."

"He warned me about the dangers of spiritual pride. . . . Do you think I am a victim of spiritual pride, Uncle Blackie?"

"Arguably it might be said that you had more reason for that than do most of us, but I doubt that you are capable of spiritual pride. You are far too ready to laugh at yourself."

"So what do you think my most serious fault is?"

"That's easy. You're likely to be too impatient with yourself for not being patient enough with those who don't share your gift of laughter. . . . And, oh yes, you should listen more closely to God when He tells you, chill out!"

I switch the genders in these matters in the name of balance and political correctness.

"Good points! You'll be a great spiritual adviser, Uncle Blackie."

"Thank you! I'm happy that I passed the test."

In fact, I am mortally scared of the blessed ones. In their presence God becomes very close. In Margaret's case, however, the transcendent presence was simply charming, forgiveness, and love, as Therese has told us.

EPILOGUE
(Blackie)

"*My failure from* the start was that I did not see that the assault on the sometime angel to the church of Laramie was in fact aimed at his niece. Everyone kept repeating that she was the obvious target, but I did not realize that was literally the truth until I heard about the dead-stick landing on Highway 31."

"Why attempt to kill a bishop to get rid of Margaret?"

"As I should have realized when Loretta endeavored to blame Margaret at the time of the first police investigation, she planned to eliminate Margaret by convicting her of assault on Malachi. The sabotaged aircraft was a fallback she had already prepared in case it was necessary."

"It would not have worked, would it?"

"Sergeant Munster was prepared to charge her the second day of his loopy investigation. The Nolan lawyers might well have successfully impugned such charges, but the board of AVEL would have hesitated to vote such a one to their fellowship."

"It would have been clear at the trial, would it not, that Loretta was crazy?"

"Mr. Sumner Butterfield would have destroyed her testimony, but you can never tell what a jury will do."

"Maybe I should have a Gulfstream 4 of my own."

"You will hold me excused from flying in it."

"Well, you get a 'W' on this one, though I'd say just barely."

"As the sainted Vince Lombardi once said, losing isn't anything."

As to the loose ends, Margaret did move to New Orleans and prospered as a teacher of the poor and powerless and continued to build up flying miles toward her two-engine aircraft. E-mail flashed back and forth between her room in New Orleans and Joseph's apartment in Hyde Park, where, having been admitted to the Div School, he listened to David Tracy on God and Margaret Mitchell on Jesus. Margaret Nolan also found time to fly (in the company's Gulfstream) to New York for board meetings. Michael and Juana Maria continued their tender care of Nolan's Landing, to which Spike and Lady Anne returned frequently. Josie and Margaret continued their reconciliation via e-mail. Consuela gave birth to a son, Francis, and her husband became an assistant district attorney for Kings County. The board named Brendan Kelly executive vice president of AVEL. After eight months of therapy, Loretta Nolan was released from the hospital, tentative and uncertain. At last report she takes her meds every day. Archbishop Malachi Nolan, with considerable publicity in the English press, ensconced himself as Archbishop in Residence at Ampleforth Abbey. Sean Cronin, his health still excellent, continued to preside over the Archdiocese of Chicago. His innocuous Coadjutor still specialized in cleaning up messes.

EPILOGUE

(Joseph)

I saw her a couple of more times before she flew off to New Orleans and I moved into Hyde Park for graduate school. We went to a Woody Allen film in Three Oaks and water-skied several more times on the *Mary Kathleen.* We did not manage a rendezvous on the Lake at night, which was probably just as well. Next summer maybe. I took her to dinner at a restaurant in Three Oaks that was sufficiently special that she wore nylons and heels—and a touch of makeup—and I a sports jacket (no tie, not yet).

"This could be considered a date," she remarked over dessert.

"I guess so."

"That means you have to kiss me good night."

"I think I can manage it."

I extended my hand on the table and covered hers. She pulled away and then quickly seized my hand.

"I need time, Joseph."

"As far as I'm concerned, Margaret, you have all the time in the world."

She frowned.

"I don't need *that* much time."

"How much do you need?"

She took a deep breath. This would be a serious promise.

"Till next summer would be enough."

"We can communicate by e-mail?"

"Sure, even an occasional cell phone call."

"That's fine with me. . . . But why do you need time? To be sure about me?"

"No way, Joseph. To be sure about myself."

"I'm already sure about you, Peggy Anne. So are my mom and dad."

She squeezed my hand.

"Sure they are. Your family is adorable. . . . Still I need to be a little more sure about me."

"Like I say, take all the time you need. I'll wait."

"You don't *have* to wait."

"That's up to me, isn't it?"

"Shunuff!"

Holding her hand, I walked with her down the beach from our house to Nolan's Landing, resplendent and funny under the masses of stars, as if the stars were laughing with us.

I managed a relatively skillful kiss.

"Uncle Blackie says," she informed me, "that next summer always comes even if this one should be the last summer of our lives."

Then she kissed me with lots of feeling. She turned and hurried up the stairs to Nolan's Landing. I walked home, or perhaps I should say, I floated home.

Shunuff.

Turn the page for a preview of

THE
ARCHBISHOP
IN
ANDALUSIA

A Blackie Ryan Novel

———◦◦◦———

Andrew M. Greeley

Available in November 2008

A FORGE HARDCOVER

ISBN-13: 978-0-7653-1590-8   ISBN-10: 0-7653-1590-4

1

"*So, Don Juan,* I am told that your presentation this morning was brilliant?"

The Cardinal Archbishop of Seville was about to invite me, with the deviousness he shared with Milord Cronin in Chicago, to a dinner that would have distinctly unpleasant, if fascinating, consequences.

He honored me with the title applied to royalty and princes of the Church in this rather odd country. Even the King was Don Juan Carlos. One would hardly address the Cardinal Archbishop of Chicago as Don Sean or even Don Juan Patricio. It would be thought a pretentious affectation, much as if one referred to the putative president of our own republic as Don Barack.

I must respect the wisdom of the dictum "When in Rome . . ."

"Call me Blackie!"

Not Ishmael surely, not in al-Andalus where it might be a fighting word.

The Cardinal, always effervescent, clapped his hands enthusiastically, though not as the flamenco groups in this part of the world clap, and permitted his dark-skinned face to erupt in a smile as bright as the Andalusian sun.

"Bravo! Bravo! Don Nero!" he exclaimed in his rich baritone. "It conveys perfectly the persona. But Nero is Italian. So we will call you El Padrecito Negro—the little priest called Blackie."

Which is what my siblings and my friends call me. Also my fellow priests, such as these may be, and my parishioners, when I had such, and my lay staff, and even the ineffable Megan, the porter persons in what used to be my rectory and now is the house where I live, and almost everyone else, save for deadly serious religious women for whom the name indicates an absence of seriousness, call me Blackie. The name fits me perfectly.

As in Boston Blackie and Black Bart and the Black Prince and the Black Knight, though not as in the Black Death and the Black Sox.

Said serious religious women choose to call me "Jack," a name that depresses me. I only vomit, however, when that is changed to "Jackie."

But what could "Blackie" convey to this tiny (at least four inches shorter than I) prince of the Church, resplendent in his watered silk crimson cummerbund, cape, and zucchetto (looking very much like "the fool" in a Renaissance painting of a royal family), as he struggled to make sense out of me.

"I do not fully understand you, Padrecito Negro. You wear black jeans, a black clerical shirt without a collar, a blue and red windbreaker celebrating the Chicago Cubs, whoever they be, and a baseball cap that depicts a fearsome *toro*, but not one of ours." Don Diego was finding it difficult to sort me out. "You do not act like a coadjutor archbishop with right to succession and a distinguished enough philosopher to be invited to a conference in Seville on American Philosophy. Still, I find the whole image charming."

I should not have put the man in such an awkward

position. When Milord Cronin heard that the conference would be in Seville, he absolutely insisted that I had to live in the home of his good friend Don Diego. "You and he will hit it off perfectly. He's just like you."

I was not at all sure that I wanted to hit it off perfectly with someone who was just like me.

Don Diego sipped his superb sherry with the respect it deserved. He was a bright and quick man—he had dismissed my adversary at the morning conference as a "Dominican and they haven't had a decent philosopher since Aquino. You will, how do you say in America, crush him. That would be a good work if only he could realize that he had been crushed."

His grin was especially impish against his black face which earned him the admiring nickname among his priests of "El Moro"—the Moor.

El Moro and El Padrecito Negro.

"It is true that my ancestors were Moriscos, people who pretended to be Christian but in fact kept the faith of the Prophet. But that ended a couple of generations ago, I believe."

He laughed again, a deep, solemn laugh, somehow inappropriate for a man of his size.

"Touché, Don Diego."

We were sitting in the study of his rose-colored palace whose broad windows faced on the Cathedral Plaza. On one side was the Alcazar Royal, a network of palaces rebuilt by Don Fernando and Doña Isabella, and then again by Don Carlos, the first Hapsburg king. On the other side was the immense gothic cathedral which El Moro had claimed was the largest in Europe (a claim which my friends in Cologne would deny). Next to the Cathedral loomed the Giralda, the giant bell tower with the one-ton weathervane which had begun life as a Muslim minaret and appeared in the set of the Tyrone Power TCM favorite *Blood and Sand*.

It had been, as I told him upon return from the conference (in Carmen's tobacco factory, now the locale of the philosophy faculty), "a piece of cake."

This had delighted him and occasioned his first spasm of joy.

"You are not a serious man! That is excellent."

"It said in the islands, which were originally populated by migrants from Spain at the end of the ice age, that for the English a situation may be indeed serious but never desperate, while for the Irish the situation is always desperate, but never serious."

He celebrated again, toasting me with his sherry.

"You are, then, a desperate man, no?"

"In the land of my ancestors that would be a high compliment. Life is too short ever to be serious."

Though my worries about Milord Cronin these days violated that principle.

Don Diego did not look like an African. Rather he had the appearance of a Moor, the folk who had run this part of the world for hundreds of years until the arrival of Ferdinand III, a pragmatist who thought that the local folk, a mix of Arabs and Persians and Berbers, were brilliant architects and builders and should not be chased away. He also believed that the Jews were clever and ingenious and sometimes even wise. Tolerance had ebbed and flowed during the half millennium in which Christians and Moors had fought over the Iberian Peninsula. Pragmatic leaders on both sides were not as tolerant, perhaps, as political correctness would require today. But in many places and many times under Moorish and Christian monarchs the three religions of Spain lived together in relative amity.

Appropriately therefore in this new ecumenical age the Cardinal of Seville (Is BE ya) would be a Moor.

Sometimes a new dynasty of Berbers would sweep across the Straits of Gibraltar and proclaim "Death to the

Infidel!" But the modus vivendi would survive. Sometimes a Castilian king would surround a city like Toledo and threaten "death to the infidels," and then change his mind. However, finally, one of San Fernando's descendants, Isabella the (so-called) Catholic, toppled Granada, the last Muslim city-state, and celebrated in due course (having dispatched Cristobal Colon, the Admiral of the Ocean Seas, to New York City) by banning all who were not Catholic from her brand-new kingdom.

It was in this very Cathedral Plaza that priests baptized Moriscos and Marranos by the thousands by the simple expedient of strolling about and sprinkling them with water while pronouncing the sacramental words. It was an act of blind folly, not to say horrific injustice, and was at least one of the causes of the terrible murders which have afflicted Spain ever since. Since there was some reason to suspect that not all of these converts were sincere, the local Holy Office of the Inquisition was set loose on those who might be heretics.

Why else would Don Diego be lifted from his comfortable chair of Philosophy at Salamanca and deposited here in Andalusia?

"But you did indeed crush that nasty English Dominican this afternoon! So I am informed by my best spies!"

"One can but try," I murmured with false modesty.

"You told him that William James's pragmatism converged with the reflections of his fellow Englishman Cardinal Newman. And when he asked you about the President of the United States, you told him that you were no more responsible for that gentleman than he was responsible for Ms. Thatcher."

"Cheap trick," I said.

"And the audience cheered like you were a matador in the bullring."

"I don't attend bullfights."

"Nor do I. Quite inappropriate."

It was a triumph that I would not dare remember for long, lest I fall victim to the temptation of morose delectation.

"Your nephew, I am told, is residing currently at the Alfonso XIII Hotel. He is the *novio,* I believe, to the young woman also residing there who flies her own jet plane."

"A *novio* in separate hotel rooms," I insisted.

My virtuous sister, Mary Kathleen, so impatient for a marriage date to be settled upon, had confided to me, "They won't sleep together, but I wish they would."

I understand nothing of these matters. I am at her own request the spiritual director of the good Peggy Anne. She had, however, on one occasion drifted away from addressing her prayer life, to explain the situation.

"We still love one another, but we have some things we have to tidy up first. Like he has to finish his dissertation and I must finish my term as president of ACE Fellowship."

ACE is the remarkable Notre Dame missionary effort to provide teachers for poor Catholic schools. They are an attractive, dedicated, and enthusiastic bunch of young men and women. The Fellowship is an alumni group, most of them still teaching in Catholic schools. About a third of them marry one another. A new form of a religious order? Why not?

"Peggy Anne," I had said, lapsing into a vernacular I rarely use with young women, "that is, you should excuse the expression, a crock of bullshit! You both are losing your nerve."

She blushed and then laughed.

"I guess you're right . . . we don't want to give up our last bit of freedom."

I left it at that.

"I understand," Don Diego continued, "that both of the young people speak Spanish?" He took on a crafty look, like someone who had a plot. Only difference from Sean Cronin's plots is that Milord is much less obvious.

"No, they speak a Mexican dialect thereof, just like I do. None of this effete Castilian lisping for us."

"I understand also," he continued, "that they were at your lecture? I would have liked to be presented to them. Señorita Margarita and Don Jose are apparently striking people. But I was bound by the University rule that they don't want Cardinals at their academic events."

"Good rule. Too many Cardinals getting in over their heads."

"Though several times a week I walk over to one of the campuses and chat with the young people. They seem quite friendly despite the general hostility of all professors to the Church."

"A tendency for which they have some historic reasons."

"God knows." He made a reverent sign of the cross. "I would like to offer a dinner in your honor this evening. I will try to invite interesting people."

"That would necessitate my presence?"

"I fear so. Unfortunately we descendants of the Vandals eat our evening meals rather late in the day when the heat of the sun has cooled . . . perhaps nine thirty? And I would instruct Don Pedro to invite your nephew and Señorita Margarita, if that would not displease you?"

"We will be honored." I tilted my head in what was the closest I could come under the circumstances to delight. Joseph and Peggy Anne (as she is called in our family) might be too much for the locals, so it could even be an amusing evening.

"Incidentally is that Gulfstream 560 really hers?"

"Oh, no," I said, as if I were horrified at the thought. "Her personal aircraft is a modest Cessna Citation 310 Bravo which does not have intercontinental capabilities. However she recently has been cleared to act as copilot on the Gulfstream. Actually it is a company plane. She is using it to demonstrate for European airlines the merits of a new radar system for intercontinental flights."

"Interesting."

You better believe it, Don Diego.

"And she writes articles on spirituality too."

"*Very* interesting."

And in the unlikely event the conversation wanes tonight she will intervene to save the party.

"May I have Don Pedro tell them that the dinner is in your honor?"

"Certainly, but they'll come anyway."

Don Pedro, whose last name I never learned, was the perfect cardinal assistant. He possessed all the admirable qualities that I lack for such a role—charm, youth, discretion, wit, enthusiasm, and a wonderful smile. He lacked, however, two indispensable qualities which I possess in super-abundance—cynicism and skepticism.

"Now, since you have been traveling, you might wish to avail yourself of the afternoon siesta after you join Don Pedro and myself for some tapas and a sip of a different sherry, drier than this, but very interesting."

Tapas are a variety of fascinating snacks offered on a single plate, a small but vigorous version of the Swedish smorgasbord.

I confessed that his suggestion was very pleasant.

I don't believe in siestas or naps, but I do think it imperative that at certain times and on certain days one rests one's eyes.

None of the Ryan clan of my generation enjoy traveling. I think that the Notre Dame football stadium is the outer limit of my tolerance for a journey. Name all the troubles which affect the jet flyer and I have them— motion sickness, altitude sickness, jet lag, troubled digestive track, irritability. "How long does it take you to get over an intercontinental flight, Uncle Blackie?" she demands as she aims the Gulfstream toward Andalusia (land of the Vandals, who were the first wave of invaders who attacked Roman Iberia, enjoying a brief interlude of destruction before the arrival of the Visigoths, moderately more civilized but also Arian heretics).

She laughs as she contacts the Santa Justa (pronounced Husta) Airport to announce our arrival.

The only aircraft problem I don't have is the classic fear of flying, perhaps because a crash would put an end to my various afflictions.

Nor did I particularly like Seville after less than a day. It was one more modern city with a million or so inhabitants, traffic problems, abundant graffiti, and swarms of tourists from every nation under heaven, not excluding Kazaks, Icelanders, and Micronesians, each equipped with digital cameras and sunscreen. What did the New Testament say, "Parthians and Medes and Elamites, Irish and Turks and Swedes and, oh, yes, Yanks."

The sun was bright and the white buildings in the old Jewish Quarter glowed. The gardens around the Alcazar dazzled. The gold in the Cathedral glittered until you realized it was stolen from the Aztecs. The outside of the arena where the bulls were killed looked like a set the Lyric Opera of Chicago had lent to Seville from its *Carmen* production. The souvenir shops were like all others around the world, and there was no one dancing the flamenco around the restaurants on the Avenida de la Constitucion. It was clean anyway and the cops in their gray baseball caps were polite and tried not to smile at my Mexican accent.

Seville did not conform to the image of Arturo Perez-Reverte or Pierre Beaumarchais or Prosper Merimee. No one was singing Mozart arias in the steets. My late mother, God be good to her and he'd better or he'll hear about it, used to complain that the TV version of *The Lone Ranger* ruined the story because no mortal white horse could live up to the image of the "great white horse Silver!" One would not find the cruel passion, tragic romance, ill-fated love, and fierce hatred which had allegedly marked Spain and Spanish culture since the Romans replaced the Celto-Iberians in this city with an Arabic name.

I could not have been more wrong.